Unraveled

THE GATEKEEPER CHRONICLES
Book Two

DINA M. GIVEN

This book is a work of fiction. Names, characters, places, and incidents either are products of the author's imagination or are used fictitiously. Any resemblance to actual persons, living or dead, events, or locales is entirely coincidental.

Printed in the United States of America
Publisher: Team D Enterprises, LLC
ISBN: 978-0692505342
Cover Design by Hang Le
Editing by C&D Editing
Copyediting by Sue Soares

Formatting by Pink Ink Designs

Chapter One

EMMA

Even at this height, perched high above New York City, my senses were bombarded with the sounds of car horns, cab whistles, and police sirens. I thought I could even detect the faint smells of soft pretzels and roasted peanuts floating up to me on the hot, evening breeze. My mouth watered thinking of those sweet and salty flavors on my tongue, washed down with an ice cold, sour beer from Proletariat, my favorite craft beer bar in New York's East Village.

A bead of sweat slipped down my temple as I caught a whiff of my own overheated body and crinkled my nose at the smell. *What I wouldn't give for a cold shower right about now*, I thought.

Fanning the black leather vest I wore, I tried to get some cooler air to touch my skin. Even though the jacket was sleeveless, it trapped heat against my body like steam in a pressure cooker. Unfortunately, the jacket was a necessary evil to conceal the large weapon I carried on my back.

My pacing did little to calm my nerves or lower my body temperature. Stepping up to the low wall that surrounded the rooftop, I leaned forward and peered over the side of the fifty-four-story building. A small flutter clenched my stomach, and I quickly stepped away.

The anticipation was always the best and worst part of any mission. My nerve endings were raw and tingling with pent-up energy. I was hyper-focused, my senses on alert, like a lion just before springing into a herd of prey. Still, doubt and fear also crept in, flitting around the corners of my mind where I couldn't dispel them. Those shades whispered to me. *You're not good enough, not strong enough. This is finally the mission you will fail on. You won't make it out of this one alive.*

I closed my eyes and quieted my mind then reached out with my senses. I had been practicing this little trick for the last couple of weeks and was finally starting to get the hang of it. I could feel the hot currents of air swirling around the skyscrapers, hear the clip-clop of heels on the pavement below, and smell cigarette smoke and car exhaust.

Then I found what I was searching for, and that all too familiar tingling sensation bloomed on the back of my neck, sending a shiver down my spine. It signaled what I now knew to be the presence of magical energy. It was something I had felt many times before, but only recently learned it was my own magic reacting to that of others near me.

Whatever it was I sensed the thing was close.

I threw back the flap of my jacket and reached for my lower back. With a quick flick of my wrist, I unsnapped the leather binding that held the wooden shaft snug against my body. After a practiced tug, I heard the light click as the axe head came free from its locking holster between my shoulder blades.

It had taken some time to perfect the design, working with a medieval weapons expert and a leathersmith I met online. Battle-axes weren't normally sheathed. They were usually held or slipped into a loop on a horse's saddle. Since riding a horse around New York City, or walking the streets carrying a three-foot double-bladed battle-axe was a bit too conspicuous, I had to find a better way.

The axe was too large to swing freely at my hip. I had tried it, and the shaft constantly banged into my knees and shins. I had tried holstering it upside down on my back like a sword, with the shaft at my shoulder, but the head swung like a pendulum, throwing me off balance when I fought. The answer was a locking mechanism that held the axe head in place by my shoulders and easily came free with a tug, and a strap at my waist held the shaft snugly in place.

I held the axe, waiting, listening. Then I heard it: a soft puff of air, followed by an almost imperceptible increase in the heat at my back. With my eyes still closed, I spun, swinging upward with the axe and encountered a satisfying resistance, followed by a pained screech.

Not giving the creature time to recover, I pressed my advantage, swinging the weapon from right to left and back again in repeated figure eights. It scrambled away from the blade as I moved forward, twirling and spinning the steel so fast it was just a blur.

I could sense that I was approaching the edge of the roof. Therefore, in one final move, I landed a roundhouse kick to the creature's chest, sending it hurtling into the wall that surrounded the roof. Hearing the brick crack as mortar gave way under its weight, I poised the axe above my head, prepared to strike the killing blow.

Opening my eyes, the victorious smile slipped from my face when I saw a manticore crouched before me. It was the same type of monster that had attacked my friends and me in Citi Field a few short weeks ago, slaughtering almost an entire clan of elves.

That's not what turned my blood to ice, though. The manticores in Citi Field had been manipulated, genetically and physically, by the U.S. Government, using the bodies of the many Monere they had slaughtered and autopsied. The Monere were monster-like creatures from the realm of Urusilim, a parallel universe to Earth, only accessible by slicing open a rift between worlds using the very axe I now held. I had been attacked by one such creature that surgically bore the head of my elven friend, Lockien, gruesomely sutured to a monstrous manticore body — that of a mutated, oversized lion with a scorpion tale. A part of Lockien had been trapped inside that disembodied brain. He had begged me to kill him, and I had obliged, but that moment continued to torment my dreams.

The all-too-familiar eyes within this manticore's face locked me in place. It got back to its feet, and all I could do was stand there as panic flooded through my immovable limbs.

No, no, no, no. That word just kept repeating itself in my head as I took in the features of my foster brother Daniel.

My greatest fear had manifested before me, even while a small part of my brain tried to convince me it wasn't real. The last time I had seen Daniel, he had been unconscious, carried through the gateway to Urusilim on the orders of Gabriel Marduk, the man who had sent monsters and one hot yet crazy mage to hunt me down. Oh, and Marduk also claimed to be my real father. I felt an odd kinship with Luke Skywalker.

The manticore hesitated a moment, but then realized it had the advantage and sprang. The sudden movement was like a slap across the face, kicking my training and muscle memory into gear. I held the axe across my body to block the manticore's talons from slicing open my abdomen.

The impact forced me backward, and the manticore pressed its advantage, Daniel's sweet face twisting into an unnatural sneer. The scorpion tail lashed at me, and I twisted away, only barely dodging impalement. It immediately struck again and again, keeping me off balance as I tried to avoid the poisonous stinger.

If I didn't gain some space to gather myself and jump back on the offensive, this thing would turn me into a shish kabob. *What I wouldn't give for my Glock right now.* I didn't bring the handgun, knowing I needed more experience fighting with the axe. That's the last time I ever put Baby in a corner.

Spinning on my heel, I sprinted away from the manticore with no plan for how to escape it on this open rooftop. A sharp twinge pierced the back of my neck, like my usual tingles on steroids, and I dropped flat to the ground as the manticore passed over me in a flying lunge, landing and skidding to a stop a few feet from my head. I scrambled to my knees, preparing to make another run for it as the manticore spread a pair of black, leathery wings wide.

"Oh, shit."

I didn't even make it to my feet before the manticore leapt at me again, pumping its wings. Talons tore into the back of my coat, shredding the thin leather yet leaving enough material for it to get a hold. Claws scratched across my skin, and I could feel something hot and wet trickle down my back. Then the manticore lifted into the air, dragging me up with it.

I hung in mid-air as the creature gained altitude, soaring above the New York City skyscrapers. My coat began to slide off my body with no closed buttons or zippers to secure me, and I clawed at the material, desperately seeking some purchase, but to no avail. When one arm slid free of the sleeve, a short scream tore free of my throat as the coat slipped off my other shoulder.

Still clutching the axe in my right hand, the coat bunched up around my right wrist. The cross-wise axe handle was the only thing stopping me from plunging to my death.

Dangling hundreds of feet above Manhattan's bustling streets, I was buffeted by searing winds as the manticore flew through the canyons created by the city's tall buildings. When we came to the cross streets where there was no protection from the skyscrapers, the wind shear threatened to rip my hand from its already precarious grip on the axe handle.

My palm burned and grew slippery with sweat. I gritted my teeth, trying to force strength into my hand through sheer will, but as my flesh grew clammier, my grip failed me. I fell into the void, my stomach lurching into my throat as I became weightless. The axe fell with me, spinning end over end, fated to shatter on the asphalt below, or get crushed by passing taxicabs.

I took a moment to thank the universe that it was only a practice weapon, and I had decided to keep Sharur, my magical battle axe, safely locked away.

Time to fly, I thought, spreading my arms and legs, allowing the wingsuit I had been wearing under the jacket to catch the air current. Suddenly, falling turned into gliding. It was exhilarating.

I couldn't gain any altitude in the suit, only cut through the air horizontally. I craned my neck, looking for the manticore and finding it a few dozen feet behind and above me. It spotted me at the same time, dropping what remained of my tattered coat. With an angry shriek, it folded its wings back and dove directly for me.

I pulled in my arms to increase my own speed, trying to outmaneuver the creature by banking sharply around corners and cutting through alleyways between buildings. However, the manticore was a natural flyer, whereas I had only practiced with the wingsuit a couple of times. I couldn't shake the creature, so I took a different tack.

I turned down 5th Avenue and picked up more speed by sacrificing altitude, forcing the manticore to increase his velocity, as well. Hopefully, I could take care of the manticore before crashing into the street below. After all, I wasn't wearing a parachute, and there was no other way to safely land.

Just when it came within reach of my legs, I spread my arms wide and arched my back, creating as much surface area as possible, giving me lift and sharply slowing my momentum. When the manticore overshot me, I immediately poured on the speed again and caught the manticore easily, landing on its back.

I wrapped my forearm around its human neck and squeezed while reaching into my boot with my other hand to pull out the knife I kept sheathed there.

Pressing the blade to the creature's throat, I purred in its ear, "You always said you wanted me to mount you." Then I gave him a kiss on the cheek.

The manticore laughed deep in his throat. "This isn't what I had in mind."

"Well, it's as close as you'll get. Can we go get a drink now?"

Chapter Two

EMMA

The manticore landed on the rooftop of the building we had taken off from, its body melting and bones popping loudly as they reformed into a new shape. The transformation began almost before I could jump off its back and was complete in mere seconds. After a moment, Eddie stood before me in his birthday suit, doubled over and panting from the effort of shifting, and I'm sure the pain, although he would never admit it to me.

I found the black duffle bag he had stashed on the roof when planning our training session and pulled out a change of clothes. He dressed quickly into jeans and a black T-shirt printed with a fake prescription drug ad that said, *Ask your doctor if MYKOC is right for you.*

I had lost my jacket during our treacherous flight high above the city, but no longer had need of it since I had lost the axe too. I reveled in the feeling of wearing nothing more than a thin, black tank top as we descended through the cement and metal stairwell until we emerged onto 42nd Street.

"Raines?" I asked hopefully, referring to my former home-away-from-home — a speakeasy-style cocktail bar in Greenwich Village, hidden behind an unmarked door on an unassuming street. I hadn't been there in weeks, trying to lay low and stay away from the places I had frequented. I missed it almost as much as I missed my apartment. It felt like the best pieces of my life were slipping away from me.

I didn't even wait for Eddie to answer before hailing a taxi. Then Eddie and I scrambled into the yellow cab, relieved to be out of the heat and immersed in the ice-cold air conditioning.

"Come on, Em. You know we can't go to Raines. Anyway, I can stomach a fancy froufrou drink every once in a while, but a man needs a good old-fashioned beer to keep the testosterone flowing."

"The last thing you need is more testosterone," I said. "All right, Proletariat it is. I was dreaming about an ice-cold beer earlier, anyway."

Eddie let out a whoop, startling the driver. Proletariat was Eddie's favorite night and afternoon spot. Heck, if it were open for breakfast, it would be his favorite morning spot too. Given his English accent — more Jason Statham than Colin Firth — I would have expected Eddie to prefer old-fashioned pubs, but apparently, froufrou beers were more his style.

Proletariat was a narrow, hole-in-the-wall bar that

served unique craft beers from around the world, and the bartender was friendly and incredibly knowledgeable. Even though I wasn't much of a beer lover, he had the uncanny ability of selecting beers for me that agreed with my less than sophisticated hops and barley palate and thank fuck didn't taste anything like Budweiser.

Once the cab let us off on St. Mark's Place in SoHo, we made our way into the small space, taking stools at the well-worn bar. A chalkboard behind the bar listed dozens of tonight's special selections.

"Hey, guys," said Chris the bartender. "Emma, I have just the thing for you tonight. I think you'll really like it. It's a scotch ale, aged on tart cherries in brandy barrels. It's dark and lightly sweet."

"Thanks, Chris. Sounds perfect. What's it called?"

Chris filled a rich, red glass of ale from the tap. "It's a Grimm Cherry Oak Shape Shifter."

I peered at Eddie, trying to choke back a laugh, so it came out like a snort instead, which threw us both into a fit of laughter.

"I like my shape shifters like my beer — dark and lightly sweet," I teased.

"Then I'm just the shifter for you, love," Eddie said, darkening his pale English skin to a rich mahogany.

I elbowed him in the ribs. "Quit it before someone notices," I hissed, and his skin lightened back to its usual pasty complexion just before Chris returned to set my beer in front of me.

"Eddie, an Owl Farm Porter?" Chris asked.

"But of course, my good man."

Chris stepped away to pour Eddie's glass. "I don't

know how you drink that stuff. It's so thick and bitter. I feel like it needs to be chewed instead of drank."

"Hey, you love Starbucks, and I don't criticize you for not being a civilized tea drinker."

"Yes, you do," I muttered.

Chris returned with Eddie's sludge, and we both took appreciative sips from our glasses. "Perfect, as usual. Thanks, Chris." He rewarded me with a wink and moved on to other customers. "So, how did I do tonight?" I asked with a smug smile, expecting only the highest praise for my kick-ass performance.

"Eh," Eddie said, shrugging one shoulder noncommittally.

"What do you mean, 'eh'?" I turned on him with wide eyes. "I kicked your ass tonight."

"I wouldn't go that far, love. You're not going to wear a flight suit every day, are you? You never should have let me get you into the air."

I knew he was right, but I wasn't about to admit it. "I almost had you on the roof. What the hell did you think you were doing, taking Daniel's face?"

"Trying to throw you off your game and it worked. You need to expect the unexpected if you are going to survive against the Monere. If that had been a real fight, any creature would have easily taken you down while you hesitated."

Shit. Way to burst my bubble.

"Well, I still won," I said, moping like a child.

Eddie turned toward me and pierced me with his warm, chocolate eyes. "Emma, love, you need to take up the axe."

I shook my head vehemently, my long, brown waves of hair slapping my cheeks. "Eddie, the mistakes I made tonight wouldn't have been solved if I had the axe. I'll do better next time."

"There may not be a next time, love. Sure, you've beaten a lot of creatures, but bullets aren't effective against all of them, and you no longer have the elves or mages standing with you. Do you really think you could beat something like a chimera alone?"

I had told Eddie about my run-in with a chimera earlier in the summer when one pursued my friends and me through the streets of Manhattan, over the Brooklyn Bridge, and through the Holland Tunnel, only to be taken down in Liberty State Park by a clan of elven warriors.

"No," I conceded. "But no chimeras came through the rift in Citi Field. I would have noticed something that large if it had. So far, I have been able to handle everything that came through that night, and I have no reason to believe that will change."

About four weeks ago, I was forced to open a gateway to Urusilim from Citi Field, the Mets baseball stadium. Dozens of creatures had flooded into this world and escaped the stadium into the city. I was only able to close the gate after a ruthless, bloody battle.

"A lot of creatures made it through the gate that night, and if you recall, we were somewhat preoccupied, so none of us stopped to take attendance."

"There is no way violent creatures will be able to go undetected in this world for very long. As soon as they raise their ugly heads, I'll know about it and will stop them."

Eddie gave me a withering look. "Oh, yeah, it's impossible for creatures to hide among humans."

"I wasn't talking about you. Your people are different."

Eddie merely shook his head, swallowing his response with another gulp of beer.

"As soon as I get rid of all of the Monere who escaped into the city that night, I'm retiring and moving to a farm in New Jersey."

Eddie snorted. "You, on a farm? I can't picture it. Although, I would like to see you in daisy dukes and a half shirt, milking a cow," he said, staring into the distance with a dreamy smile on his face.

I jabbed him in the ribs again, interrupting his fantasy. "I'm serious, Eddie. My time as the 'chosen one,'" I air quoted, "is over. I'll clean up my mess and be done with it."

"I can't decide whether your naiveté is adorable or moronic."

"What is that supposed to mean?"

"Ah, how I love a woman who is both beautiful and brainless." This time, he was quick enough to block my elbow. Becoming more serious, he said, "Emma, love, there is more going on here than you can possibly imagine. That little show at Citi Field was just the tip of the iceberg."

"Little show?" I said, gaping.

That "little show" resulted in the deaths of many friends and allies. I thought of Therran, the elven leader, and his gregarious daughter Lilly. I hadn't seen them since our escape. The elves probably thought I had abandoned them and most likely hated me for it. Instead, I had gone into hiding with Eddie and his shifters so they could help train me. As much as I missed the elves and my best friend Jason, I wanted to keep them far away from my creature troubles, and me. I couldn't stand to put them in danger again.

"Do you really think Marduk will just slink back into his hole and give up on seeking Sharur?" Eddie asked.

"I have the axe, Eddie. It is stashed away in a very secure location. No one, including Marduk, will ever be able to find it and use it to open another gateway."

"That may be so," Eddie said, sounding unconvinced, "but you still have plenty of enemies here on Earth beyond the Monere. Have you forgotten about the government's monster program or the Mage Council?"

"Benjamin said the monster program was shut down, and Connor is on unpaid leave, pending a full Congressional investigation."

Benjamin was the head of Procurement for the U.S. Military, and his control over military spending put him in a unique position of power and knowledge. Benjamin was an ally who had helped us take down Ed Connor. Connor led the Committee on Superhuman Research, and not only had he ruthlessly experimented on Monere, but he had captured and tortured me, trying to learn my secrets.

"No," Eddie countered. "Benjamin said he wasn't *aware* that the program was still active. The program could have been taken deeper undercover, beyond his reach. It could still be going on under all of our noses."

"That's not very likely. Benjamin is the most well connected man in the government. Nothing happens without his knowledge. After all, he controls the money, even the secret funding."

"And the Mage Council? What story have you told yourself about them that has you convinced they are no longer a threat? Alcina wants Sharur and your head on a pike for good measure."

"She doesn't know where I am," I said, sounding uncertain even to my own ears.

She might not know where I was right then, but that little brat was nothing if not shrewd and resourceful. Alcina was an ancient mage and the leader of the Mage Council, not to mention a downright bitch, cloaked in the body of an adorable seven-year-old.

"Really? You think the most powerful mage in existence can't locate one lone woman in New York City who frequents the same hangouts night after night?"

"If she knew how to find me, then why hasn't she come after me yet?" I challenged.

"Ah, now that's the question that should worry you."

If Alcina had been monitoring my movements, she could have seen where I stashed Sharur. She wanted that axe more than anything. She claimed it was to ensure the powerful magical weapon remained in the hands of those strong enough to protect it and keep it safe. As a result, if she knew where it was, she would go after it in a heartbeat with all of the formidable resources at her disposal, and I wouldn't stand a chance. The fact that the axe was still safely tucked away was the best evidence that she hadn't located me yet.

When I didn't respond, Eddie continued. "And let's not forget your boyfriend."

For a moment, I couldn't figure out whether Eddie was sarcastically referring to Alex or Zane. However, thinking of them made me realize I had the dubious honor of having one "boyfriend" desperate to kill me, and the other "boyfriend" recuperating because I almost got him killed. No wonder I was still single.

"Zane made it out of Citi Field that night, and the barmy bugger of a mage will find you sooner or later."

"I can handle Zane," I said, lowering my eyes. I didn't want Eddie to see the fear, sadness, and desire that warred within me at the thought of Zane. Part of me wanted to be found by him, but the other part of me knew being found could result in my violent death.

"Face it, Emma, this thing isn't over yet. You've gotten better in your creature fighting, but you need to gather your allies around you. Call Therran. He will come to your aid."

"No, Eddie. His sons and clansmen died the last time he tried to help me. I will not ask him to sacrifice anymore." My guilt wouldn't let me face Therran right now, maybe not ever.

"Then Jason."

Jason had been my best friend and partner in the mercenary business for years, but I hadn't seen or spoken with him in a while. After I escaped Citi Field and left him behind with the elves, I assumed he had either stayed with them or gone his own way. I intended to find him, but not yet, not until all of this was behind me.

"I already lost one friend, Eddie. With Daniel gone, Jason is all I have left; he's my only tie to humanity. I need him to keep breathing. If anything ever happened to him…" My voice hitched. Clearing my throat, I asked, "Are you going to suggest Alex next?"

"No. Don't get me wrong, love. Alex has been a strong ally and is a good man, but he can't be trusted." I didn't try to hide my surprise. "He is a mage, aligned to Alcina, and she demands nothing less than complete loyalty from the Council members. I don't think he has it in himself to betray her, and I'm not sure I would trust him if he did. I would always wonder whether we were being double-crossed."

Cold settled in my stomach at the thought of Alex possibly betraying me, but I shook off the thought. Alex and I were friends. He would never do anything that would cause me harm, especially after everything we had been through together and all he had risked to keep me safe.

"But he saved your life," I said, thinking of when Alex had helped fake Eddie's death so the shifter could escape from servitude under Marduk.

"Don't mistake aligned goals with loyalty or friendship, love. Alex needed the shifters to turn against Marduk, and the price for our betrayal was you. We would never ally ourselves with those dodgy mages, but you, on the other hand … I have a talent for backing the winning horse." Eddie winked. "Anyway, enough about Alex. No one has seen him for weeks, and after the injuries he sustained at Citi Field, who knows when he'll be back in play?"

I took another swig of beer, finishing my glass. "You head on home without me, Eddie. I'm going for a walk." I slashed him a warning look when he opened his mouth. "I'll be fine. I don't need a babysitter. I'll see you in a couple of hours."

I walked out of the bar before he could utter a word, leaving him to pick up the check. I figured he owed me after dropping me off a skyscraper tonight.

Chapter Three

EMMA

It was a thirty-minute walk to my destination, and even though the air was sticky and stifling, it still felt like a welcome relief after that conversation with Eddie. That line from *The Godfather III* kept ran through my head — *Just when I thought I was out, they pull me back in!*

I wanted nothing more than to forget the last couple of months ever happened. My life wasn't exactly full of joy before this — being a mercenary and hired assassin is pretty lonely and doesn't exactly come with a lot of laughs — but at least I lived it on my terms. Now, it just felt like things were happening *to* me, and all I could do was react to them.

I turned onto my favorite street in Manhattan — 5th Avenue. On any other night, I would have gazed longingly into the windows of Michael Kors, Kate

Spade, BCBG Max Azria, and Lucky Brand, strategically planning my next purchase. Tonight, though, my thoughts were a million miles away from shopping.

I did, however, step into a few of the more crowded stores and wove almost aimlessly through the people, tables, and racks. I even slipped in and out of a few changing rooms and restrooms. If anyone followed me, I did my best to shake them off my tail. It was a habit I formed a long time ago, and it had saved my ass more than once.

As I slowly made my way uptown, I eventually came upon the iconic, triangular shape of the Flatiron Building. Taking a short-cut through Madison Square Park, I passed by its reflecting pool, which lived up to its name, casting the full moon's glow back into the sky. I continued my trek up Madison until I finally came upon my destination—the soaring columns of Grand Central Station.

Moving into the vaulted main terminal with its ceiling depicting the night sky, I couldn't help thinking about my first meeting with Eddie. He followed me through Grand Central that night, and I purposefully led him into an elevator that descended to an abandoned train terminal, having no idea what he was. He shifted in the elevator, scaring the ever-living shit out of me, and we had an epic brawl. I got the upper hand and detained him for interrogation. When we got to know each other better, I realized that he was funny, sincere, and trustworthy. He had been on my side ever since. I had moved into his place a month ago because it was too dangerous for me to stay in my apartment where I could easily be found. *God, I miss my apartment*, I thought.

I walked briskly, weaving around people and ducking in and out of train terminals. It was unlikely anyone still followed me, but one could never be too cautious. I finally found the unmarked door that led to the locked service elevator and rode it fifteen stories underground.

Stepping out of the elevator, I flipped the nearby light switch, casting a dim illumination throughout the walled-up and forgotten train station with its lone subway car rotting away on tracks to nowhere. This hidden place was my refuge. I came here when I wanted privacy, whether that was to interrogate a suspect, as was the case with Eddie, or just to be alone and think.

It was also a good place to hide something valuable. No one ever came down here because very few people knew of its existence. I pried open the doors to the subway car and stepped into my haven.

I had been making the car homier ever since I had been forced to abandon my own apartment. I had taken a sledgehammer to the hard plastic subway seats in a cathartic moment and replaced them with a small futon, beanbag chairs, a papasan chair, and floor pillows. I couldn't very well drag large pieces of furniture down here, so I had to select items that were more portable, and carry them in one at a time. It took weeks to finish the redecorating.

The result was a space crammed with a hodgepodge of overstuffed, mismatched garage sale rejects in a variety of clashing colors and patterns. It looked like a rainbow had thrown up everywhere, and I loved it.

It was everything I wanted to be, yet wasn't—joyful, carefree, fun. Sometimes when I was here, I could almost pretend I was those things...until I walked back through the doors of the subway car into the gloomy darkness of the underground cavern, which was more a reflection of me.

Moving aside a mound of cushions and blankets, I unearthed an original Chubb Sovereign safe, built in the United Kingdom in 1979 and designed to be the strongest private safe in the world. Its walls were an impregnable fortress of thick alloy plates of copper, aluminum, and carbon steel, protecting its contents from an arsenal of burning, breaching, cutting, and even explosives. It had two locks: one biometric and the other a mechanical key lock. That meant someone had to kill me, chop off my hand for fingerprints, and find the key. Not impossible, but pretty damn difficult.

I pulled out the chain I wore around my neck and had tucked inside my bra for extra safekeeping—*no one would find it there*, I thought wryly. A small key dangled from the chain. Kneeling down, I inserted it into the safe's lock, turned it, and then placed my thumb on the pad of the fingerprint reader. A small green light clicked on, informing me the vault was unlocked and safe to open.

My hand clutched the handle, but I froze, unwilling to pull the door open. Each time I found myself in this position it became more difficult to take that next step. Maybe I should just walk away and leave the vault's contents hidden in this dark corner of the old train car, lost to time and memory. I couldn't, though. It called to me, like the inexorable tug of a siren's song.

Part of the reason I kept it here was in the hopes that burying it miles away and fifteen stories underground would quiet the incessant ringing in my blood. Regardless, it grew stronger each day, as if it was increasingly desperate to reach me.

Taking a deep, steadying breath, I pulled open the vault door to reveal the ancient, double-bladed battle axe called Sharur. The first time I had laid eyes on it, I had been less than impressed. It had been dull and scarred with time and wear. Even though I hadn't made any effort to clean the axe, it seemed to get brighter and sharper every time I saw it, as though it fed off my energy to renew itself.

The metal gleamed, as if illuminated from somewhere deep inside. The intricate scrollwork etched in the blades was now prominent where it had previously been faded and barely visible. Its three-foot long handle was made of a smooth, black hardwood that ended in a wicked spike I had used to impale a vampire who had almost drunk me dry a few weeks ago. I still bore the scar on my neck from that encounter, a constant reminder that I would be dead now had it not been for the axe.

I rubbed the spot absently, feeling the puckered flesh under my fingers.

Yet, for all of its beauty, the most stunning feature of the axe was the aquamarine gemstone embedded into a circular depression in the center of the axe head. The gem was the deep greens and blues of a tropical sea, and deep inside the heart of the stone, subtle movement could be detected, like the ethereal swirl of smoke and shadow.

I knew inside that stone was my blood, taken from me and absorbed during the ritual in Mexico the night I first learned of the Monere's existence. My blood in the stone powered the axe's ability to open a sustainable gateway to Urusilim.

Reaching into the vault, I lightly caressed the axe. It was warm and thrumming with energy, the vibration reverberating through my body and tickling my nerves. The connection was almost immediate. I had only visited Sharur a few times since I had hidden it away, but each time I came, it felt like our connection grew stronger. Maybe that had something to do with its improving condition.

You have returned.

The words were as clear as crystal in my head, spoken in a male voice with a deep, coarse accent, somewhat like a cross between Russian and German. I had heard it for the first time in Citi Field, driving me to stay alive and fight back against the vampire. At the time, I had chalked up the disembodied voice to exhaustion, poison, and blood loss. However, each time I touched Sharur since then, the voice came back.

Thus far, I couldn't bring myself to respond to it, to acknowledge its sentience.

You have naught to fear from me, it said, as if reading my thoughts.

"I'm not afraid of you," I shot back too quickly then jerked my hand from the axe as though I had touched a hot stove. I hadn't intended to speak to it.

My hand hovered over the weapon, hesitating to

touch it again, realizing I was afraid, but of what? It couldn't physically harm me, could it? It might be able to speak, but it certainly didn't have arms or legs to attack me.

But could it get into my head? Maybe it was able to read my mind, uncover things in the darkest recesses of my brain. Could it find those memories that were still hidden from me? Did I want it to? Even though Zane had cracked the wall blocking my past, it wasn't showing any signs of crumbling just yet.

Even worse than digging through memories, could Sharur poison my mind, manipulate me, or drive me insane like poor Zane? The things I would be capable of doing under someone else's control made me shudder. I had no idea who owned the loyalty of the axe and what its true motives were. Then again, I would never learn the axe's secrets if I didn't take the risk of speaking to it.

A slight tremor shook my hand as I reached for the weapon. It only took the barest brush of my fingers to re-establish the connection. It didn't say anything, but I could feel its presence in my mind: patient, eager, and suspicious.

"What do you want?" I asked aloud.

No response.

"Who do you take your orders from?"

Still nothing.

"If you have nothing to say, I might as well just lock you away again."

Wait. Its sharp tone and spike of emotion startled me. *The more important question is what do you want from me?*

I narrowed my eyes. Sharur sounded as uncertain about me as I felt about it. If that was the case, it wasn't going to be easy to get information.

"What would I want from you?"

It didn't take the bait.

"I don't want anything. If I did, I wouldn't keep you locked away."

It was silent for a moment, as if thinking through my argument.

Where am I? Which world am I on?

The question took me aback. There were more worlds than just Earth and Urusilim? If there were two realms, it made sense that more would exist, but how many more?

"Earth," I answered.

Earth? How did I get here? This isn't one of the Primary Realms.

"What's a Primary Realm?"

Why am I here? It challenged, avoiding my question.

We were at a stalemate.

"That's a long story, one we can save for another time." I didn't want to reveal too much of what had happened until I knew more about Sharur, but I had to throw it a bone, or we wouldn't get anywhere with this conversation. "I don't know exactly how you got to Earth. All I know is that you were in the possession of a man named Nathan Anshar before you were stolen from him."

Ah, Anshar, it said, as if Nathan's name alone revealed the answers to all of its questions.

"Do you know Nathan? How? Do you speak to him

too?" The questions came out in a rush before I could stop myself. Coming across as too desperate for information would put me in a poor negotiating position. Sharur seemed to realize this, as well, and didn't respond. "Okay, time to go back in the box."

Please, don't. I felt its desperation acutely. *I have been asleep for far too long. There is no need to keep me locked away.*

"You are too dangerous. If you fell into the wrong hands…It would be bad."

But I am in your hands now. Do you not trust yourself? Without knowing it, Sharur had just voiced the question I most feared to answer. *You used me the night I awoke. I helped you then, and I can help you again.*

I had a feeling this was what the voice of the Devil sitting on one's shoulder sounded like.

"I don't need your help. I do just fine on my own, and I won't be in the creature-killing business for much longer, so why don't you just go back to sleep in your cozy, little box?"

You wouldn't be alive today if I hadn't helped you kill that vampire, it said. *There are more vampires out there and other things even more dangerous, and you cannot hope to defeat them without me.*

I rolled my eyes. It sounded just like Eddie, and I couldn't help wondering if the two of them were right. Were they underestimating me, or was I in denial? Sharur was just a weapon, after all. How was it any different from carrying around my Glock except for the whole sentience thing?

I didn't want to ask it, but I needed to know. "Can

you take over my mind?"

No, it said with a trace of amusement. *I can speak to your mind, but I cannot control it. Your stubbornness is safely intact.*

"Very funny," I said, eyeing the weapon, not trusting its answer.

Maybe I should just pick it up. Part of me craved to feel the warm, smooth wood in my palms, the weighted heft of the blade, and the power of the axe as it coursed through my veins, making me feel invincible.

My hands grasped the shaft, and I lifted it out of the vault. Feelings of elation, trepidation, and freedom washed over me, and I knew they weren't mine. I absently wondered whether Sharur could similarly feel my eagerness, fear, and desire. I gently lifted it out of the vault and rose to my feet.

Words weren't needed between us anymore, only actions. Stepping outside of the train car onto the open platform, I hefted the axe in my right hand and gave it a test swing. It felt good—perfectly balanced, light enough for easy wielding, but solid enough to provide deadly momentum.

The shaft thrummed in pleasure as it cut through the air. I danced through a series of practice moves: ducking and weaving, rolling to avoid pretend enemies, and lightly leaping to my feet, cutting them down. The axe was an extension of my arm, allowing me to move effortlessly, almost without thought.

I felt stronger, faster, and more graceful than ever before, as if I could vanquish even the most deadly creatures with ease. The train platform blurred with the speed of my movements, and the cool, underground air blew across my heated skin. I was hyperaware of every sound and sensation. Yet, at the same time, my mind felt a million miles away, wanting only to hold onto the sensation of euphoria that came from strength, confidence, and a feeling of invincibility.

Pulsating energy radiated from the axe into my hand, up my arm, and moved throughout my body. Eddie had been right all along. No one could stand against me when I wielded Sharur. The heat flowing through my veins pooled in the palm of my empty left hand as I twirled on the balls of my feet, slicing the axe through the air.

As if guided by some unseen will, I dropped into a crouch, ducking an invisible blow, and threw up my left hand like a shield. A flash of searing blue light temporarily blinded me, followed by the deafening sound of silence. Looking up, an entire section of tunnel wall was simply gone. It hadn't exploded; it had just ceased to exist. A searing heat dragged my attention to the palm of my left hand. It glowed, and pulsating color shifted under the skin: blue, purple, and silver.

"Holy fuck!" I jumped to my feet then threw the axe away from me, and it clattered against the cement, coming to a stop about fifteen away. "What did you do to me?" I screamed at it, knowing it couldn't respond since we weren't physically connected.

I examined my hands, turning them over. A faint glow illuminated the blue threads at my wrists and moved up my arms until they disappeared under the thicker flesh at my biceps. Then the energy receded back into my veins.

When the glow subsided, exhaustion slammed into me. It was a good exhaustion, though. Not like the kind I felt after getting my ass kicked, but more like how it felt after pulling that amazing all-nighter with Zane a few weeks ago. It was the after-glow of something sinfully delicious, but no less tiring. I wanted to curl up in a ball under something warm and fluffy, and drift off to sleep with a smile on my face.

The recovery was almost as euphoric as the build-up, and it scared the hell out of me because I wanted more.

Chapter Four

ALEX

The harsh tones of angry voices coming from the parlor downstairs broke through my sleep-addled mind. I had been unconscious more often than not these past few weeks, and I could almost feel my muscles atrophying as I lay there.

Get the fuck up, I urged myself silently.

With a groan, I sat up in bed then sucked in a sharp breath as pain shot through my right knee and hip that had been severely fractured.

My recovery after that night on Citi Field had been arduously slow, but I supposed that could only be expected when one was brought back from the brink of death.

I didn't remember much from that night, but the moment I decided to throw myself into Zane's path to give Emma a fighting chance at killing Marduk was crystal clear. My gamble might have saved her from Zane, but Marduk had gotten away. The Council was still livid that I hadn't simply grabbed the axe and left Emma and the elves to die.

They were down there right now, arguing about their next move as they did every night. I had joined them a few times, but didn't have the stamina to keep up with the heated discussions. They merely expected me to go along with whatever they decided, anyway, as I always did, I supposed.

It wasn't that I was a pushover by any means, but I was loyal and committed to the cause. The Mage Council had taken me in after I was cast out by my own family for being different. The Council raised me, taught me, cared for me. They were my family. Without them, I would likely have starved to death on the streets, been killed by humans who mistrusted magic, or killed by creatures who simply enjoyed killing. Instead, I was safe in a warm bed, recovering from my wounds.

I pulled on a gray T-shirt with plaid pajama pants that hung low on my hips then padded out of the bedroom on bare feet. I didn't know why I felt the need for stealth, but I stepped lightly and slowly, not wanting to divulge my presence. After gliding down the stairs, I hid in the shadows outside of the parlor.

"There hasn't been any sign of her for weeks," Ronin grumbled. He was a grizzled veteran on the Mage Council and Alcina's right-hand man. He had an angry scar that cut down the right side of his face, beginning on his forehead and ending at his jaw, passing over his now blind, white eyeball. He was hard as nails and terrifying in his intensity. "She hasn't returned to her apartment, nor to the elves' compound upstate. We haven't been able to locate the shifters, and even if we did, they wouldn't exactly be forthcoming with us."

"Fucking shifters," came the voice of a small child. Such language was still startling to hear coming out of Alcina's sweet bow of a mouth. She had blond curls, creamy skin, and a button nose with the cruel eyes of an ice princess. "How is it that we didn't know they would betray Marduk? What good are our spies if they can't find out the truly critical information?" she demanded.

"There is always the possibility that the shifters are still working for Marduk and trying to gain her trust or that Emma has allied herself with Marduk," Ronin said in an even tone, as though restating something he had proposed several times before.

I hadn't told the Council that I'd had a hand in the shifters' change of heart. I wasn't exactly friends with Eddie, but their goals were aligned to ours. I needed to reduce Marduk's allies, and Eddie needed a savior he could truly trust. The gods knew that wasn't Marduk or the Mage Council. A few well-placed lies and Eddie was prepared to hand over his soul and his people to Emma.

I hadn't revealed my plans to the Council, because I knew they would never allow me to negotiate with creatures. The Council lived and died by their ideal of magical purity. It wasn't necessarily because the mages thought they were better than everyone else was; it was because history had proved creatures and humans were dangerous and unpredictable if given access to magic. The Council only wanted to protect the people of Urusilim and bring peace to our world by ensuring magic and all of its ill effects were controlled by those responsible enough to use it. It was why a parent would never allow a child to play with a loaded gun.

"I suppose we can't discount any possibility at this point," Alcina conceded. "But that still doesn't help us find her and, more importantly, find Sharur. Somehow, she is shielding herself from our seeking spells. We need to find a way to draw her out."

"Maybe I can help," I said, limping into the room.

Alcina eyed me up and down, as if she could see through my skin to the damage beneath. "You're not in any shape to help right now."

"I'm feeling better. Maybe I can draw her out. She trusts me."

"You wouldn't even know where to start looking for her. You told us you don't know where she hangs out, who her friends are, what she likes to do, so how do you intend to find her?"

Alcina's words cut deeper than I expected. She was right. What did I really know about the mysterious Emma? I had known her when she was a child, but even then, it was only in passing. Sure, I spent time with her over the past several weeks, but how much had she really revealed about herself? How much had I revealed to her about myself? Not much. How could I expect her to open up to me when I wasn't prepared to reciprocate?

But Zane knew her...intimately. Zane had taken the time to discover the person within; what made her tick, what incited her passions, what she believed in, what turned her on. A knot formed in my gut at the thought.

Alcina's face softened when she noticed my stricken expression. "Alex, we know you want to help. Once you are fully recovered, and we determine the best way of locating her, we will be sure to include you in our plans. For now, why don't you go back to your room and rest?"

Knowing that was an order, not a caring suggestion, I turned and made my way back up the stairs, using the railing to help pull myself upward. Before reaching my closed bedroom door, I felt her presence, and my skin warmed, as if the ambient air temperature had increased a couple of degrees.

It was a sensation that most people would ignore or write off as a hot flash, a temperature fluctuation, or just increasing humidity during this already sweltering summer. However, I felt this before and knew exactly what it was.

My heart rate increased, and an unbidden smile crept across my face as I picked up the pace, limping heavily. As I flung open my bedroom door and found the room empty, disappointment crashed over me in an unexpected wave. I stepped into the room and closed the door behind me, my shoulders slumping.

Click. The sound of the door's lock engaging caused me to spin around, and there she was.

Emma stood with her back to the door, arms crossed over her chest, looking uncertain. Her dark hair hung loose in a tangle of waves cascading over her shoulders to the middle of her back, and the dimly lit room cast her in dramatic shadow, accentuating every curve. By the gods, she was beautiful, and the fact that she didn't seem to know it made her even more attractive.

She wore black, skinny jeans, tucked into those shit-kicker boots she loved so much, and a vintage *Star Wars* T-shirt that was tight across the chest she hid behind crossed arms.

"Hey," she said softly.

"Hey," I repeated without making a move, as if I was trying to reassure a wild animal.

"How are you feeling? You look a little better. The limp isn't so pronounced."

"I'm good. As long as I keep walking and stretching the muscle, I should get full function back in my leg."

"Good." She nodded, crossing the room and taking a seat on the edge of my bed. "You need to get your lazy ass back out in the field and help me fight." She gave me a teasing half smile, testing out the humor to see if it would be accepted.

"I don't know. I rather enjoy lying in bed all day, watching *Days of Our Lives* and eating bonbons," I remarked, taking a seat next to her.

"Oh, yeah? Is Stefano still trying to kill John and Marlena? You would think, after thirty years of trying, he would give up."

"That's the benefit of not growing up on Earth: *Days of Our Lives* still seems original to me." The smile slipped from my face, and I grew serious. "What are you doing here, Emma? You are taking a huge risk of getting caught by Alcina. If she ever found out you have been visiting me…"

"That spoiled brat can kiss my ass," Emma said, but we both knew she didn't stand a chance against Alcina.

"I'm here because something happened tonight, and I need to talk to you about it."

Her response caught me off guard. She had never volunteered information before and certainly never asked for my help or advice. Either this was something truly disturbing, or maybe, just maybe, she was beginning to open up a bit.

"I went to see Sharur tonight," she said, looking at her feet.

"You did? Why? I thought you hid it away forever." When she had told me Sharur would never be seen again, I had thought she might have buried it at the bottom of the ocean, thrown it into a volcano, or dropped it into the money pit on Oak Island. The fact that she had ready access to the axe told me that it was nearby and recoverable.

"I don't know," she sighed. "I just had to see it, maybe to prove to myself that I didn't need it."

"And do you need it?"

She fell into silence for so long I was afraid the conversation was over, and she would leave without bringing me any closer to learning more about her.

"It did something to me," she said, twisting her hands as if trying to wash them, but they wouldn't come clean. "It pushed power into me."

I reached out and gently took her hands in mine, stilling them. Then I turned them over to examine her palms yet saw nothing unusual. I was hyperaware of her in that moment: the feel of her warm hands in mine, the patches of rough skin telling the story of recent battles. Her thigh brushed against me, causing my abdomen to clench as my mind wandered to places it shouldn't. I rubbed my thumbs in circles on the center of her palms, and she didn't pull away.

"The weapon used me as a weapon," she said with a mirthless laugh, clearly not affected by our contact in the same way I was. "The worst part is it felt so good. I want to feel that kind of power again."

When she looked at me with terror in her eyes, it reminded me so much of the small child I once knew that a shiver ran down my spine. I released her, sitting back slightly to put some distance between us. As much as I wanted to be close to her, was drawn to her as a planet caught in the gravitational pull of a bright sun, I knew she didn't feel the same way.

"Emma, the axe is dangerous. It will control you if you allow it. Please think about turning it over to Alcina. I promise you, the mages can secure it so it can never harm anyone again. Just tell me where it is."

"Can the axe cause catastrophic destruction like what happened in Urusilim?" she asked.

I noticed she purposefully avoided admitting that she had been the cause of that destruction in Urusilim when she had lost Zane. "I honestly don't know what it can do, but I do know what *you* are capable of when you have access to power of the sort the axe can give you. I'm not saying you would do it again—you were young then, emotionally unstable…" I shrugged, leaving the rest of the sentence unspoken.

I could see fear, anger, and stubbornness warring within her, wanting to deny vehemently my allegations, yet also knowing the truth in my words.

"I just want you to be safe," I said. "It will be safer for everyone if we turn Sharur over to the Council. I give you my word that they will do the right thing with it."

Her eyes narrowed with suspicion. "And what is 'the right thing,' Alex? Why do the mages really want the axe so badly? If Alcina's motive really is to hide it away, then why does it matter who does the hiding? She doesn't need it to cross worlds. I would think there are probably several mages on the Council strong enough to open a rift for her and a select few to get through. That is how she got here, after all, isn't it?"

"She believes only the mages are strong enough to protect it and keep it out of the wrong hands. You know that."

"And who decides who 'the wrong hands' are? I'm sure her hands aren't clean of wrong-doing," Emma said, her back rigid and fists clenched in agitation.

"The Council exists to protect the people of Urusilim against those who could use their abilities to do harm. If her hands are unclean, they got that way for the right reasons."

"The ends justify the means and all that jazz? That sounds very noble, but let me ask you something, Alex. When you say, the 'people' of Urusilim, does that also mean the creatures, or are we just talking about humans?"

I could hear the accusation in her tone, and it confused me. Why was she questioning what was clearly an admirable purpose, one I had been training my entire life to uphold?

"Of course that doesn't include the creatures,"

I said. "They are the ones we are protecting people against. You've seen them yourself. They are strong, bloodthirsty, and unpredictable. Humans don't stand a chance against them."

"Would you put shifters into that category?"

"You mean like Eddie?" I asked with disdain. "Look, Emma, I allied with him temporarily because I had no other choice, but make no mistake, he and his kind are dangerous. I told you that when you first met him, and it was the truth. You can't trust him. He keeps you around because he hopes you will lead him to the axe. Then he'll take it for himself and use it for leverage to get what he wants."

"And what does he want?"

"How would I know?" I said, throwing up my hands in exasperation. This is not how I wanted this visit to go. "Maybe he'll go running back to Marduk with it to get back into his good graces, or maybe he'll use it as leverage against the Council to get them to end their protection of the humans."

"It seems a bit odd to me that everyone and their mother are fighting over this axe. Sure, opening a gate between worlds is powerful stuff, but I can't help thinking there is more going on here. Tell me, Alex, what else does Sharur do?"

The question took me off guard. Could it be that the axe might do more than open a rift between Earth and Urusilim? Although I had never contemplated the question, I wasn't naive enough to trust entirely that Alcina meant to secrete the axe away somewhere forever. Even if she did have intentions to use it, I always assumed she would use it primarily as a bargaining chip against Marduk. Was there more to the axe than she was letting on?

"Emma, I think you're making a leap in logic." I held my hands out toward her and spoke in low tones, as if trying to talk a jumper off a ledge. "First and foremost, it's just an axe. Its primary function is to cut and hack. The magic allows it to cut a tear between worlds instead of just cutting physical matter. It might be a magical weapon, but it's still just an inanimate object with limited utility. Believe me, there are lots of magical objects out there, and one thing they tend to have in common is that they were created for a singular purpose."

Emma looked at me askance. "You really believe it's just a mindless weapon that opens rifts," she asked, more as a statement than a question.

Before I could answer, she shook her head, and her entire body language changed. She transformed in front of me, relaxing and slipping back on her emotionless mask.

"I have to go," she said, standing abruptly.

"Emma, wait. I'm sorry if I said anything to upset you. That wasn't my intention."

"You didn't upset me, Alex. It's important for friends to be honest with each other." She leaned in and pressed her warm lips to my cheek, but before I could enjoy the sensation too much, she pulled back. "I'll check in on you again soon."

"Just be careful, Emma."

"I always am." She winked then was gone through the window.

Peering over the sill, I watched her dark form gracefully rappel down the wall on the grappling hook she had shot over the sill. When her feet touched the grass, I released the hook and dropped it down her. It retracted into a harpoon-like gun, and then she silently slipped into the shadows, heading for the forest that surrounded the sprawling property.

Once she was out of sight, a pang of emptiness filled my chest. I missed her already.

Chapter Five

EMMA

I left behind the old foreclosed mansion in which the mages had been squatting. The building was vacated months ago and lingered on the real estate market. It was surrounded by a heavily wooded property so none of the neighbors noticed the activity occurring in the house. They were holed up in the upper crust Long Island suburb of Cold Spring Harbor, a town that would forever make me think of Billy Joel and the first solo album he released of the same name. I started singing *She's Got a Way* quietly under my breath.

I heard Billy Joel's frequent concerts at Madison Square Garden were nothing short of fantastic, but my memory loss meant I had no nostalgic connection with the Piano Man. I had only recently learned his music when Jason downloaded every single Billy Joel album for me. Jason had been appalled when he found out that I didn't know who the singer was.

When I came out of my coma ten years ago, I spent most of my recovery time watching movies, not listening to music. Movies taught me about popular culture and helped me to feel more connected to a world that seemed so strange and foreign to me.

Now I knew the world had seemed so unfamiliar, not because of my memory loss, but because I had never been to Earth before then. The thought made me feel like a stranger who didn't belong anywhere, stuck between worlds, floating in the void of space. Alone.

I took the train from Long Island to Brooklyn. It was a long ride back to Eddie's row house in Bushwick, but it gave me plenty of time to think. I stared out the train window at the darkened streets and well-lit strip malls, while I continuously replayed the conversation with Alex in my head.

I believed he told the truth about his knowledge of the axe, or lack thereof. He didn't know that Sharur was sentient, but I had a feeling that Alcina knew and kept most, if not all, of the Council in the dark. But why?

Unfortunately, I couldn't even take an educated guess as to what she wanted with the axe since I didn't know the motives that drove her. I also didn't have a clue as to what the axe was truly capable of doing. I had been too afraid of it to even think about questioning it, let alone exploring its full potential.

What should I do now? I could go back to Eddie's place and get some sleep, hoping a new day would bring new clarity around my next move. I could go back to Grand Central Station and wring every last secret out of Sharur, even if it meant the literal death of me. After all, my death was probably more acceptable than the risk that I would destroy those around me by trying to wield a weapon I didn't understand. On the other hand, I could hunt some monsters and blow off this full head of steam that burned me up from the inside and, in the process, prove to myself that I didn't need that goddamn axe.

Maybe I should just turn it over to the mages. This didn't have to be my fight anymore. I could hunt the Monere with a good old-fashioned Glock as I had been doing for weeks and leave the magical bullshit to the bullshitters.

I got off the train and walked the four blocks to the building I now shared with eight other shifters—all male, by the way. I hated living there. I missed my very beautiful and very private apartment in Manhattan. Living in this building was like dorming with frat boys. Eddie was the most mature of the bunch, which wasn't saying much.

The 'Frat Boys,' as I liked to call them, lived in an old brownstone. It was gorgeous on the outside, with a red brick facade and white crown molding trimming the black front door and windows. A short flight of stone steps led to a small front stoop. I couldn't help myself and had installed planter boxes on each of the windows that dripped with petunias, verbenas, and daisies. I had thought the Frat Boys would have a collective heart attack when they saw the flowers, but they had let me have this one splash of pretty in their slob palace.

The inside of the building was almost devoid of furniture with the exception of a faded black, pleather couch; an old rear projection television that was the size of a small truck; three different video game systems; and mattresses on the floors of each bedroom. Their idea of decor was dirty laundry strewn about every room, and the place smelled of alcohol and stale pizza.

I snuck up the three flights to my room in the renovated attic. The sloping ceiling required me to stoop, which was why none of the guys wanted the space. It was annoying, but at least it was a shifter-free zone. It neared one a.m., and the clubs would just be getting started, so I had better hurry. I needed to blow off some steam with a few kills.

Quickly stripping off my uniform of black jeans, a retro T-shirt, and black shit-kicker boots, I changed into something much more club appropriate. I hated dressing like this, but if I expected to be let into Club Outpost, I had to dress the part.

I wore skinny black jeans that were so tight they looked painted on, and a pair of four-inch black stilettos accentuated the sleek curves of my calves and thighs. My matching black top was form fitting and cut low to my naval, exposing some generous cleavage. The back of the top was loose with folds of fabric that hid the bulge of the Glock holstered at my lower back. The outfit was sexy as hell; however, I thought the jeans made it slightly less sleazy than some other options. Of course, I might have been wrong about that.

Tiptoeing down the steps with my black stiletto sling-backs dangling from one finger, I managed to get out of the house unnoticed. When I reached the street corner, I breathed a sigh of relief and slipped on my fuck-me shoes. My feet immediately complained as the four-inch heels caused my entire body weight to shift onto my toes.

I hailed a cab to take me to Williamsburg, and when I gave the driver my destination, he appraised me in his rear view mirror.

"Are you sure that's where you want to go? Alone?"

I forced myself not to snap back that I could damn well take care of myself. This stranger was actually concerned for the well-being of a woman going into a questionable club alone; being out alone on the sometimes sketchy streets of New York was the least of my worries.

"I'm meeting my boyfriend there," I lied, which seemed to appease him.

A few blocks later, he dropped me off in front of a squat, unmarked building on a nondescript street corner in Williamsburg. The cement walls of the building were painted black, and the only thing that hinted at what might lie inside was the long line of scantily dressed young people that lined the front of the building, wrapping around the corner.

At the front of the line, standing next to a steel gray door was a man the size of a Mac truck holding a dainty clipboard. It looked like he could snap the thing in half if he so much as sneezed on it.

Club Outpost was an underground rave club that hadn't done very well at staying underground. It might not advertise itself, but word-of-mouth via social media had quickly made this "hidden gem" very high profile. The club was also quite selective about those who were let in, which caused demand to skyrocket even more; hence the line of Disney World proportions.

Moving toward the long line, I groaned, convinced I would never get in tonight. Not only was Club Outpost a favorite nightspot for twenty-somethings looking for a thrill, it was also a hot bed of creature activity. Eddie occasionally brought me here for our training sessions because of the greater than normal presence of Monere. They seemed to be drawn to the desperation, addiction, and greed rolling off many of the humans who frequented the place. I guessed it had something to do with predators picking off the weakest members of a population.

I looked dejectedly down the long line of tramps, degenerates, and wannabes when a sharp whistle turned my head to where the bouncer waved me closer. I looked around, thinking for a moment that he must be beckoning someone else. When I realized I stood alone, and he was actually addressing me, I stepped toward the door.

"Yo, Angel, you can go in," he said in a voice that sounded like sandpaper rubbing against gravel. He wore a tight AC/DC T-shirt that showed off every muscle on his massive, almost seven-foot frame. His bald head shone in the single spotlight above the door, yet for all of his physical presence, I thought his expression might have softened a bit when he looked at me.

"Hey, John," I greeted the big man I had met once before when I had been here with Eddie, surprised that he remembered me. "Angel?" I asked.

He simply winked and opened the door for me.

I didn't expect to be let in so easily, but I wasn't about to pass up the opportunity; therefore, I stepped through the black curtain hanging on the inside of the door. It blocked the view into the club for those waiting on the street, probably to keep the club shrouded in mystery and increase the patrons' desire to get inside.

The sights and sounds of the club unfolded before me. Club Outpost had set up shop in a converted warehouse, so it was spacious and airy. The ceiling soared two stories above the dance floor with zigzags of industrial pipes. Along the perimeter walls of the second story were catwalks where professional dancers gyrated around stripper poles, clad in bright-colored masks, feathers, tiaras, and other accessories that made them look like they belonged on a Mardi Gras float.

Below the dancers, the floor stretched out toward a raised stage against the back wall of the building. On the stage was the club's DJ Lex, rocking a pair of cans on his ears as he slid and shifted the knobs on his control board. Along the wall to the right was a long bar, lit up in blue and pink neon. Backlit glass shelves holding every brand of alcohol known to man reached about twenty feet above the heads of the bartenders. Clearly, it was mainly for show because there was no way anyone could reach that high without a ladder.

The club was packed with sweaty bodies grinding provocatively to the heavy thump of the techno music. I pushed through them, trying not to jostle anyone too hard, but some of the women seemed to enjoy being bumped into. They used it as an excuse to fall forward into the arms of the guys they flirted with.

I was here to work. If I could bag myself a Monere first thing, I might be able to spend the rest of the night enjoying myself on the dance floor. Closing my eyes, I tapped into that spot at the back of my neck that always seemed to know when an otherworldly presence was near. I had never done this before except in training with Eddie, but I had to try.

The tingling sensation exploded down my spine and rushed into my skull. I cried out in pain, but was drowned out by the thumping music. I immediately released my focus until the feeling subsided. There were too many Monere here—at least five, but maybe more. They overwhelmed my senses, making it difficult for me to get a clean read on any one of them.

I decided to give up that effort and hope I got lucky luring them in as a single girl alone at the bar. I finally reached the bar after elbowing my way between a group of clean-cut jocks in baseball T-shirts and a gaggle of girls in slinky, black dresses, one of which wore a fuzzy tiara that proclaimed this was her bachelorette party. The girls were clearly getting their drink on, and it was starting to show. The boys eyed them appreciatively, trying to decide who would hit on which girl. None of them looked very happy when I stepped between them.

I raised my hand to get the attention of Ivy, the bartender. She wore low slung, leather pants with a glittery belt that showed off her curvy hips and a half top revealing her diamond-stud belly ring, and her blond hair fell in waves around her shoulders. She was stunning and got hit on by patrons constantly, but she turned them all down with gentle humor. She was in a serious relationship with the club owner, whom I had never met.

"Hey, Angel," she shouted above the din with a broad smile.

"Why does everyone keep calling me that?" I yelled back, leaning farther across the bar so we could better hear each other.

She shrugged. "It just seems fitting." My brow furrowed in confusion, but before I could question her further, she asked, "The usual?"

The thought of a strong drink distracted me for a moment, and I nodded my head. She turned and began making my dirty martini. She made one hell of a good drink, just the right amount of salty to balance the burn of the vodka.

"It's a crazy night tonight," she said, pouring the briny liquid into a frosted martini glass. "There are always weirdos sneaking around the club on nights like this, like that guy over there." She nodded her head down the bar, and I followed her direction.

Although the bar was jammed, I easily found the guy she meant. He stood out in the crowd at six feet tall with wavy, black hair and piercing, amber eyes. He wore dark jeans that hugged his perfect ass and a tight, white T-shirt that defined every muscle. Cords of veins snaked up his arms, giving him a strong, dangerous look. He leaned with his back against the bar in a casual stance, but his eyes were alert, scoping out the dance floor as if he was looking for someone specific.

He must have felt my eyes on him because he turned and met my gaze, and a slow smile crept across his full lips as he pushed off the bar, stalking toward me with a graceful fluidity. It was hard not to drink him in from head to toe, admiring the way his jeans clung tightly to muscled thighs and his V-neck shirt revealed just a hint of smooth, tanned chest.

When he reached me, he leaned down, placing his lips close to my ear. "Dance with me," he said in a rich baritone.

His sweet and spicy scent flooded my senses, causing my skin to flare with heat. He was just the type of guy I would have gone home with a few weeks ago, but now things were different. I had too many other men in my life who left me spinning as if I just got off a carnival ride that was thrilling and sickening at the same time. However, it couldn't hurt to enjoy one dance before I had to get to work.

Chapter Six

ZANE

I noticed Ash the instant she walked through the door of the club. She calls herself Emma now, but she will always be Ashnan to me. My sweet, fiery, stunningly beautiful Ashnan.

I stood against the wall of the club near the door as she walked right by without noticing me; the breeze she left in her wake carried the faint scent of jasmine and vanilla. I breathed deeply, trying to capture it before my senses were once again overcome by the haze of sweat and alcohol.

I wasn't entirely surprised to see her here. After all, what better place to hunt Monere than at the source? If I was being honest with myself, perhaps I had subconsciously arranged my meeting to take place at the club in the hopes that I might see her.

Now that she was in the same room with me, so close that I could reach her in only a few steps, I could do nothing except stand there and drink her in. It had been a long time since I had seen her wearing anything other than tactical combat gear, and the sight of her in those tight jeans and low-cut top that revealed every delectable curve was enough to ignite a war in my brain.

I knew what I was supposed to do, what I had been ordered to do, but I didn't want to. I wanted to touch her, take her, but not in the way my brain screamed at me to do. The beast that had been planted in my mind tried to crowd out my consciousness and take over, but if I let him, Ash would be as good as dead.

The world began to take on a red tint, a telltale sign that the beast was winning. It had a thirst for blood and liked to remind me of it. While that familiar blinding rage welled up inside, my heart pounded, and sweat broke out on my forehead. With clenched teeth, I forced myself to take deep, calming breaths until I pushed the beast back into its cage. My vision cleared, and the world was no longer the color of blood.

The beast grew harder to control every day, but thoughts of Ash could sometimes subdue it. By the gods, I missed her. Some days, the longing was so acute it felt like I had been gutted, heart and soul. The memory of her and the fruitless hope that we might be together again was the only thing keeping me connected to the last thread of humanity I had left. I clung to it like a drowning man thrown a life preserver. Regardless, the beast whispered to me that it would just be easier to slip under the waves of its influence and let it take over, and

I knew he was right. I didn't know how much longer I could hold on.

I took a step toward my Ash when a woman moved in front of me, barricading my access to the only person in the room who mattered. The woman was smoking hot in a Barbie doll sort of way: tall, blond, breasts the size of balloons — and just as plastic — and wearing a hot pink mini dress with matching lipstick. Thanks to the effects of the air conditioning, it was obvious she wasn't wearing a bra.

She might have looked like a vacant Barbie doll, but her eyes were bright and laser-focused. She struck me as the type who couldn't resist a challenge. She moved in close, pressing her artificially enlarged breasts against my chest, and leaned close to my ear. "Can I buy you a drink?" she asked in a throaty, seductive voice. Then she had the fucking nerve to touch me, placing her hand on my bicep and running it down my arm.

I jerked away and threw her a threatening glare before I sidestepped Barbie, trying to get my eyes back on Ash. However, she was no longer standing at the bar, talking to the bartender. Every muscle in my body tensed, thinking Ash might have left while this plastic bitch tried to get my attention. My eyes darted around the packed dance floor, desperate to find her.

Barbie wouldn't accept the brush-off and stepped in front of me again, ignoring the fact that I had just rejected her.

"Or we can just skip the drink and go back to my place," she said, raising her hand to touch me again.

Before she could make physical contact, I snatched

her wrist. I could snap her bones so easily and snuff the life out of her with no more effort than it would take to kill a fly. A tint of red bled into my vision, and the beast growled at me to do it, yet the fear in Barbie's eyes stopped me dead.

What kind of monster have I become? I don't want to be the beast. With a herculean effort, I willed my grip to loosen, gritting my teeth with the effort of overcoming Marduk's programming. It took several long seconds for the beast to recede and my hand to respond. It wasn't always possible for me to influence the actions of the monster in my head, but it worked this time, letting me set the woman free, and she ran into the crowd shaking. No doubt, she would find a man in the club to comfort her in her time of need.

I knew I should leave the club. I couldn't risk losing that fine thread of control I currently had. I would only put Ash in danger.

I turned to leave, taking one step then two toward the door, but the third step wouldn't come. I froze. I couldn't bring myself to walk away from her, knowing she was so close.

Before I could even consciously register what I was doing, I spun on my heel and marched deeper into the club, scrutinizing the crowd for a glimpse of her dark hair and olive skin. There she was, on the dance floor with… *Shit!* What the fuck was she doing dancing with that thing? Did she even know what it was? Her casual smile and ease around him told me she didn't have a clue. I had to get to her.

Rather than delicately pick my way through gaps in

the crowd, I unceremoniously jostled bodies out of my path, making a beeline for my woman. When I reached the couple, I stood behind Ash as her dance partner looked up, noticing me for the first time, and his face blanched, turning a pasty white. His mouth opened and closed, as if he was about to offer an explanation then thought the better of it. Then he simply turned and disappeared into the crowd of gyrating bodies.

Ash didn't seem to notice his departure, and I realized her eyes were closed as she let go and allowed the throbbing beat of the music to wash over her, her hips swaying while her arms were lifted over her head.

My eyes drifted down to her perfect ass, and I took a moment to admire the way she moved. She was all sleek muscle and soft curves, and my mouth watered at the thought of placing my hands on her waist and sliding them underneath her top.

As I stepped in close, pressing my front to her back, she stiffened for a moment then inhaled deeply, relaxing under my touch, and began moving again. This time, we moved together. I placed my hands just below her breasts, but the temptation to cup those soft globes was too great, so I slid down to her hips instead, holding her against me.

She lifted her arms and wrapped them around my neck, arching her back and resting her head against my chest. I buried my face in her neck and breathed in her jasmine scent deeply. I wanted so badly to place small kisses along her throat, tasting every inch of her skin, but I didn't want to alert her to the fact that she wasn't with her original dance partner. I wanted this moment to last forever.

A rare moment of peace descended over me, and the ever-present growl of the beast in my head quieted. I could think of nothing except how much I wanted to rewind time to when we were both young and madly in love, when my mind had been my own.

I thought back to our last moments together on Urusilim before all hope for a future together was violently ripped away. So brave and so foolish, Ash had escaped her father to find me. I stayed in the village after yet another failed negotiation attempt with Marduk. Alcina had just learned of my secret relationship with Ash and had forbidden me from seeing her again. I had been ordered back home, never to return. However, when she found me, I realized I couldn't let her go.

She might have been only a teenager at the time, and I wasn't much older, but I asked her to marry me, aware we needed to find another way to be together. That was the first time I took her to my bed. I remembered the feel of her naked skin against mine, the taste of her body, and the way she responded to my touch.

As the past and the present crashed into each other, I knew she must have felt my arousal, but it didn't stop her from grinding into me. I growled deep in my throat at the sensation, her hips moving rhythmically against me. Unable to control myself any longer, I buried my face in her neck and pressed my lips to her overheated skin.

She dropped her head to the side, inviting me to continue, so I did. I kissed that sensitive spot right behind her ear and drew a moan from her. Giving into the temptation, my hands travelled from her hips, up her waist, and settled teasingly just below her breasts. She arched her back, silently willing me to keep moving upward as her fingers tangled in my long hair and tugged me even closer.

I could take her right now; she wouldn't resist. Images flooded my mind of pulling her into a dark corner of the club, peeling off those sexy jeans, and sinking deep into that sweet flesh. My muscles twitched as I struggled to stop my body from acting on those thoughts. I knew I wouldn't be able to control my actions if I let my baser instincts take over. The beast could get control. I was still under orders to capture her — kill her if necessary — and I wouldn't be able to defy my programming for very long. It was time to go.

In one smooth movement, I pulled away and disappeared into the anonymous mass of sweaty, gyrating bodies. It was only then that I realized I was late for my meeting.

Shit. Duncan isn't known for his patience, I thought with more annoyance than concern.

I slipped behind the stage and found the metal stairs to the catwalk above. Picking my way along the narrow walk, I found the black painted door that blended in with the walls of the club and knocked twice. It cracked open then swung wide after a moment, and the creature stood aside, allowing me entry.

I stole one last glance back at Ash, standing alone and beautiful on the dance floor as she spun in a slow circle, searching for her lost dance partner.

Chapter Seven

EMMA

I turned in confusion, not entirely certain who I was actually looking for. I had gotten myself so lost in the music and my imagination that, for a moment, I had been sure I was dancing with Zane. That strong body and amazing spicy scent had been so familiar. God, my mind was playing crazy tricks on me.

When I had first walked onto the dance floor with the mysterious stranger, I had turned my back to him and closed my eyes, trying to block the strange guilt I felt. Who did I really think I was betraying? Zane and I had no future together. I would mourn that loss maybe for the rest of my life, but I accepted it. Then Alex was always so distant, giving nothing away. We had grown to trust each other, and were now close allies, but even if I might be interested in something more with him, I just didn't think he was that into me. And Jason would never be more than a friend.

I had no reason to feel guilty. Even so, I started moving my hips tentatively, still uncomfortable. Then when the stranger's body pressed against my back, he had felt bigger and more solid than I expected him to be. The hard muscle and heat radiating from him felt sultry against the bare skin of my back, and the scents of mint and sandalwood floated to me, smelling like Zane. My mind then went into a tailspin, and I lost myself in the sensations of touch and smell, imagining it was Zane at my back.

I wanted it to be him, so I pretended it was and let myself go. It was fucking hot, and I would have gone anywhere, done anything with him in that moment. Then he was gone.

Noticing movement on the overhead catwalk, I looked up as a figure disappeared through a door that had been camouflaged against the black walls. It was dark in the club, and the spinning colored lights never illuminated that particular area, so I didn't get a good look at the large man. Nevertheless, for a moment, I thought I saw a blur of long, dark hair. Then I blinked and he was gone.

Shit, my imagination was running away with me. I had Zane on the brain. It couldn't have been him, though. If he ever saw me again, he would be more likely to try to kill me than dance with me. I needed to focus back on the real reason I had come here.

I moved back to the bar, ordering another dirty martini from Ivy while observing the crowd. It wasn't long before my attention landed on the guy who had asked me to dance. He had a steel grip on the arm of a sexy blonde in a hot pink mini dress, and it looked like she was yelling at him to let go of her. He clearly didn't understand that no meant no.

Something darted out of his mouth so quickly that I almost missed it. Then the blonde stopped her struggling and went limp, her head lolling to one side. I had intended to intervene, anyway, but now I left my drink behind on the bar and urgently pushed my way toward the couple.

The man draped her arm across his shoulders and held her around the waist, dragging her to the exit of the club. Anyone would mistake her for a chick who had partied too hard with too much alcohol and maybe some X, but I knew that wasn't the case.

I rudely shoved sweaty bodies out of my path, getting plenty of curses and dirty looks in the process, but I couldn't reach the couple before he whisked her through the door and into the humid night air.

I made it outside several seconds after them, fearing I was already too far behind. I hit the sidewalk at a run, my head frantically swinging back and forth, looking for them, but as I suspected, they were gone. That poor girl.

If I was right about what I thought I had seen coming out of his mouth, her captor was clearly Monere. What would it do to her? I didn't even know what it was, but there was something disgusting living inside of that human facade. I couldn't just stand here and let it get away, but I had no idea which way to go.

Now that I was outside of the club, away from the interference caused by multiple Monere, I might have a chance at detecting this one creature. I took a few deep breaths to still my pounding heart and racing mind, and concentrated my mysterious sixth sense on the target.

The tingling sensation bloomed to life as soon as I called on it, as if it had been waiting for me. I gathered the energy and pushed it out into the city, searching for the creature. In my mind, I could visualize the streets and buildings as my senses moved through the neighborhood. About three blocks to the left, the tingling sensation spiked, and I knew I had found them.

Snapping my eyes open, I broke into a full sprint, and it didn't take long to catch up with them. The girl moaned and whimpered softly in protest, seemingly unable to control her muscles well enough to put up any sort of resistance. I debated stopping the Monere right then and there, yet I wanted to know what it planned. What if it was bringing her back to a den of creatures? Now that I had eyes on her, she was in no immediate danger. I could use this opportunity to gather some intel and possibly get a chance to kill more of them.

I slowed my pace and kept to the shadows, stalking my prey as the creature turned down a set of cement steps into a below street-level restaurant. With no name on the outside of the building, just a small, nondescript placard sat on the sidewalk that said *Sushi*.

When he pushed the girl through the front door, I crouched at the top of the steps to peer in through the front windows. Always prepared, I slipped off my heels and pulled the Glock from its hiding place underneath the back of my top.

The restaurant only fit ten cheap, wooden tables with folding chairs that were placed toward the front of the room. The back of the space was taken up by a small sushi bar lined with four stools. The room was sparsely decorated with only a set of crossed katana swords hanging on the wall behind the sushi bar. The swords looked more than simply decorative — the handles had a well-worn appearance as if they had been used often, but the blades were sharp and polished showing they had been cared for. Perhaps they were the chef's family heirlooms. The remaining walls were bare, and the floor was cracked, white linoleum. A few tables contained patrons, and one sushi chef manned the bar, intently slicing up something red and raw.

Once the creature dropped the woman into a chair closest to the front door, she would have fallen limply to the floor, but she managed to gather the strength to shift her weight so she fell forward onto the table. The kidnapper waved his hands, yelling something I couldn't make out to the patrons. They stared at him dubiously, making no move to leave. Then he reached up and put his fingers into his mouth, pulling his face wide open. It cracked and split until the hole was large enough to allow another creature's mouth to emerge, soft and wet with teeth as thin and sharp as needles.

That got the patrons' attention.

I dodged out of the way as terrified guests stampeded past me in a desperate scramble to escape, and the chef was right behind them still holding his sushi knife in one hand and a piece a raw flesh in the other. However, one diner remained, sitting calmly, dabbing his sweaty forehead with a napkin. He was rotund, easily over three hundred pounds, with a balding head and beady eyes.

The kidnapper closed his mouth, looking human again, and took a seat across the table from the man I decided to nickname The Blob. Jerking his thumb in the girl's direction, the kidnapper said something I couldn't hear. The Blob eyed the girl salaciously from head to toe, licking his lips as if she was a steak dinner, and then slid a paper bag across the table.

Her captor fumbled in haste to open it and pulled out a wad of cash. I could almost feel the excitement rolling off the creature in waves, like an addict who had just gotten the means to score his next hit. He gave The Blob a salute then stood to leave. It was time to make a move.

I practically flew down the small flight of stairs and burst through the front door, my Glock aimed and the safety off. The tingling at the nape of my neck confirmed the obese man was a creature, as well, but he didn't seem capable of making any sudden moves, so I decided to ignore him for now and focus on the more immediate threat. I aimed my gun at the kidnapper.

That was a mistake. The Blob opened his mouth and hacked up a ball of bright green phlegm, spitting it in my direction. I ducked, and it splattered the wall behind me. I expected acid, but instead, the phlegm began to wriggle and move.

I stepped to the side, keeping my gun on the kidnapper while watching the progress of the ooze. It crept to the floor, and slimy tendrils reached for my boot.

"What the hell?" I yelled, hopping back. I didn't know what that thing did, but I was sure I didn't want to find out.

Taking advantage of my distraction, the kidnapper opened his mouth wide to release the monster inside. As before, he pulled his mouth open, but this time, he kept going and drew the human skin fully back to completely uncover another head.

The thing inside was sickly gray and coated in a thick, glistening substance like oil that probably helped the human skin slide off more easily. The head was bulbous on a thin stalk of a neck, and it was almost all mouth and tiny razor teeth with insect-like eyes that were so small they were easy to miss. This thing's priority was clearly eating.

It came for me just as The Blob spewed three more gobs of phlegm in my direction. I threw myself forward in a dive, and they landed in thick, wet plops where I had just been standing. I managed to avoid the mini blobs yet landed right at the feet of the kidnapper, pretty much serving myself up to him on a platter. *Fucking perfect.*

As he stepped on my gun hand, grinding it into the floor with his stiff dress shoes, I cried out in agony, my pained fingers releasing the Glock. He then grabbed me by the biceps and, with surprising ease, lifted me clear off the floor. Feet dangling, he drew my face to his hideous, slavering mouth, and a tongue reached out with a barb on the end, glistening with a drop of the paralytic poison he had injected the girl with. Damn! I had forgotten about the girl.

I kicked out, crushing his knee joint, and he fell to the floor, dropping me on his way down. I scrambled for my gun, grabbing it and spinning around just as one of those green gobs propelled itself toward the now semi-conscious girl, still seated at the front of the restaurant. She saw it coming and let out a shrill cry.

After years of practice shooting guns at moving targets, I managed to hit the mass on the first shot. It splattered in mid-air, droplets of goo spraying across the floor and spattering the front window. I had to get this girl outside before coming back and finishing off these creatures.

I sprinted for her just as another ball of goo hurtled toward her face. With a spin kick, I caught it with my boot and sent the thing flying toward the kidnapper, still clutching his knee on the floor.

When the ooze landed on the kidnapper's hands, he immediately screamed in terror, waving and rubbing his hands, trying to get the substance off, but it was like glue. It slid up his arm toward that open maw, and the kidnapper clawed frantically at the ooze, but to no avail.

The gob slipped its way into the Monere's mouth, and he seized on the floor, shaking and thrashing violently. Clear mucus leaked from his eyes as the substance attacked his brain.

I should have been dragging the woman out of the restaurant by that point, but I couldn't tear my eyes from the sight, and neither could she as she screamed bloody murder at the scene unfolding before her. I couldn't blame her, but God help me, I still wanted to slap her and tell her to shut the hell up. Some savior of the human race I was.

The kidnapper's seizure stopped after a few seconds, and I thought he was dead, but then his body twitched. He slowly rose to his feet with uncertain jerky movements, like a newborn fawn trying to walk for the first time. His face was slack and eyes vacant. The gob had taken over his body, turning him into a zombie of sorts.

As the possessed creature lurched toward me, I aimed my weapon and put three bullets into his head. He staggered backward at the force, and then straightened and kept coming. I glanced to my side briefly to see two more globs sliding closer to my feet, and the one I had shot was reassembling itself, the splatters sliding back down the walls and windows to rejoin their siblings.

There was no winning this one. Shooting the mini blobs and the zombie kidnapper had absolutely no effect. My best strategy was to cut my losses, grab the girl, and run out the door.

As I turned to do just that, I saw that the gobs had combined to form a single gooey mass, and it tried to pull itself up into a vertical shape close to my height. It had also positioned itself directly in front of the door, cutting off my only means of escape.

Chapter Eight

EMMA

With the living glob of phlegm ahead of me and the zombie kidnapper behind me, I had to pick my battle. I chose the zombie, emptying my gun into the oncoming Monere to slow him down and buy me a few extra seconds.

The zombie fell backward, smashing into a table and turning it to splinters. While he flailed, getting back to his feet, I leapt over the top of the sushi bar and dropped into a crouch on the other side.

My shaking hands flew over shelves and yanked out drawers, scattering soup bowls, sushi plates, and plastic take-out containers in my desperation to find something, anything I could use as a weapon. There was nothing here except serving items, a small gas stove with a tempura fryer, and a few bottles of alcohol to make a limited selection of mixed drinks. Somehow, I didn't think chopsticks were going to cut it, either. I silently cursed the chef for running out of the restaurant with the only sushi knife in the damn place.

Shuffling and scraping sounds alerted me to the zombie heading my way. The top of his bulbous head came into view, as did the table leg he held over his shoulder like a baseball bat. It came swinging down, smashing into the refrigerated glass case that housed the raw fish.

I threw up my arms, shielding myself as best as I could from the shards raining down around me. Something wet and cold dropped onto my arm, and I jerked back, trying to fling the slimy thing off me. It landed at my feet, swollen and weeping fresh blood. It looked like some sort of organ, though none I had ever seen before and I ate a lot of sushi. Maybe it was some weird, exotic fish.

Tearing my eyes from the gruesome delicacy, I looked up and saw my salvation. Mounted on the wall behind the sushi bar were the two crossed Japanese swords.

Another blow from the table leg rained down on the bar, almost slicing the flimsy counter in half. The next strike would obliterate my shelter completely, leaving me exposed and vulnerable. Bunching my muscles and focusing all of my energy into my thighs, I leapt straight up from my crouched position. Then I grabbed the hilts of each sword and, still airborne, lifted my knees, pushing off the wall with both feet. With a graceful back flip, I soared over the shattered sushi bar and the zombie, landing in a loose fighter's stance, holding a deadly katana in each hand.

With complete disregard for the danger he was in, the zombie lurched around to face me then attacked. He swung the table leg at me as if he was Babe Ruth. I caught it between the blades of the swords and, with a quick twist, wrenched the club from his hands. It clattered to a stop at the feet of The Blob, who continued to eat his meal, watching the proceedings with only mild interest. I would deal with him later.

The swords felt light and comfortable in my hands, thanks to Eddie's training. It pissed me off to admit he had been right about my gun not being the solution in every situation.

I twirled the swords, familiarizing myself with the feel of them. Then the zombie lunged at me again, reaching out with his hands. In two quick slashes, his oily balloon head fell to the ground with a dull thud, and the top half of his body slid from the bottom half where I had cut cleanly through his torso.

That might have taken care of the vessel, but the ooze wasn't affected. It poured forth from his eyes, nose, and mouth, sliding across the floor to join the larger mass that had moved into the center of the restaurant. It seemed to be waiting for a command from The Blob, who had his hand held up, signaling for it to wait.

My eyes shifted to the girl who was still in a chair in the far corner by the door. With gritted teeth, sweat beading her forehead, and mascara running in rivulets down her cheeks, she was intent on willing her body to move. Her face was terrified, but the paralytic effects of the poison seemed to be slowly wearing off as her fingers twitched.

Turning to The Blob, I said, "Why don't you call back your mucus monster, and I'll let you walk away from this in one piece, not like your friend there?" I nodded toward the wet, bloody pieces of the zombie littering the floor.

He chuckled deeply. "Why don't you leave, and I'll depart peacefully with the girl and my pulmonata?" he said, referring to his gooey offspring. "The way I see it, I have the distinct advantage here. Your flimsy swords cannot harm my child."

Yuck. He just referred to that giant ball of snot as his child.

"What do you want with the girl?"

"There are plenty of desperate Monere out there who aren't as fortunate as I am to have a human-like form. Some need a human to wear so they may come out of hiding and live a normal life. Others just need to eat or mate," he said, eyeing me from head to toe. I shuddered, knowing he was picturing me naked. "My job is to supply them with what they need."

Bile rose in my throat at the thought of what could have happened to that poor woman. How many other humans had already suffered the same fate? And here I was, practically playing games with these creatures, refusing to take up the most powerful weapon I had against them because of my own fear. How many had died or been sold into slavery already because of my own cowardice?

Enraged, I spun my dual swords and lunged toward

the smug bastard. Fear flashed across his face, but he was too big and lumbering to even attempt an escape. Instead, he spat mucus globs at me, one after the other. My spinning swords sliced them to ribbons before they could touch me, splatters of goo flying across the restaurant and landing on almost every exposed surface.

By the time I reached him and split him open, chest to pelvis, spilling his innards onto the floor between his feet, he had let loose almost a dozen zombie-making children.

Pausing to catch my breath, I heard the woman by the door scream, "Behind you!"

I spun around to see every last droplet of ooze moving down the walls and along floors. If that stuff escaped the restaurant, it could infect hundreds of humans. Given the disgusting filth that already stuck to public streets and sidewalks in the city, green ooze would just be more globs stuck to the bottom of shoes and carried home to infect entire families.

I had to kill it, but how? Slicing through it with a sword or shooting it with a gun just splattered it into smaller, harder to fight pieces. Would Sharur have been able to kill it?

I thought back to the incident in the subway tunnel. Somehow, the axe had affected me, causing that surge of power throughout my body. It had turned me into an explosive force. I was willing to bet that force could have taken care of this creature, but I was fresh out of magical axes at the moment. I needed another idea.

What could kill without tearing through a body? Poison would do it, but I was also fresh out of arsenic.

Fire. It was my only chance. It would hopefully burn those things to ash. However, it wasn't as if I had matches on me.

The slime finally made its move once it realized the signal would not come from its father. I leapt back, swinging one of the swords, trying to block the creature, but mostly succeeded in making more of them. The gobs I had cut off the main body kept coming for me, their numbers increasing as I tried to fight them off. Soon one would slip past my defenses, and I would become nothing more than a mindless vehicle.

I stepped back, almost tripping over the remains of the smashed sushi bar. Dodging another phlegm projectile, I stumbled and reached back to steady myself on a part of the bar that remained standing. Then I looked over my shoulder, my eyes landing on the single gas burner stove and pot full of cooking oil for frying up tempura. That would work.

I grabbed a bottle of cheap tequila from the shelf and crouched low, trying to use the remnants of the sushi bar for cover. Opening the bottle, the sharp odor of alcohol stung my nose. I stuffed the neck with paper napkins picked up from the floor where they had scattered. Crawling over to the gas burner, I was reaching up to ignite the flame when slime hit the bare skin of my shoulder with a sickening splat. I tried prying it off, but my fingers couldn't get a grip on the slippery mass. A green tendril reached toward my ear, probing for an opening into my body.

It took all of my courage and willpower to release my grip on the ooze, praying I would be faster than it would. I jabbed the neck of the bottle into the burner, and the napkins caught fire immediately.

Placing the flames to the ooze on my shoulder, the heat scalded my neck and face, but I gritted my teeth and bore the searing pain. The slimy critter shot off my shoulder, giving me hope that my plan would work.

I tossed the crudely constructed Molotov cocktail over the sushi bar as I would a live grenade, aiming for the main body of ooze in the center of the room. The bottle hit the floor in front of the creature, splashing it with fiery liquid.

It let out a high-pitched shriek, gyrating violently. Pieces of it separated from the main body, seeking safety from the flames; however, the surrounding tables and chairs caught fire, engulfing the nearby escapees.

I had to let the entire restaurant burn. It was the only way to ensure no remaining globs would be left. My eyes moved to the table near the door, concerned for the woman. However, I shouldn't have been.

She had regained control of her body, but instead of immediately getting the hell out of there, she had taken the time to take out her cell phone, and I could hear the furious camera clicks as she photographed the entire scene. Then she slipped out the door before I could reach her and smash that damn phone. That couldn't be good.

Looking around me, I saw my plan had worked. The gobs of ooze bubbled in the searing heat, liquefying until even the liquid burned off, leaving behind a sticky black residue. There was no coming back from that.

Choking on smoke and the pungent smell of fried green ooze, I slipped and fell on fish and other unrecognizable flesh as I made my way over the sushi bar debris on my hands and knees. The fire was spreading rapidly through the restaurant, fueling itself on napkins, paper bags, kitchen towels, and wooden chopsticks. I crawled blindly, my eyes burning and watering from the thick, roiling smoke. I lost all sense of direction, praying I was moving toward the front door.

Fear flooded my system as oxygen was sucked from the room. My lungs burned and seized as I gasped for air, only pulling in acrid, foul-tasting smoke. The flames licked at my clothing and jumped to my jeans, and excruciating pain lanced up my thigh.

Rolling to my back, I looked down at my leg and saw that my pants were on fire. I screamed and frantically swatted at the flames with my hands, barely noticing blisters forming on my fingers.

The expanding flames would eventually engulf my body before I could find my way to the door. Hell, I didn't even know if was crawling in the right direction. This was it for me. I was done for, and this was not one of the better ways to go.

Chapter Nine

EMMA

Just when I thought I would be consumed like so much dry kindling, a cool, wet sensation poured over my body, and the relief was so intense I went limp, savoring the beautiful respite. Then arms slid under my knees and behind my back, lifting me off the floor while trying to avoid rubbing against the burns on my leg.

Even with the close proximity, I couldn't make out my savior through my smoke-tortured eyes. At that moment, I didn't care if it was a mass murderer or bloodsucking vampire—same thing, really—taking me out of that building. I rested my head against a strong chest, grateful for the arms cradling me gently.

When we exited the building, even the thick, humid air felt cool and refreshing, soothing my raw throat. My lungs were locked up tight, and it took every ounce of effort just to pull in a breath. Once I finally did, I gagged and coughed until my stomach ached and my lungs screamed with every inhale.

My rescuer set me down on the sidewalk across the street from the restaurant and gently rubbed my back until the coughing fit subsided. Looking back at the building, I saw that the restaurant was fully consumed in flames, and the fire was spreading to the surrounding storefronts. I felt the weight of guilt on my shoulders at the immense loss that would be suffered by those business owners. If it hadn't been for the Monere and me, the livelihoods of those business owners would not be in jeopardy.

The heat from the ravenous flames pressed against my raw skin while billowing clouds of smoke poisoned the air. The pain of my burns returned as the cool water on my skin evaporated under the oppressive temperatures. Gritting my teeth and trying to bare it in silence, an involuntary moan escaped my lips, and my vision went white at the edges as my brain sought to escape the searing agony.

Just as I felt consciousness slipping away, blessed relief returned as something ice cold was applied to my injuries.

I blinked rapidly until my vision cleared and looked up at my rescuer for the first time.

"Alex," I breathed.

He smiled in relief, but the concern never left his eyes. "I'm glad I decided to look for you tonight. I didn't like the way we left things earlier and wanted to apologize."

"How…? How did you find me?" I asked, struggling to sit up.

"As I told you once before, I wouldn't be much of a mage if I wasn't able to pull off a few tricks here and there."

I smirked. "Still as cryptic as ever."

His grin widened, and I couldn't help noticing how his ice blue eyes sparkled when he smiled, his dimples punctuating his cheeks. He was a good-looking guy, but the intensely serious demeanor and stoic expression he always wore were intimidating and off-putting to many people. When a smile broke out across his handsome face, though, it was as if someone had pulled aside a curtain and let brilliant sunshine into a darkened room. He was beautiful and electrifying.

Alas, the smile slipped from his face as the sirens grew closer. The police and fire department would be here in minutes. "Can you stand?" Alex asked. "We should probably get out of here. We don't want to be on the scene of an arson fire with two dead bodies inside. Not to mention, you are covered in the blood and other stuff of the victims." He eyed my blood stained and burned clothing, crinkling his nose at the smell and sight of me.

"Good point," I said, allowing Alex to help me unsteadily to my feet, which was made more difficult from the inability of my burned leg to bend.

Fear pierced me at the realization that my leg wasn't responding to commands from my brain. Looking down at it, I saw that a coating of thick ice encased me from thigh to ankle, immobilizing my leg yet holding the burn pains at bay.

Locking eyes with Alex, I said, "Thank you," trying to put the full weight and sincerity of my gratitude into those two simple words.

He didn't respond for a few seconds, letting the intensity of my appreciation wash over him, and then he gave his head a small shake. "I'll always be there for you, Emma, no matter what. There are no thanks necessary. Now let's get out of here."

"Wait," I said, suddenly remembering the woman I had come here to save. "There was a woman."

"Don't worry. She made it out. I saw her get into a cab and leave just when the fire started."

"That's great, but she got a ton of photos of me in there, killing creatures and setting fires. If she sends those to the cops, I'm in big trouble." When working as a mercenary, I hadn't worried much about the authorities because I was always meticulously careful about ensuring I wasn't seen, and I cleaned up after myself so no evidence was left behind. In years of doing that kind of work, I had never once come even close to being caught.

"Shit," Alex said, hesitating over our next move, probably trying to figure out if there was still a chance we could catch up with the woman. The sounds of sirens drew closer, and flashes of red lights reflected off storefront windows on the far corner of the block. "We'll deal with that when we can, but right now, we need to move."

He draped my arm across his shoulder and wrapped his other arm around my waist, pretty much dragging me down the street, away from the lights and sirens. When he got to the corner, he picked a random direction and kept moving. He maintained a steady pace for a good twenty minutes, snaking our way through Brooklyn and putting as much distance between us and the first responders as possible.

Just when we thought we had lost them and slowed our pace, a set of headlights bloomed at our backs. As with all of the other cars that had driven past us during our escape, I tensed, praying it was just a random driver and not a cop car searching for any suspects that might have escaped the fire.

Alex moved us into the shadows between two buildings just to be certain. Then he pressed me against the brick wall, hoping to block me from the view of any cars on the street. Needing to rest anyway, I welcomed the brief pause.

"This brings back memories," I said, thinking of the first night I met Alex in a dark New York City alley and witnessed a mind-bending magical battle between him and Zane. That was the night I first learned that magic was real, and it changed my life irrevocably. However, since my life wasn't so great before that defining moment, the jury was still out on whether this new life was better or worse.

Alex smiled at me again, making warmth flood my body, pooling in my abdomen. I actually fucking blushed at the effect he had on me, but I didn't think he noticed in the dark.

"That was one crazy night," he agreed, his voice deeper and rougher than usual. "I've never been the same since."

Was he flirting with me? It was so hard to tell with him since he was perpetually stuck in serious mode. His response could have been a solemn observation, or it could have meant I affected him in a personal way. Maybe I should say something flirty in return and see if he engages.

I opened my mouth to test the theory when the car we hid from moved very slowly past us. It was unmarked and black with lights on the roof. At the next corner, it turned, and Alex relaxed his embrace. I immediately missed the comforting weight of his large body pressed against mine.

"Maybe we can find a cab or a subway station," he said, unaffected by the loss of our close proximity. "We need to get off the street."

He helped me out of the alley, but we didn't make it more than another five steps before the unmarked car came screeching around the corner and ground to a stop beside us. It had obviously been waiting for us to reveal ourselves.

The driver's door flew open, and a man leapt out, stretching his arms across the roof of the car, training a Remington 870 12-gauge shotgun on us.

Since when did the police carry FBI SWAT weapons?

Chapter Ten

EMMA

The rear driver's side door opened, and a man stepped out. Something about him felt... familiar, but I couldn't put my finger on it. Maybe it was that he reminded me a little bit of Nathan Anshar. They were both tall, handsome older men who carried themselves with quiet confidence. However, whereas Nathan earned his reputation as a media darling by being warm and approachable, this man exuded mystery.

The dangerous glint in his eyes didn't invite any personal questions, and the smirk on his lips seemed to dare someone to even try it, at their own peril. He had more muscle than Nathan did, and I knew immediately he wasn't the type to back down from a fight. Hell, he might even relish one.

Similar to Nathan, it was almost impossible to pin

down this man's age. His skin was flawless and wrinkle-free, and his dark hair didn't hold a hint of gray, but his eyes and overall demeanor reflected life experience, not all of which was good.

"Ms. Hayes," he said in a deep, velvety voice with just a hint of an accent that I couldn't place. "Mr. Griffin, I didn't expect to see you here."

I could feel Alex stiffen against me and tighten his grip on my waist. He was clearly as surprised as I was that the man knew him.

The man eyed me up and down, taking in the blood and gore staining my shirt and skin. I expected him to whip out the handcuffs and read me my Miranda rights, but he just said, "My name is Sam Powell. I'm with the U.S. government, and I'd like to ask you both to step inside the car, please." His tone was polite but firm, brooking no argument.

"If you think I'm going to let Emma get into an unmarked car with a stranger and a bunch of guys with guns, then you will be seriously disappointed," Alex growled, turning our bodies slightly to position himself between Sam and me.

If either of the gunmen opened fire, they would hit Alex first, giving me a chance to run. However, in my current condition, I wouldn't get far, so Alex's attempt at chivalry was pointless.

"I can assure you, I just want to talk. In fact, I am here because I need Emma's help. She's in no danger from me."

My eyebrows drew together. Why did the government need my help? When I worked for them,

I was with the military, not intelligence, and that was years ago. I couldn't imagine I had information or skills they couldn't get from someone else unless this was about my current profession.

"What department did you say you are with?" I asked.

"I didn't," he said simply, not attempting to answer my question.

Two could play at this game. I put my free hand on my hip and cocked my head, letting him know I wasn't going anywhere until he answered some questions.

The corner of his mouth quirked up and he gave in. "I believe you know my predecessor, Edward Connor."

"Oh, hell no!" I said, trying to pull Alex with me as I prepared to storm away. "Now I'm definitely not getting in a car with you. The last time I saw Connor, he tried to kill me. How do I know you don't plan to do the same?"

"Look, Emma, I know Connor did some horrific things, but just because I have his job, it doesn't mean I am anything like him. In fact, the Committee on Superhuman Research has been temporarily disbanded, pending a Congressional hearing. All of the committee's files were transferred to the FBI, and I was assigned to look into them. After that debacle at Citi Field, Connor is going before Congress soon."

"So he's still alive," I said, more as a statement than a question. "The last time I saw him, he was being sucked dry by a vampire."

"Yes, well, he survived the experience, but he will likely live out the rest of his days in a nursing home as a result."

I wasn't sure if Sam expected me to feel sympathy or pity for Connor, but I didn't. I felt that justice had been served. Connor deserved nothing less than to live the rest of his life knowing he had created his own fate.

"Good," I said simply, and Sam gave me a slight nod of agreement.

Maybe this man isn't so bad after all, I thought.

"And what are you planning to do with these files now that you know what Connor was working on?" My mind flashed back to the horrific labs on North Brother Island where Monere were sliced and diced for scientific, Frankenstein-style research.

"My goal is to show those stuffed suits in Washington how effective I can be in this role so they never put a guy like Connor back in charge. This agency is too important to be placed in the hands of a self-aggrandizing douchebag like Ed Connor."

Sam had me at douchebag. I could also tell he was being sincere, if not entirely truthful. Something about him still itched at the back of mind, but any enemy of Connor's was a friend of mine.

"So what do you want from me, a witness statement to his douchebaggery?" I asked.

"Not exactly," Sam said. "I need your… special expertise. If I am going to keep this job, I need to solve a particularly challenging case, and I think you can help me do that."

"You know I'm not an investigator, right? My 'special expertise' lies in a very different area."

"I suspect you don't even know yet what you are capable of." That statement hit home and made me think about the incident on the subway platform at Grand Central when I generated a palm full of blue light. Of course, he couldn't know about that, but before I could open my mouth to respond, he continued. "Your Facebook fans certainly think quite highly of your talents."

"My what?" I asked, surprised. I didn't even have a Facebook account or any social media presence, for that matter. It's not as if I had friends to keep in touch with or had anything socially acceptable to tweet about. What would I say? *Slaughtered a zombie-creating blob and burned down a sushi restaurant today #anotherdayattheoffice.*

"Didn't you know you are an internet sensation or, at least, in a very small subsection of a corner on the internet? A Facebook group was created a couple of weeks ago, dedicated to creature sightings in the New York City area. Any random visitor would think the group is full of criminals, addicts, and conspiracy theorists, and maybe it is, but some of the posts seem to ring true. We have been monitoring it closely to track the locations of dangerous creatures. Then we started to see a lot of posts about a mysterious female monster hunter who was nicknamed *Angel.*"

That was the name John and Ivy had called me at Club Outpost. Is that why they gave me the VIP treatment? They knew I was the one trying to keep humans safe from the creatures roaming their neighborhood?

"How did they find out about me? And why Angel?" I asked.

"I'm guessing they chose Angel because they see you as their savior, their protector. As for how they found out about you, how many people have you helped in the weeks since the creatures came through the rift? A dozen? More?"

I shrugged noncommittally.

"Have you heard the saying that some secrets are fires so scorching the only way to quench the burn is to tell someone? You, my dear, are an inferno."

I looked down at my leg. "Well, I almost was, anyway." I squeezed Alex's arm in a gesture of gratitude, and he rewarded me with a fleeting upturn of his mouth.

"A few people got some grainy photos of you in action and posted them online, which is how I figured out who I was dealing with. We've been monitoring Facebook, Twitter, Instagram, and other sites for sightings of you. Then, only a few minutes ago, a woman posted to Facebook that she had been drugged and kidnapped from a nearby club by an alien. She put up a photo of you setting a jelly-like creature on fire inside a building right before the 9-1-1 call came in about a restaurant fire a few blocks away. We check out all leads, and this one finally panned out."

"Are you going to arrest me for arson?" I knew he couldn't pin me with the murder of an inhuman creature—the government would never come clean about their existence, and I doubted they actually had any constitutional rights—but arson could put me away for a while. *Shit!* I knew I should have tracked down that woman and taken the damn phone away from her. Figures she would thank me for saving her sorry, bleach blonde ass by outing me.

"No, I'm not going to arrest you. In fact, we removed

the photo from Facebook, so the fire can't be attributed to you."

"What? Why would you do that?" Maybe my first reaction should have been more along the lines of 'Holy God, thank you, thank you, thank you!' But all I could think about was what he wanted from me in return for this favor.

"Like I said, I need your help, and I can't get it if you are in jail."

"And why would I want to help you? Your agency didn't exactly leave the best impression on me."

"Because I am not Connor. We are on the same side."

"And what side are you on? The last time I checked, I wasn't running Dr. Frankenstein's secret laboratory and slaughtering innocent creatures in the name of science."

"Emma, please get in the car," he urged under his breath, losing patience. I wasn't about to make it easy for him, but at the same time, I knew I didn't have much of a choice.

"Don't you dare, Emma. I don't trust him," Alex said.

"I don't trust him, either, Alex, but I'm also not in a position to outrun him, even with your help, and there is no point in both of us getting killed."

"We need to move this little shindig off the street," Sam said.

A group of college kids had stumbled out of a nearby dive bar, laughing loudly, and falling all over each other. They moved toward us and, even in their inebriated states, took notice of the man leaning against the car, gun still drawn. One girl gasped, coming to an abrupt stop, and grabbed the arm of the boy next to her to get his attention. He barely seemed to notice her reaction, but if we didn't get out of there, we would draw everyone's attention soon.

"Let's go," I muttered to Alex, urging him past Sam and into the car.

Alex got in first then helped to gently lift my stiff leg, allowing me to slide across the seat and lean against him. After Sam followed and closed the door behind him, the driver holstered his weapons and got in. Soon, we were traveling through the darkened streets of Brooklyn.

"Where are we going?" I asked.

"There is something I want to show you. If your Facebook fans are right about you, I think you can help me track down a killer."

"Let me guess; you're trying to find a creature that is hunting down humans. Join the club," I said, unimpressed. This was going to be easier than I thought. "Just put me on the scent and I'll find and kill the thing within twenty-four hours, guaranteed. Then we can part ways, and I'll go back to my epically fantastic life."

He looked at me as if he wanted to roll his eyes. Even a complete stranger could tell there was nothing fantastic about my life. That sucked. The rest of what I said was true enough, though.

"Actually, we're not hunting a human-killer. We're hunting a creature-killer," he said.

Alex and I turned our heads sharply in unison to stare at Sam. Somebody else was out there killing creatures besides me? That meant someone knew about monsters, magic, and alternate realities. Was it Jason, the elves, or even the mages, or was it someone else entirely?

I turned to Alex. "Do you know anything about this? Is it the mages?"

"No," he said immediately then amended, "At least, I don't think so. Alcina doesn't tell me everything, but it doesn't sound like her style. She wouldn't leave bodies lying around for humans to find."

He was right. Alcina would never be so sloppy. She was a bitch, but a smart one. It also sounded like she no longer trusted Alex as she once had, and I couldn't help feeling responsible for that. She had ordered Alex to spy on me and kill me if necessary. Therefore, I was sure she didn't appreciate that Alex had a hand in saving my life and helping me escape being captured by her in Citi Field. I couldn't help wondering if she kept him close as a possible way of getting to me. I hoped Alex made sure he wasn't followed when he snuck out tonight.

"Why are you looking for this person?" I asked Sam. "It seems to me that he or she is doing you a favor, and you might want to let them do it."

"Do you really believe that?" he asked with disappointment in his eyes.

Why would he feel disappointment in me when he didn't even know me? Disappointment was an emotion felt when someone you cared about or believed in let you down. What surprised me even more was that my cheeks burned pink at the thought that I fell short of his expectations.

I shrugged, not knowing what to say that would redeem me in his eyes and not knowing why I cared.

"You don't kill all creatures that you come across, do

you?" he asked. "What about your friend Eddie? You trusted him enough to put your life in his hands when he helped you escape Citi Field, yet he is a dangerous creature from another realm. Why did you choose to let him live?"

How could I explain my relationship with Eddie? Sure, he tried to kill me when we first met, but he quickly won me over with his devilish charm and sophomoric sense of humor. More than that, I just had a feeling, certain to my core, that he didn't mean me any harm.

"I trust him," I answered simply.

"What makes you think Eddie is unique? Did you ever stop to think there might be more creatures out there who are worthy of your friendship or, at the very least, who don't deserve to die? What about Alex here?"

"Alex isn't a monster," I snapped with more vehemence than I meant. Compared to most of the men I had known, with the possible exception of Daniel, Alex was a boy scout. I didn't think he had a brutal bone in his body.

"Mages aren't exactly normal humans, and he has dangerous power. He poses as much a threat to the human race as any of those other monsters."

"You don't know anything about me. I'm here to protect humans, not harm them," Alex said, his eyes flashing with anger as he took offense to his character being questioned. I was pretty sure he had followed the rules and been on a straight and narrow path his entire life, and he was damn proud of it.

"Is that really why you're here?" Sam asked in a low voice. "To protect humans?"

Alex's mouth drew into a tight line, refusing to respond.

This car wasn't big enough to hold all of this testosterone.

I thought about Sam's argument. Most of the creatures I had been exposed to until now had been trying to kill me or trying to kill other humans. However, maybe those were the only ones I met because they were the ones I looked for. I supposed it was possible there were creatures out there, trying to fly under the radar and live quietly among humans. Just because I hadn't seen them, it didn't mean they didn't exist.

"I suppose there could be Monere out there that aren't all bad," I said grudgingly, trying to diffuse the tension between the two men flanking me. "I haven't met very many of them, though."

"Be that as it may, they are out there, and they are being picked off," Sam said, turning away from me to gaze out the car window. "I know it isn't my place to defend these creatures. Hell, killing them isn't even a crime technically since they aren't human, but I don't intend to stand by and allow living beings to be senselessly murdered."

"Why not?" I challenged. "Those things don't belong in our world, and they don't seem to have any interest in returning to their own."

"Did you ever stop to ask yourself why that might be?" He looked back at me, his face illuminated by the glow of a passing street light, and I thought I saw sadness in his expression. Then his features fell back into shadow, and I couldn't be certain what I had seen.

"No, I can't say that I have," I said, starting to get defensive again. Why the hell was this guy standing up for those things? If it wasn't for the Monere and their leader—my father—Gabriel Marduk, Daniel would still be here with me, and many other humans would be alive and safe rather than the victims of the horrific creatures that escaped Citi Field.

"Maybe one of these days you can ask your friend here what's really going on in their world," Sam said, incriminating Alex.

I could feel Alex tense at my back, but he did not attempt to make an excuse or offer an explanation.

I clenched and unclenched my fists, wanting to hit someone, but I couldn't decide whether I was angrier with Sam or with Alex. I had been trying to find out from Alex what was going on in Urusilim, but he was frustratingly tight-lipped, no doubt at Alcina's orders. I also wasn't about to throw my friend under the bus in front of a stranger, so I would deal with Alex later.

"Excuse me for not stopping to ask them their personal stories and refugee situation while they tried to rip me in two, turn me into a zombie, or bleed me dry."

"I think you are painting an unfair picture. They can be the victims of violence too. Maybe this will start to change your mind," he stated as the car slowed and came to a stop next to a barricaded section of street guarded by three men in black suits.

We had pulled up to the entrance of a private, underground parking garage on Park Avenue in Manhattan. In one of the city's more affluent neighborhoods, the garage was for the residents of the sleek and modern apartment tower that proudly soared over fifty stories above us.

"Hang on," Alex said, commanding Sam's attention. "Emma has an injured leg. She needs medical attention."

I had almost forgotten about my leg, still encased in soothing ice, but Alex was right. Even if he could keep reapplying ice as it melted, I couldn't walk well on it. If trouble arose, which it usually did when I was around, I wouldn't be able to fight or run away.

"Can't you just use your hocus pocus to heal her?" Sam waved his hands dramatically like a stage magician.

"My magic doesn't work that way," Alex said between clenched teeth. "But I know someone whose magic does." He pulled a cell phone from his pocket and typed out a quick text. In a few seconds, there was a tinkling chime, indicating he had received a response. "Someone will be here soon. In the meantime, let's get this over with. Show us why you dragged us here."

Alex helped me out of the car, and I leaned against him for support as we followed Sam. The suited men saw us approaching and, without asking for identification, moved aside one of the wooden barricades to let us through.

Alex's arms held me tighter as Sam led us down a short but steep ramp into the parking garage. I tried not to think about Alex's muscles bunching and flexing beneath my hands as he helped me walk or the warmth of his touch where he gripped my waist, but I was losing the battle.

I didn't want to think about Alex that way, though. I

valued his friendship too much to want anything more than that, and a physical hook-up would destroy this fragile balance we had settled into. Besides, he was at the center of a tug-of-war between Alcina, and me and I did not intend to drive him away by coming on to him when I believed it was something he didn't want.

The parking attendant booth was empty. The parking spots closest to the entrance were taken up by an extensive array of luxury vehicles that probably rivaled Jay Leno's collection. I recognized the emblems of Lamborghini, Bugatti, Bentley, and Ferrari gracing the sleek hoods of the red, black, and canary yellow vehicles. The cars belonged to residents who purchased the parking spots for their babies at tens of thousands of dollars a year.

Beyond the exotic automobiles, a plastic tarp lay on the garage floor, covering a large lump. The smell of gasoline, plastic, and something more organic filled the air. I had become all too familiar with the ripe scent of rot. Even so, I crinkled my nose against its stinging odor.

Sam walked up to the tarp, grabbed one corner, and yanked it back. The smell that had been wafting through the air immediately spiked in intensity and hit me full in the face, and I turned away, coughing and gagging.

Alex made a choking sound next to me, and I could hear him swallowing hard, probably trying to prevent himself from puking on me. Sam was unaffected, standing still over the body that had been revealed.

Chapter Eleven

EMMA

J looked down at the remains of the creature. "Oh, God. What the hell is that?" I covered my mouth with my hand, trying unsuccessfully to block the smell.

"It's hard to say, given the condition of the body, but based on the color and texture of the skin that's left and the size of the mass, we're guessing it was a stone giant. We took some samples for genetic testing to be sure," Sam responded.

"I'm glad all of those murders and autopsies really paid off in your ability to identify creature remains," I sneered, remembering that nightmarish laboratory filled with body parts floating in jars and tanks. That made me think of Lockien again and the horrific things the agency had done to him: shooting him dead, decapitating him, and then bringing his head back to life, attached to an animal's body. I still saw his eyes in my nightmares, filled with horror and torment, right before I killed him.

"The agency doesn't do that anymore. Shutting that project down was my first priority when I got this position. I believe we can learn a lot more about these creatures by observing them and maybe even communicating with them directly."

"Oh? Are you building a Monere zoo now?"

Sam sighed, shaking his head, clearly not in the mood to engage in my snarky attitude. It wasn't any fun if I couldn't get a rise out of him, so I let it go.

"What killed it?" Alex inquired in a slightly nasal tone, as if he was trying not to breathe through his nose.

"We don't know, which is exactly why I need Emma here," Sam answered before looking at me. "Emma, we are hoping you can help us figure it out. You are very good at tracking down Monere. So good, in fact, it's almost like you have a sixth sense."

Actually I did, but I wasn't about to tell him about my minor magical ability.

"This isn't the first body you've found like this, is it?" I guessed.

"What makes you say that?"

I shrugged. "I can't imagine you would come running to me for help with every dead creature you came across, so there must be something unusual about this particular case. What aren't you telling me?"

The corners of his mouth quirked up in approval. "This is the third creature we have found in a similar condition, and the bodies have all been located in wealthy neighborhoods where you wouldn't expect to find monsters. These creatures tend to prey on the lost, the weak, and the addicted, hanging out in places like that club you were at earlier tonight. This kind of neighborhood isn't their typical stomping grounds."

"Don't tell me you are only investigating this because some rich asshole is upset that the riffraff is moving into his neighborhood, and the body might stink up his Ferrari." I nodded my head toward the line-up of eye candy.

"No. I'm looking into it because there is a pattern here, and I don't think the killer is human. I don't see how a human could cause this kind of physical damage. How long do you think it will be before we start finding human remains in this condition? This killer is way too dangerous to be allowed to roam the streets."

"And for a minute there, I thought you were worried for the safety of creatures."

"I am, but that's not a popular opinion to have. If I want to keep my job and get the resources needed to do it well, the people I work for need to hear something they can get behind."

I stared at him hard, looking for anything in his expression that might reveal whether he was lying to me. His steady eyes met mine, and I saw concern, compassion, and a steely resolve in his gaze.

"Why do you care so much about these… things?" I asked, confused and more than a little curious.

"You may not understand this, but I believe at my core that all law-abiding beings deserve to live in peace. This country was built on the backs of immigrants and refugees seeking a better life, a safer life. Doesn't everyone deserve to live in peace and security? I don't believe the Monere are inherently evil, and I certainly don't believe they should all die simply because of what they are."

"What do you know about it?" Alex challenged. His eyes flashed, and his face flushed with barely repressed anger. "You've never lived in a world surrounded by them, had to negotiate with them for a peace they don't want, had your family slaughtered by them…" He choked on those last words, releasing his grip on my waist and stepping away to compose himself.

With the loss of his body for support, I swayed a bit on my feet until Sam reached out to steady me.

I watched Alex's back with a mix of astonishment at him having revealed something so personal and a sad feeling of kinship with him, knowing exactly how it felt to be orphaned. I had no idea that Alex and I had that kind of loss in common. I thought we were friends, but in that moment, I realized how very little I knew about him. Was he purposefully keeping himself closed off from me, or was I so wrapped up in my own drama that I had never even bothered to ask him any personal questions? Maybe it was a combination of the two.

I was just as guilty for keeping up that wall between us as he was. Standing there, watching Alex struggle to wrap that cloak of secrecy back around his shoulders, I was determined to try harder to get him to open up to me, which probably meant I needed to be prepared to open myself up to him in return.

"I'm sorry for your friend's loss, but he shouldn't condemn an entire species for the acts of a few. If there is something out there, murdering innocent creatures, I'm going to stop it."

"And what makes you think this creature was innocent?" I questioned, pointing at the lump on the floor. "Maybe it deserved what it got."

"I happen to believe in innocence until proven guilty and all that jazz." He gave me a tolerant smile.

"How the hell did you get your job?" I asked, finding it impossible to believe the same people who hired Connor would ever consider a man like Sam for the job. "I thought immoral asshole was part of the job description."

"I can be very persuasive." He winked at me, and I froze, not sure how I should interpret that wink. It wasn't flirtatious. Instead, it communicated that he had a secret he wasn't going to share with me. I shouldn't be surprised; he wouldn't be the only one hiding secrets. However, if I wasn't prepared to divulge mine, I wouldn't push him to reveal his.

Alex returned with his expressionless mask firmly back in place, but when I reached out my hand, he didn't hesitate to take it. I gave him a sympathetic squeeze, and he acknowledged it with a quick tightening of his grip.

Turning my attention back to the body, I leaned down to get a closer look at the gray and pink matter, and Alex moved his hands to my waist, securing me so I wouldn't topple forward. I was starting to go nose blind to the smell, thank God.

The skin was rough and pebbled, like stone. Where it touched the asphalt, the color shifted to black, and the texture became finer so it blended into the ground it lay on. I guessed it was called a stone giant because it had the ability to camouflage into a rock-based environment. Where better to do that than in the concrete jungle of Manhattan?

I straightened, thinking over what Sam had told me about this case and his concern that humans might get hurt. How did we know they hadn't already? If any humans had been victims, the call and subsequent investigation would go to the NYPD, not the FBI. Why were these creatures prowling around wealthy areas unless they were looking for something or someone that could be found in such places?

"Have you checked with the NYPD to see if there have been any attacks on people in the surrounding area?"

"Yes, we checked, and there haven't been any unusual deaths."

"And what about other crimes? Maybe we're not necessarily looking for a murder."

Sam was quiet for a moment then pulled a cell phone from his pocket and walked a few feet away to dial. With his back to me, I could only hear low murmurs of conversation, but I knew he put in a call to the police department.

Although I didn't know Sam's background, I was willing to bet he didn't have a career in law enforcement prior to his current job. I wondered once again how he had landed this position. Maybe he was a bright-eyed politician who was still naive enough to think he could make a difference in the world.

Sam returned after a few minutes. "You were right.

At the last two locations where we found a dead creature, a human was reported missing. Neither person has been found yet. There was no evidence of a struggle at any of the scenes, and no bodies were recovered, so the police haven't ruled them foul play yet."

"And in this building?" I asked, looking upward.

"A call came in to report a missing person who lives in this building while I was on the phone with the detective. I offered to follow-up since we are in the area, but he doesn't want the FBI stepping in on his investigation. The missing person case is not my jurisdiction... yet. The detective was just on his way out to respond to another call across town, so I'd say we have about an hour before anyone gets here."

I gave him a sly grin. "So, what are we waiting for?"

Sam called out to the suits at the top of the parking garage ramp. "Hey, Charlie, bag it and head out. I'll be behind you in a bit."

"Yes, sir," came the reply as the three men trudged down the ramp, sliding on plastic surgical gloves they probably kept in their pockets for just such occasions.

Kinky, I thought with an inside smile.

I threaded my arm through Alex's. With Sam, we headed back up the ramp. Sam flashed his FBI badge, and the doorman let us into the heavily ornate lobby. It all but screamed, "Pretentious rich people inside." The floor and walls were covered in black marble threaded with gold veins and polished to such a high shine I could see my reflection in the tile. Corinthian columns supported a gilded ceiling painted to depict cherubic angels floating in a blue sky.

When my eyes lowered from the ceiling, they landed on two figures standing up from uncomfortable-looking, red velvet chairs. I sucked in a breath at the sight of Lilly and Jason, tears springing unbidden to my eyes. I hadn't realized how very much I missed them until they stood before me.

Lilly's eyes also shone as she sprang forward, arms wide, engulfing me in an enormous hug.

"Emma, where the heck have you been? I was so worried about you. We didn't know if you were dead or alive after Citi Field. I was sure you would have called us if you had been able to. Then I thought maybe you had lost your phone in the battle and had no way of getting in touch with us, so I figured I would give you a few days to get to an Apple store so you could buy a new phone, but then you still didn't call…"

"Lilly, take a breath." I laughed at my elven friend. I was glad to see even a bloody battle couldn't dilute Lilly's personality. "I'm fine. I'm sorry I never called. I was trying to keep you and your family safe. Too many of your clan died that night."

"And what about me?" Jason asked quietly from behind Lilly, not making any move to step closer. "Why didn't you call me?" The hurt in his eyes was like a living thing, permeating the air around him and saturating his entire being. I knew our separation would hurt him, but I hoped that, with some distance, he would get over me and move on. Apparently, I had been wrong.

"Jason, I…" I couldn't find the words that would take away his pain and disappointment. I felt like a horrible friend. What would I do if Jason didn't want to be a part of my life any longer? Would I still be human if I had no ties to humanity?

Sam saved me by stepping forward and jutting out his hand in introduction. "Hi, I'm Sam Powell with the FBI. Emma and Alex are helping me with an investigation."

Jason shook Sam's hand reluctantly, suspicion and curiosity warring in his expression, but he was still too angry with me to ask any questions. Lilly didn't seem at all phased by the FBI's presence. She shook Sam's hand enthusiastically then greeted Alex with a warm hug.

"Lilly, Emma's injury…" Alex gently reminded her.

"Oh! Oh, my gosh. Emma, are you okay? I'm sorry. I completely forgot. I was just so happy to see you. Where are you injured? Are you in pain? Alex didn't give me any details. What happened?"

"Lilly, it's all right. I've got burns on my leg from a fire, but I'm not in any pain right now. Alex took care of it temporarily."

Alex helped me to a small sofa positioned in a secluded corner, with its back to the main lobby, giving us some privacy. It looked soft and luxurious yet felt like it was stuffed with cardboard. He gently lifted my leg onto the cushions.

Alex's face was a mask of concern as he looked at the injury. "I need to remove the ice so Lilly can heal the skin underneath. It's going to hurt." *That's the understatement of the day*, I thought. "Are you ready?"

Once I took a deep breath and nodded, Alex placed his hands over my leg, and the icy crust melted away. Searing pain welled up to reclaim its rightful place at the forefront of my senses. I sucked in a breath and bit back a scream, and it came out as a gurgled moan, instead.

As Lilly knelt by my side and examined the charred and blackened ruin of my leg, the men stood in a protective circle around the sofa, trying to block the view from any curious onlookers. Lilly's hand hovered over my wounds as her lids drifted closed in concentration. A soft, moss green glow emanated from her palms and absorbed into my skin. The relief was almost immediate and I breathed easier, the tension releasing from my body. Tingles filled my leg and grew in intensity. Just as they were becoming more than slightly uncomfortable, the sensation was gone, replaced by soothing warmth.

Lilly dropped her hands to her lap and swayed precariously. Jason leapt to her aid, holding her until the dizziness passed.

Lilly did amazing work. My skin was smooth and pink, unmarred by even the smallest scar. Without Lilly, those burns would have resulted in weeks of hospitalization, multiple skin graft surgeries, and months of rehabilitation.

I sat up and gave her a bear hug, whispering thanks into her ear. When I released her, Sam was at Lilly's side and said to her, "You have a very special and rare ability, Lilly. I don't think I've ever met a healer quite as powerful as you." He looked at her with respect and admiration.

"You've met other healers before?" Lilly questioned, her eyes wide and hopeful. "I thought I was the only one."

"Oh, I... um... Well, I read the government's files on

all of the Monere they've come across and recall seeing one or two about creatures with minor healing abilities, but nothing like yours."

I knew Sam said he had *met* other healers. Why would he lie to Lilly about that?

Lilly seemed to accept his explanation, so I decided to let it go for now yet promised myself I would question Sam further at a more convenient time and place.

"Emma, we really need to get moving. The police detective will be here in about thirty minutes."

"Yes, right," I said, getting to my feet and tentatively putting weight on my newly healed leg. It felt good. "Sam and Alex, why don't you grab an elevator, and I'll be there in a minute."

After the two men departed, Lilly gave me a final hug and told Jason she would wait for him outside. She gave me a sympathetic smile as she left the building.

"Jason…" I started, but didn't get far, completely running out of words.

"What the fuck, Emma?" he hissed. "You drag me into this bat-shit crazy world filled with monsters, magic, and elves, and then you abandon me when things get tough? Or did you decide to push me away because you already have too many men in your life? I noticed that Alex didn't get the same blow-off treatment I did. What the hell is that all about? Are you sleeping with him?"

I had been weighed down by guilt at the start of Jason's tirade, knowing he was entirely justified in his anger. I had abandoned him. I thought I was doing it for the right reasons, but I should have talked to him about it. Instead, I had been seriously avoiding him for weeks, knowing this conversation was coming and dreading it. Yet, in all the ways I had imagined this conversation unfolding, I had never expected Jason to pull the slut card. When he did, all of my self-reproach melted away, and I could feel my cheeks burning with indignation.

"I get that you're angry with me, Jason, but dragging Alex into this is out of line and none of your damn business." Jason had the good sense to look ashamed at his outburst, breaking eye contact and lowering his head, so I softened my tone. "You're right; I shouldn't have bailed on you. I did it because I was trying to keep you safe from all of this. I don't want you to have to live in my hellish version of reality. This is not your burden to bear."

His head snapped back to me, and some of the fire returned to his eyes. "It might not be my burden, but it is my choice. We have been through hell and back together. Remember Pakistan? And how about Nigeria? We always had each other's back. I'm not about to leave you alone in all of this."

Tears sprang to my eyes, though I refused to allow them to fall. "Jason, you are my last tie to my former life. You remind me that I am, or maybe once was, human. Sure, my life wasn't always easy — in fact, pretty much none of it was — but it was mine. I knew where I stood in the world. I was in control of my own destiny. Now I feel like I have lost who I am, and I can't lose you, too."

Jason didn't hesitate; he stepped forward and engulfed me in his strong arms. It felt familiar, comfortable, and good. I leaned into him and returned the embrace, laying my cheek against his chest.

"I'm not going to leave you, Emma, ever," he said, resting his chin on the top of my head.

We just held each other for a moment, and all I could think about was how there were no guarantees in life.

Chapter Twelve

EMMA

After Jason left, I met up with Sam and Alex at the elevators. I could tell Sam was growing more anxious with the limited amount of time we had to interrogate our witness.

"Let me do the talking," he said. "This is my investigation, and we'll need to wrap this up quickly. Just signal to me if you notice anything out of the ordinary."

"Yes, sir," I said with a mock military salute, trying to shake off the melancholy of my moment with Jason. He frowned and I smirked

The elevator brought us to the top floor of the building, and the doors slid open to reveal a lone door directly in front of us. Sam knocked, and after waiting almost a full minute, Sam raised his fist to knock again when the sound of a series of locks releasing signaled someone was on the other side, so he lowered his arm and waited.

Pinpricks bloomed at the base of my skull. I braced myself, preparing to shove Sam out of the way of impending danger, not knowing what hideous monstrosity lay in wait on the other side of the door.

I trusted that Alex had also sensed the danger and could use his magic to take care of himself. He didn't seem to have the same confidence in me, though, because he shifted to position himself between the door and me.

I attempted to grab Sam and shove him to safety when the door swung wide. My eyes widened at the sight before me, and I could feel Alex stiffen and saw Sam's jaw go slack.

Leaning against the doorframe was the most stunning woman I had ever seen. She made Sophia Vergara look plain and frumpy. She was tall and voluptuous with soft curves in all the right places. She wore a blood red, silk camisole and matching boy shorts that hugged her rounded hips and small waist. Her bare legs were long and lean and looked like they went on forever. The strap of her camisole slipped off one shoulder, drawing attention to her full breasts that threatened to spill out of the top. Then she shifted her weight, jutting out one hip and lowering her shoulder even farther, so the top slid down ever so slightly, giving us a tantalizing glimpse of her deep cleavage.

Jet-black hair cascaded in soft waves over her shoulders and spilled to the curve of her lower back.

The color complimented her golden skin. However, her most striking feature was the bright violet of her eyes. They curved slightly, reminding me of a cat, and held a natural, seductive gaze.

"Um… I've noticed something out of the ordinary," I said to Sam under my breath, squeezing his arm. I needed to tell him she was Monere, and we were in danger, but he completely ignored me, unable to take his eyes off the woman.

"Can I help you?" she purred in a throaty voice that sent a pulse of warmth down my spine. It was delicious and silken, like melted chocolate.

Heat pooled in my abdomen, and I clenched my legs together, trying to dispel the feeling. If she had that kind of effect on me, what were Sam and Alex feeling? I glanced at the two men and noticed Alex shifting uncomfortably as he tried to conspicuously adjust his pants. Sam appeared only slightly less affected. His face was flushed with a sheen of sweat breaking out on his forehead, but at least he could still put two words together.

Clearing his throat, Sam made a valiant effort to act normal. "Yes, ma'am. We're with the FBI and need to ask you some questions about the missing person you just reported. Can we come in?"

"Yes, of course, please." She stepped aside and motioned us into the apartment.

It was sleek and modern, all clean lines and no clutter. The entire apartment was white: white walls, white carpets, white furniture. Clearly, she didn't have kids or dogs.

"Can I get you something to drink or anything else that might make you more… comfortable?" Her eyes swept over Alex's body, lingering on his biceps as she noticed what had been distracting me throughout the evening—Alex clearly worked out, and the short-sleeved T-shirt he wore showed off the definition in his arms and chest.

Alex noticed her checking him out, and when her eyes lifted to meet his, they locked in place.

"I'm Emma Hayes." I thrust my hand toward the woman, trying to break that enraptured gaze.

She looked at me, catching me in her web just as easily as she had with Alex. Her startlingly purple eyes trapped me in their bottomless depths and made me want to fall into them. When she took my outstretched hand, electricity ran up my arm. I wasn't sure if she pulled me closer or if I moved of my own volition, but I found myself pressed against that soft body of hers, our faces only inches apart.

"Gwendolyn Cubare, but please, just call me Gwen. It is a pleasure to make your acquaintance." Her sweet breath kissed my cheeks, and I breathed in the scent of her. She smiled in invitation, continuing to hold my hand for longer than was generally appropriate.

I wasn't immune to Gwen's charms any more than Alex was, though I had never felt desire for a woman before now.

When she finally released my hand, it left me feeling cold. I wanted her touch back. Then she turned back to shake Alex's hand and learn his name, and a streak of jealousy stabbed through me. I had a hard time understanding whether the jealousy was caused from being slighted by Alex or by Gwen.

"Please, sit." Gwen gestured to the white leather sofa.

Alex and I took a seat next to each other, while Sam remained standing in the at-ease position with his hands clasped in front of him. I guessed he was trying to hide Gwen's effect on his nether region.

Gwen stretched out on a settee across from us, resting one arm over her hip and the other holding up her head. The pose accentuated her lean legs and the curve of her hip as her generous cleavage threatened to fall out of her top.

"I assume you are here to help find Bill."

"Yes, ma'am," Sam answered. "We are responding to the call you placed earlier. The victim's name was Bill?"

"Bill McNeill. I'm sure you've heard of him. He's the CEO of Global Mechanix, the world's largest engineering firm. He's my boyfriend," she said with a hint of pride in her voice.

The name sounded vaguely familiar, but I had a hard time thinking straight. I couldn't stop looking at Gwen, wondering what it would feel like to run my hands over her soft skin.

Squeezing my eyes shut for a moment to regain my composure, I asked, "When was the last time you saw him?" I told Sam I would let him do the talking, but I needed to distract myself from my own sordid thoughts.

"He never came home from work last night. Lately, he has been so wrapped up in work he's spent the night in the office, but when I called his assistant today, she said he hadn't been in at all today or last night. It's not like him not to come home to me."

"Did the two of you get into an argument recently? Maybe he needed some space and decided to stay at a hotel or with friends?" Sam offered.

She laughed, and the sound sent a pulse of pleasure racing to my most sensitive nerve bundles. I gasped at the sensation as her laugh settled into quiet giggles.

"No, he has no reason to stay away," she said, emphasizing her point by playing with a strand of midnight black hair that drew attention to her ample breasts.

The only thing that broke my gaze from her cleavage was the shrill ringing of a cell phone.

Sam pulled his phone out of his pocket and put it to his ear. "Yes… I see… Okay… Give me a minute. I'll call you right back." Sam hung up and turned to us. "I apologize. I have to make a very important call. It should only take a few minutes. Is there somewhere I can take this in private?"

"Yes, of course," Gwen said. "Just go down that hall. Bill's office is the first door on the right."

"Thank you, ma'am." Turning to me, he said, "Emma, do you think you can continue the questions until I get back?"

The look of surprise must have shown on my face, but I merely nodded and said, "Sure, no problem." Then Sam walked out, leaving Alex and I to conduct an illegal interview under false pretenses. Awesome. "You mentioned he's been working late. Is something going on at work?" I continued, squirming in my seat, trying to find some relief from the heat between my legs.

"We don't talk about work too much." She winked. "All I know is that his company landed some kind of big government contract, and it's been taking a lot of his time lately. The funny thing is he doesn't even know what he's building."

"Do you have a picture of Bill?" Alex asked.

"Of course." She stood, her muscles moving with a cat-like fluidity that conveyed grace as well as danger. She walked to a bookcase across the room as if she was a model at Fashion Week, picking up a black and white photo in a simple silver frame. She returned to us and leaned forward at the waist, handing the photo to Alex while giving him a clear view down her camisole.

I took the photo from Gwen since Alex couldn't manage to lift his hands. He didn't even attempt to glance at it. The photo was of Bill and Gwen on a pier with the ocean waves crashing below them and the sun setting on the horizon. Her dark locks swirled around them, whipped by the wind, and Bill had his arms wrapped around her to share his warmth. They both wore enormous smiles.

Bill wasn't what I expected. He was middle-aged, lean, and balding with pale skin and frameless glasses. I wouldn't have been surprised if he wore short-sleeved, white, button-down shirts with a pocket protector in the breast pocket. Regardless, Gwen looked genuinely happy with him. Maybe she was just an amazing actress or was in it for Bill's money.

I looked up as Gwen slid to her knees in front of

Alex. She placed her hands on his thighs and gently spread his legs, fitting herself between them, and her hands slid up his thighs, kneading them as she moved higher. The bulge in his pants twitched as her long fingers drew closer.

All I could do was stare while a sultry heat hung in the air with a sweetly cloying scent that reminded me of exotic spices from far off lands. It was intoxicating. My lids grew heavy as a deep relaxation settled over me. I could feel my inhibitions slipping away and wondered if I could join Gwen and Alex in what I expected was about to happen.

Gwen leaned forward, parting her lips as if preparing for a kiss, but she stopped only centimeters from Alex's mouth. Alex's breath came out in ragged pants, eager for her touch. She inhaled deeply through full lips, and a soft glow seemed to be pulled out of Alex. She sucked the white light into her mouth and moaned as if the taste alone was the ultimate pleasure.

Alex's eyes rolled into the back of his head, his arms falling limply at his sides and his shoulders slumping.

Chapter Thirteen

EMMA

Alex's skin grew ghostly white and thinned into tissue paper as deep shadows blossomed around his sunken eyes and cheeks. The warmth and light that emitted from this wonderful and vibrant man faded, died. In minutes, he would be nothing more than a withered husk.

With Gwen's attention diverted to her feeding, the influence she had been exerting lessened. It felt like a little bit of pressure had been let out of an over-inflated balloon, and I could take a breath. I shook my head to clear the cobwebs, and realization finally dawned on what I was witnessing. Oh, God, she was feeding from him.

I threw myself forward, slamming my full body weight into Gwen, knocking her aside, and breaking that deadly contact with Alex. I landed on top of her in a heap, hyperaware of the lean lines of her body and bare skin pressed against me. I could feel her hard nipples through my thin T-shirt as we wrestled for the top position.

I won, straddling her and pinning her arms under my knees. She continued to struggle, her strength close to that of a male body builder until I bitch-slapped her hard, stunning her into stillness beneath me. Gwen looked at me, wide-eyed and slack-jawed. I didn't imagine she had ever been rejected before, and that realization probably hurt more than my backhand.

"Things are going to get a lot worse for you if you don't shut down that sex mojo shit you're giving off," I said, reaching around to my lower back as if about to pull a gun. She didn't know I was bluffing since I had lost my gun in the sushi restaurant fire.

Her eyes tracked the movement, and then the air cleared as the tension disappeared. When my shoulders sagged with relief, I realized how taut my entire body had been, every muscle straining with desire, anticipation, and resistance.

"What the fuck are you?" I asked, sounding less threatening and more exhausted than I intended. "Is this how you treat people who are trying to help you?"

"I'm a succubus," she said, lowering her eyes. "This is pretty much what I do. I need to feed on life force, or I'll die, and I use sex to do it. It's pretty much who I am. I'm sorry." Her voice cracked at that apology.

"Alex, are you okay?" I called back to him without taking my eyes from the succubus.

"Yeah," he said from behind me, his voice weak and winded.

Relief poured over me like a spring rain, and the weight that had been pressing on my chest lifted. As I debated the easiest method of killing Gwen, Sam came back into the room.

"It's okay, Emma. Let her up." Sam had his gun drawn, but it was pointed toward the floor. Even so, I didn't trust her.

"No fucking way. What if she turns on her mojo again and convinces us to let her go, or sucks us all dry, and walks away clean?"

"I won't. I promise." Her eyes were shining with unshed tears.

"I'm not in the habit of taking the word of monsters," I spat.

"I'm not a monster," she said so softly her words were almost inaudible.

"Emma, let her up," Sam said slowly and soothingly, as if talking a jumper off the ledge. "If we start to feel… aroused, I give you permission to take her out, but this is still my investigation, and we need to question her."

I reluctantly got to my feet yet made no attempt to help Gwen up. She didn't need the help, managing to make standing up look sexy. Sam asked her to cover up before we got down to business and followed her into the bedroom so she could put on something more appropriate. When they stepped out, I turned my full attention to Alex.

Lowering myself next to him on the sofa, I gently stroked his cheek. "How do you feel?"

His eyes fluttered open. They were glassy and unfocused, but a smile pulled at his lips. "I'm good," he said in the husky voice of someone who just woke up from a deep sleep or just experienced a very satisfying roll in the hay.

"Really? How good are you?" I asked, my mouth quirking up at the corners. I was rewarded with a flush of color spilling across his cheeks, chasing away that deathly pallor. Apparently, there were worse ways to die than at the mercy of a succubus.

Alex sat up, his eyes clearing and the shadows leaving his face. "I'll be fine, but I have a strange craving for chocolate. I'm starving."

"Don't worry, loverboy. We'll get you some food when we get out of here."

Sam and Gwen emerged from the bedroom a minute later with her wearing a thick terry cloth robe instead of the filmy, silky number I expected to see.

"Alex, you're looking better. Are you good?" When Alex nodded, Sam ordered everyone to take a seat. "Okay, Gwen, let's try this again without you putting the whammy on us. We don't have a lot of time. When was the last time you saw Bill?"

"When he left for work on Thursday morning. His assistant said he was at work all day and left the office to come home around seven o'clock at night, but he never made it home." Her lower lip quivered, and she had to take a deep breath to compose herself. Either she was a good actress, or she was genuinely upset about his disappearance.

"Afraid you'll miss a meal now that he's not here

to feed from?" I questioned with a childish sneer to my voice. I didn't know why I was acting like a five-year-old, but I just didn't like this woman.

Anger flashed in her eyes as her jaw tensed. "You don't know anything about my relationship with Bill. I care about him."

"Yeah, sure you do," I said in as casual a tone as I could muster.

Now the tears did flow, streaking down her cheeks in an angry torrent. "Bill isn't just a meal to me. He took me in when I was lost and scared in a strange world. He takes care of me and keeps me safe. And before you ask, yes, he allows me to feed from him, but I only take the minimal amount needed for survival. It may ultimately take a few years off his life, but he does it willingly."

"How willing can he be when you have him under your lust spell? Seems to me he doesn't have much of a choice."

"I don't have him under any spell. I don't use my power on him unless he asks me to. He gives of himself freely and without influence."

"Why would he agree to that?" I didn't attempt to hide the disgust in my tone.

"It started as a mutually beneficial arrangement, but it soon became more than that. We care for each other."

"So he obviously knows you are Monere," Alex stated.

"He knew about the existence of the Monere before we met, and I was so happy I didn't have to lie to him or pretend I was someone else. He accepted me for who I am without question."

"How did he find out about the Monere?" Even though several creatures had entered the human population a few weeks ago, the Monere tended to keep a low profile and stay under the radar of the authorities.

"I really don't know," Gwen said. "When I asked him once, he just said he worked with some people in the government who told him about our existence."

Well, that can't be good, I thought. What was Bill wrapped up in that had him working with people in the government who knew of the existence of the Monere and felt the need to tell him about it? Could Bill have been abducted based on what he knew? Anything was possible, but it wasn't enough of a lead to go on.

"How did you and Bill meet?" I asked. I was sure Bill was a great guy, but Gwen seemed to be quite a bit out of his league.

She fidgeted with the belt on her robe, as if debating whether to answer the question. Looking amongst the three of us, a panicked look entered her eyes, like a cornered animal, and my hand went instinctively to the empty spot at my lower back where my gun should have been.

She saw the movement, though, and knew what I had been trying to do. She blanched and swallowed hard, finally deciding to talk.

"I met him through the Syndicate."

Alex, Sam, and I looked at each other, seeking signs of recognition, but we all looked equally confused. We waited for her to say more, but she didn't continue.

"What is the Syndicate?" Sam urged gently.

"It's an organization… of Monere."

"What?" I squeaked, my stomach clenching at the revelation. If there was one saving grace that helped to prevent an all-out slaughter of humans, it was that the Monere tended to operate alone or, at most, in small groups. Even within creature circles, there seemed to be little trust or loyalty. If the Monere were finally getting their acts together and organizing, they could plan another coordinated attack like the one Marduk had tried to pull off at Citi Field.

"It's not like that," Gwen said as if reading my thoughts. "The organization exists to help creatures assimilate into their new lives on Earth. They aren't looking to cause any trouble."

"You really expect me to believe this organization is the Creature Welcome Wagon? Maybe that's what they want you to think, but I doubt those who organized it are quite so altruistic." It also didn't slip my attention that she just revealed the existence of this group to the government. I was sure, once Sam went running back to his bosses with this tidbit of information, agents would rain down on the city, hunting for Syndicate members. I wasn't about to point that out to Gwen, though. If she realized the risk Sam posed, he could be in danger.

"The Syndicate helped me. I need to feed to survive, but I was afraid of the humans. The men I met at bars and clubs were... aggressive. There was an incident where I almost killed a man who came on too strong. Then I found the Syndicate and went to work for them. They run a number of businesses, including a dating service, and they paired me with Bill. "

"You mean a call girl service, don't you?" I was

getting the impression the Syndicate was more of a monster mafia than a welcome wagon.

Gwen chose to ignore my jab and continued as though I hadn't said anything. "Bill was lonely and looking for companionship. He's not exactly the kind of man who has a lot of confidence with women. It turned out we were a perfect match." Gwen smiled as she spoke of Bill, lost in her own thoughts of a happier time.

Sam interrupted, his demeanor was much calmer than what I exhibited, and squashed Gwen's momentary joy. "Gwen, we found the body of a Monere in the parking garage under this building. Would you know anything about that?"

Gwen blanched. "What was it?" she asked, her eyes widening in fear of the answer.

"It was in pretty bad shape, but we think it was a stone giant."

"By the gods," she breathed, dropping her head into her hands.

"I take it you knew the thing?" I inquired.

"I knew *him*," she spat, looking at me with narrowed eyes. "His name was Jace. He was Bill's bodyguard and a sweet guy. He loved to bake and used to bring me these amazing brownies every Friday." Tears filled her eyes again as she got lost in the memory of her friend.

"How did Bill end up with a Monere bodyguard?" Sam asked.

"He had been working on some secret government project, and I think all the secrecy was starting to get to him, making him paranoid. He thought he was being followed, and I hated to see him so anxious, so

I went to the Syndicate. I thought maybe if Bill had the protection of a real monster, he wouldn't be so afraid of the imaginary ones."

"When did you last see Jace?" Sam asked.

"When I last saw Bill. Jace was with Bill any time he left this apartment. They were inseparable." Upon speaking the words, realization dawned on her. "But if Jace was killed… What happened to Bill? Do you think he's dead too?" Her voice was steadily rising in pitch.

"Don't jump to the worst case scenario." Sam moved to sit next to her on the sofa and took her hands in his. "I promise we will do everything we can to find Bill and bring him back to you alive."

What the hell? Were we playing "good cop, bad cop" here? Because he was taking "good cop" a bit further than he really had to.

"Do you know where we can find the Syndicate?" I interrupted their tender moment.

"Why?" She narrowed her eyes in suspicion. "I thought you were here to investigate Bill's disappearance, not investigate the Syndicate."

"We're not investigating the Syndicate," I tried to reassure her, "but if Jace provided status reports back to his boss in the Syndicate, perhaps he told his boss something about Bill's movements or patterns that could be helpful in finding him."

It was an incredible longshot and a blatant lie. Yup, I was "bad cop" all right. I didn't really care much about Bill anymore; he was probably dead already if creatures had gotten him. My brain latched onto the Syndicate like a pit bull with a bone. I wanted to find them and destroy them. They were too great a threat to be allowed to continue. The best way to stop a criminal organization was to cut off its head, so I needed to know where to find their headquarters and the boss man.

Gwen didn't look convinced, so she turned to Sam for reassurance. I guessed the good cop ploy really did work. He gave her a small nod of encouragement.

"I don't know where they are based, but whenever I need to get in touch with them, I contact a woman named Pearl. I can give you her phone number." Gwen walked to the kitchen and scratched a phone number on a Post-It note then returned and handed it Sam.

"Thank you, Gwen. We really appreciate your cooperation," Sam said, standing.

Alex and I followed his lead and rose to leave, as well.

"We'll be in touch if we have any more questions or learn anything more about Bill's disappearance."

"Thank you both very much. Listen, I'm sorry about what I did to you earlier. Where I come from, the authorities don't treat us nearly so well, and I learned to survive by seducing my enemies. If they want to sleep with me, they are less apt to kill me — at least, most of them. Survival habits are hard to break."

"No harm done," Alex said, although he blushed so furiously I thought it might be possible he could die from embarrassment.

After we left the apartment and got back in the elevator, I said, "I'm going after the Syndicate, but first, I need to make a quick stop to pick up some gear."

Chapter Fourteen

EMMA

There must have been a glitch in the Matrix because that niggling feeling of déjà vu was hovering around the periphery of my memory. I watched Alex as he sat in the same place he had been weeks ago when he had shot Eddie in my Grand Central Station subway car. I had thought he had killed Eddie at the time, only to later learn the two had planned the encounter so Eddie and his fellow shifters could escape Marduk's control.

Although I had been preparing to march against the Syndicate, Alex had called a halt to my vendetta for the night. It was already in the wee hours of morning, and I could see the dark circles hanging heavily under his green eyes. I was still wide-awake, but it was energy born of adrenaline at almost having been sexed to death. I knew, once my anxiety subsided, I would crash, and crash hard.

Sam agreed, encouraging everyone to rest up so we were fresh for whatever we might encounter the following night. His driver had been waiting for him outside of the building. Sam stepped into the car and was chauffeured home for some needed shut-eye. I couldn't argue with his logic, but I had every intention of wrapping up one last piece of business before the sun rose.

A few weeks ago, I wouldn't have even contemplated bringing Alex with me, but now the thought of leaving him behind never entered my mind. Alex had tried to pre-empt this errand several times on our way back to midtown Manhattan, arguing for the need to rest and come back to do this in the morning. He was right; there was no immediate, driving need to visit my hideaway right at that moment. Maybe it was just my personality to be contrary in all situations.

Now, as we sat in the subway car, I was beginning to regret my decision. Alex's eyes darted around the small space, overwhelmed by the garish display of colors, patterns, and textures. After he had taken it all in, he must have found something fascinating on the floor near his feet because his gaze never strayed from the spot. His knee bounced up and down, as if dancing to its own manic, techno beat. He had his hands clasped in his lap, his fingers opening and closing, clasping and unclasping each other.

I thought he had been tired, but his rapid movements and intense fidgeting showed an abundance of nervous energy. I watched him, wondering at his mood and feeling smothered by the silence that had descended between us.

Alex sat on a small futon where hard plastic subway benches used to be. I took a seat in my favorite teal blue beanbag chair only a few inches from him. With this proximity, I could see each hard angle of Alex's face and body. I had either never had the luxury of this kind of quiet downtime with him, or perhaps I had never allowed myself to really look at him before, but I did now.

His light hair was longer than usual and mussed from the excitement of the evening. A stray lock fell across one brilliantly green eye, the color of a lush rainforest. His body tensed, showing off every taut muscle through his thin T-shirt.

He was beautiful, but he didn't know it, or if he did, he had never used his looks to his advantage. I had never seen him flirt, throw around an enticing smile, or pin someone with a smoldering stare. Although he could certainly do it, he probably thought that kind of influence was a form of cheating. He could be such a Boy Scout, but it was charming and made him trustworthy, and to trust someone was more important than a bad boy attitude any day.

This man sitting before me had sacrificed his own safety several times to save me. His job had initially been to keep an eye on me for Alcina and the Mage Council, and kill me if need be. Not only did he defy his orders, but he did so spectacularly when he saved my life in Citi Field and sided with a shifter to ensure my escape. He defied his people and his prejudice for me.

The sultry air in the subway car seemed to grow warmer and closer as these thoughts smoldered low in my belly. I thought I understood the reason for Alex's fidgeting. Being alone together wasn't something that happened often, and I couldn't recall when it had ever happened when we weren't in the midst of danger or in the lion's den of Alcina's compound. It felt like we had all the time in the world right now.

I smiled, finding his anxiety sweet and charming. He was nothing like the swaggering, overblown Wall Street guys I used to pick up from time to time at Raines Law Room just so I could feel a fleeting moment of warmth and connection with another person, even if it was mostly artificial.

A rush of longing and gratitude swept through me. Alex must have sensed it because he chose that moment to lift his head, and our eyes locked. His expression reflected everything I was feeling, and I was consumed by a desire to see whether the Boy Scout would ever explore bad boy territory.

I stood slowly, as if trying not to spook a nervous horse that was on the precipice of bolting, before lowering myself onto the futon next to Alex. His eyes followed my every movement, sweeping across each curve of my body. His expression didn't change, but his body stilled, all of that nervous fidgeting coming to a grinding halt.

Despite the futon being small, it still allowed two occupants to retain a reasonable amount of personal space between each other. I ignored such conventions and slid so close to Alex my thigh rubbed against his, and he reacted like I had electrocuted him with my touch, his leg jerking at the sudden sensation, but he didn't move away from the physical contact.

"Thank you," I said so softly it seemed as though all of the upholstered fluff in the room had absorbed the sound.

"For what?" Alex asked, his eyes now resting on my leg where the clothing had burned away to reveal the newly healed, creamy skin.

"For everything," I said with a small laugh, and he looked up then met my gaze. "Seriously, you saved my bacon a few times now, and I don't think I ever thanked you. I know you didn't have to do it, and I know it went against your orders. You put yourself at serious risk of Alcina's wrath for me." He looked away wordlessly, but not before I saw pain and sadness in his eyes. "Is everything okay?" I asked, confused by his demeanor.

He shook his head, but said, "Yeah, everything is fine." Then he took a deep breath and looked at me with a smile that didn't reach his eyes. His warm hand slipped into mine, and I embraced the unexpected touch, wrapping my fingers around his. "Emma, no matter what happens I want you to know that you mean everything to me. You always have. Even though I may have lost my way, that truth will never change. I need you to believe that."

The burning sincerity in his eyes was proof enough.

"I do," I said, squeezing his hand gently for emphasis. It felt a lot like he was saying good-bye. Maybe all of this was just too much for him.

Tears sprung to my eyes, unbidden, and I turned

away to hide them. Alex hadn't missed them, though.

With his free hand, he cupped my chin tenderly and turned my head to face him again. "I'm sorry. I didn't mean to upset you." He looked on the verge of tears himself.

"You didn't. It's just that… Well, there haven't been very many people in my life who have cared enough to want to help me, or to try to save me." Even though I didn't know exactly what Alex had meant by his last statement, I felt compelled to let him know I wanted to be there for him too. "If you ever do lose your way, I promise I'll help you find it again."

A collage of emotions flitted across his face — pain, gratitude, relief, fear — before he slipped on his expressionless mask. Silence descended once again, but our gazes were locked together in a need for connection. I became hyperaware of the sensation of my thigh pressed against his and the comforting touch of his hand in mine.

My leg shifted minutely, as if it had a mind of its own and wanted to increase the sensation of that subtle touch, calling attention to it. It had the desired effect. Alex watched me through heavy lids, and I could suddenly feel the air thicken with anticipation. We were so close. All I had to do was lean in a couple of inches.

I wasn't sure if I moved, but Alex's eyes darted to my lips, which I licked unconsciously. He sucked in a hard breath as his own lips parted, and I could see his muscles bunching under his thin T-shirt as his body prepared to move toward me, but Alex's mind hijacked his desire.

With an expression like he had just set himself on fire, he straightened his back and leaned away from me. He didn't drop my hand, only shifted his leg so we were no longer touching so intimately.

"So, um…" He cleared his throat. "Why did you bring me here?"

I was unable to respond for a moment, my brain still struggling to catch up with the sudden U-turn Alex had taken. I did my best fish imitation, my mouth opening and closing a few times while I tried to turn on the language center of my brain again.

"Oh," I finally got out with supreme eloquence. "Yeah, um…" Shaking my head to dispel the last of the quickly dissipating pheromones, I said, "I was thinking that I don't want to walk blindly into a den of Monere tomorrow without adequate protection." Those last two words made me think again of where things had been heading with Alex, and heat rose in my cheeks.

"You mean… Sharur is here?" Alex asked with wide eyes. "I thought you would have stashed it away in some high security safety deposit box somewhere, but this whole time, it's been sitting, unprotected in an old subway car?"

I bristled at the implication that I was being careless with such a powerful weapon. "It's not unprotected," I said, dropped his hand and standing up. "No one knows about this place except for you and Eddie, and neither of you are going to tell anyone about it. Plus, I keep it in a very secure safe that only I can access." I walked over to the mound of floor pillows and moved them aside to reveal the sleek, impenetrable steel of Sharur's prison.

"Good," Alex said, his shoulders returning to a more relaxed state. "So what made you finally decided to bring Sharur out of hiding?"

"Because of what happened back there in the sushi restaurant. My gun was useless. Those things couldn't be stopped by bullets, and I can guarantee they aren't the only monsters who are immune to lead. I know the Monere aren't human, but a part of me clung to the belief they were more like wild animals—dangerous, but still vulnerable to human weapons. I didn't want to truly believe they were different, otherworldly, and almost invincible.

"And what about what happened to you the last time you tried to use the axe?"

I thought back to the cold, blue light that poured from my hands and the implosion I caused that took out part of the subway tunnel.

"That's why you're here. I need you to help me understand it, maybe even control it, and if need be, stop me if it becomes too dangerous."

Alex looked thoughtful for a moment before his features hardened, becoming determined, and he nodded. "Yeah, okay. Let's do this, right now."

His eagerness took me by surprise, but I was so grateful to have his help I didn't question it. I knelt in front of the safe and went through the series of protocols required to get it open. When the door swung outward, I heard Alex suck in a breath as Sharur was revealed.

"It looks so much newer, sleeker than the last time I saw it," he said.

I didn't feel the same reverence that others from

Urusilim typically expressed when looking upon the battle axe, but then again, I supposed for them it was akin to looking upon the Holy Grail, a legend come to life. Or maybe it was that I still didn't believe anyone would entrust me with anything half so precious, so it must not be all that.

I lifted it unceremoniously out of the safe and waved it in front of Alex's wide eyes. "I'll take your picture with it later, but for now, can we get started?"

He nodded for me to proceed.

"I don't really know how it works, or if I can even recreate what happened."

"Well, let's start by stepping out onto the platform and giving you some space. Maybe if you just try to recreate what you were doing before, it will work," Alex suggested.

As we left the train car, a bundle of nerves sat like a hard pit in my stomach, sending vibrations of anxiety throughout my body. I was both afraid of experiencing that kind of power again and terrified I wouldn't be able to call it forth, so I would never feel that kind of rush again.

Giving Alex a wide berth, I took a deep breath and steadied myself. I focused on the feel of the solid ground beneath my feet, the heft of the axe in my hands, the stiffening and relaxing of my muscles, and the stillness of the stale air. When I was ready, I moved.

Fighting was a lot like dancing; it took strength, balance, and coordination. My movements were fluid and graceful and probably looked a lot like Tai Chi on fast forward. Regardless, I couldn't feel the power.

"You look too relaxed," Alex said. "Try getting more emotionally worked up."

Well, that shouldn't be too hard. I thought about this crazy night: creatures kidnapping girls, almost getting taken over by zombie-making slime, coming very close to going up in flames, and watching Alex get molested by a succubus. Then I thought about Zane and the shitty hand he was dealt, and I was flooded with grief for him. On top of all that, my new job as a monster hunter extraordinaire left me feeling lost and terrified almost all of the time. Most of all, I thought about my sweet Daniel and what he might be going through and my inability to help him.

Anger, fear, grief, and pity erupted within me at the thought of being so weak I couldn't protect or save those I cared about. I wanted to be strong and fearless, to strike down my enemies with a single blow, to provide justice for all of those poor humans who had been killed by Monere, and to make Marduk regret he had ever found me.

There you are, came Sharur's voice in my head. *I knew you were still in there somewhere.*

The power bloomed inside of me starting at my core and rushing to my limbs. It felt like drinking alcohol: burning and warming at the same time, leaving only peace and euphoria in its wake.

My hands grew incandescent, glowing brightly from within. I looked at Alex, needing to confirm whether he saw what I felt. His wide eyes and confused expression answered that question in the affirmative.

"What do I do now?" I asked him, desperation

seeping into my voice.

"Um…"

Before he could say much more than that, the soft ding of the elevator echoed in my ears. Under most circumstances, such a soft sound would have been overlooked or ignored, but I had never actually heard it here in the subway tunnel, because I was always the one in the elevator. No one else came down here without me.

Someone or something had found me.

Chapter Fifteen

ALEX

I could feel the power rolling off her in undulating waves, and each wave crested over me, filling me with wonder and trepidation. Her eyes were bright, the power coursing through her, illuminating them from the inside. Dark hair fell loosely down her back in curly tangles, and her body was taut, all lean muscle and soft curves. She moved with the grace of a dancer and the strength of a fighter.

I ached to run my hands through those long locks and explore every inch of her bare skin. The enormity of her power, which she wasn't even close to realizing, and the pull of my attraction to her were undeniable and a little disconcerting. She could destroy me with a simple rejection, yet I was drawn to her like an insignificant gnat to a black widow's web.

I wanted to help Emma learn to use and control her ability, but now that I could see it pouring out of her hands and lighting up her eyes to a bright gold, I realized this was way beyond my understanding or capability. Only a few people I had ever known possessed that kind of power, and I knew one of them was about to crash this party because I had led them here.

When the elevator door chimed and slid open, I braced myself for who would be on the other side. A little girl, cute as a button, stepped onto the subway platform, followed by a man as large and foreboding as a guillotine hovering over a stockade prisoner.

Alcina was a century's old mage who had learned the secret of immortality somewhere along the way and guarded it like a miser. It clearly involved hijacking the bodies of mortals whenever old age, disease, or injury was about to claim the body she had taken. Yet, as far as I knew, no other mage had been able to figure out how to do it.

It must be an incredibly difficult feat, which was why Alcina always chose to begin her new life in the body of a child—so she could live in it for decades before needing to make another jump.

She took her current body a few years ago in Urusilim when her seventy-six-year-old male form was failing. The girl's parents, who lived in a poor village and struggled to feed their remaining five children, had accepted gold in exchange for their daughter. Alcina claimed the little girl had been in a coma from a near drowning with no hope of awakening, but I doubted the truth of that.

Having my formerly masculine, balding, and all hard edges leader suddenly appear as an adorable seven-year-old girl with loose, blond curls and sparkling, blue eyes took some getting used to. However, that cold, calculating gaze and razor sharp intelligence was still fully intact.

Her companion Ronin was there to offer some additional protection until Alcina could physically defend herself on the unlikely chance someone made it close enough to her to do bodily harm. He was a formidable magic user in his own right, and together, the two of them were a force to be reckoned with. As a result, seeing them emerge from the elevator filled me with anxiety and regret.

As my head swiveled between Alcina and Emma, I could see Emma working it out in her head. Shock turned to rage, and then the knowledge of treachery sunk in as she met my eyes. Although I had anticipated her reaction and tried to mentally steel myself against it, the hurt and betrayal in her gaze ripped into me, tearing out my still beating heart, and crushing it to pulp. I tried to plead with her through my eyes, begging for her forgiveness and understanding, but I knew she wouldn't grant it. She couldn't understand why I had done this.

"Thank you, Alex, for showing us the way here," Alcina said in her sweet, little girl voice.

The bitch just had to rub salt in the wounds by vocalizing my deception. She couldn't just leave it unsaid what we all knew anyway.

She eyed Emma warily, like someone facing down a

scared dog that could bite at any moment. "Miss Hayes, I applaud your courage to take up the axe, but it is clearly too much for you. You will not be able to control that kind of power. I know you can feel it consuming you. You will lose yourself, and the axe will eventually take over."

Alcina's words seemed to resonate with Emma. The murderous rage slipped off Emma's face, and the light in her eyes dimmed. Then she looked down at the axe in her hands, and I thought for a moment that she would drop it, leaving it to Alcina's greed and ambition.

My heart sank at the defeat I saw in Emma, the fear and uncertainty. This was not the brave and confident facade she showed the outside world. This was a woman who struggled with self-doubt, who didn't truly understand who she was. I wouldn't have blamed her for giving up and walking away, but I would have mourned the loss of the woman she could become by taking up the axe. Therefore, I held my breath, awaiting her decision. Would she chose to walk the unknown path into darkness and hope it emerged into the light, or would she leave the path behind and turn back the way she had come, back to what was familiar?

Emma's face was a mask of stillness before her grip tightened around the shaft. When she looked up again, her eyes glowed molten gold, bright with heat and fury. She set her mouth in a hard line and fell into a fighting stance. The message was clear—Alcina was going to have to pry Sharur out of Emma's cold, dead hands. And there was a good chance Alcina would do just that.

Chapter Sixteen

EMMA

Why? The question reverberated in my head, but I couldn't find an answer that seemed to fit. Alex's betrayal was like a knife to my gut. After everything we had been through together, I had thought we were friends and could maybe even be more. That was never going to be our reality now.

I had even contemplated using the axe on him, but I couldn't make myself do it. He must have a reason for his actions. His eyes had pleaded with me to... what? Forgive him? Understand? Sympathize? I didn't have it in me to do any of those things. No matter why he had done this, there must have been another option, a different choice. There was always another way, yet he chose the path of betrayal. It was unforgivable.

Regardless, Alex wasn't my priority right now; his

bitch of a boss was. Alcina knew Sharur could speak to me, and she had just confirmed my greatest fear — the axe could exert significant influence over me, most likely not in a good way. I had fought the darkness inside of me for as long as I could remember, and now I held in my hands the instrument that could bring it forth in an unstoppable tsunami.

Would you rather I fell into the hands of the little mage? The axe whispered to me. *Is she more trustworthy than you are? Imagine what she could do with my power supplementing her own.*

Well, that was a fucking good point. There was no way in hell I was going to let Alcina grow more powerful than she already was. Nobody needed a super-charged egomaniac with a spoiled-brat attitude running around. Not only that, but I didn't think I could have handed over Sharur even if I wanted to. I didn't think I had the willpower to give up the kind of strength or control Sharur had bestowed on me. I could accomplish so much with that kind of power.

My fingers white-knuckled the shaft with every intention of blasting Alcina to kingdom come. She wasn't willing to walk away from the axe any more than I was. If I let her live, she would continue to be a threat to me and would persist in her efforts to steal Sharur, and I couldn't allow that to happen.

Alcina raised her hands, and Ronin twirled his staff, preparing to do battle. Alex looked like he was going to be sick, his skin pale, and eyes sunken with worry. He watched us as if it was a cage match to the death, his head swiveling frantically between Alcina and me.

This confrontation was a long time coming, and Alex couldn't have stopped it, no matter how hard he tried.

As my mouth curled up in an eager smile, I could taste the impending violence on my tongue, and it was delicious. A low murmur reached my ears, but I couldn't make out the words. Some deep part of my brain understood it was Sharur egging me on, talking to that primitive part of my mind that controlled my fighting instinct. For once, I completely supported Sharur working my inner beast into a frenzy. I could use all of the advantages available to me against Alcina.

I twirled the axe in my hand so quickly it was a blur, drawing their attention to the weapon and off the illumination building in my palm. Throwing out my right hand, I let loose a bolt of indigo lightning. The two mages were faster than I expected, diving in opposite directions to avoid the blast. It missed them by mere inches, hitting the cement platform where they had just been standing. The mages had been expecting an explosion, but instead, the platform simply disappeared, leaving a deep crater where the light had touched it.

I paused for a moment, gaping at the devastation I had wrought, and some of the righteous anger bled out of me, replaced by fear. Tremors rattled my hands as ice ran down my spine. I had no right to use this weapon. Its power was far too destructive for anyone to wield. It should be locked away in the deepest, darkest pits of hell where no one would ever be able to recover it. This weapon didn't just destroy; it erased. It left behind nothingness, removing its target from the world completely. Disappearing forever seemed almost worse than dying to me, like one had never existed in the first place.

The axe shook in my hands as my grip loosened, ready to drop it. Then that voice was back in my ear, talking to my primitive brain, and the anger flared once again, pushing away all vestiges of fear and doubt.

A higher reasoning part of my mind understood Sharur was controlling me, but I was unable to beat back the animal it had let loose. It felt too good to be this wild and free, unrestrained by rules and morals. I had a singular purpose: to kill, the consequences be damned.

Alcina and Ronin recovered while I was frozen in internal conflict and attacked in perfect synchronicity. They had clearly done this before because their timing was flawless. Ronin used his staff to rip free chunks of concrete from the platform and send them hurtling in my direction. At the same time, Alcina punched her staff into the ground, causing a tremor beneath my feet, trying to throw me off balance so I couldn't dodge the concrete.

I braced my feet wide and managed to keep my balance. Without any conscious thought, I hefted the axe and sliced it downward, cutting open a rift in midair to who the hell knew where. Expecting resistance, I leaned my full body weight into the movement. It felt like trying to move through water, but it worked and the objects hurtling in my direction passed harmlessly through the rift only inches from my face. For a moment, I wondered where they had gone and who might be on the other side taking the brunt of the attack, but then I shifted back into battle focus.

Instinctively seeking out the weaker prey, I took several bounding steps toward Ronin with the axe pulled back over the top of my head. Bringing it forward, I intended to split his skull in two. The weathered old man had been in a fight or two in his day and wasn't about to fall under my attack so easily, though. He lifted his staff in front of him, blocking my blow.

We twirled away from each other and swung again, axe and staff clashing with a solid *thunk* that reverberated to my elbow. Shifting my weight, I swung the axe with one hand to Ronin's left side. As anticipated, Ronin saw the axe as the greater threat and tried to block that blow while I reached out to touch him with my glowing right hand. I had no idea what would happen if I touched him, but I couldn't seem to stop myself from doing it. It was as if I watched myself from the outside, unable to reign in my actions.

I clamped down on his shoulder and willed the light to flow into him, and it eagerly obeyed my silent command. The power flowed through me and into Ronin, but he couldn't contain it. The energy sought to fill him from head to toe, and even when he was full, it kept flowing, seeking an exit through his eyes, nose, mouth, and even the pores of his skin.

Ronin screamed as the power he couldn't contain shredded his cells and tore apart his physical form. The solid, muscular shoulder under my hand crumbled and disintegrated, and in moments, nothing was left of the old mage except the smoldering ruin of his clothing.

Silence descended as Alex, Alcina, and I stared in shock at the empty space that Ronin had occupied only moments before as shame and horror slammed into me like a sledgehammer.

I killed him… just by touching him. All of my worst fears had come true. I could feel the bile rising past my throat as the truth hit me. I was no one's savior; I was their destroyer. The axe owned me, not the other way around. Sharur could make me evil.

I doubled over and emptied the contents of my stomach. Alex rushed to my side, but before he could offer me comfort, I stumbled away from him, holding up one hand to ward him off and wiping my mouth with the other.

"Stay away from me," I croaked through my raw throat.

He had caused this to happen. If he hadn't brought the mages here, I wouldn't have had to take up the axe against Ronin, and the old man would still be alive. Alex indirectly made me Sharur's puppet, and I was furious with him.

"This is all your fault," I choked out, trying to swallow the sobs threatening to escape.

Alex knew it, too, given the stricken look on his face. My words skewered him, and I didn't care.

That deep, accented voice was back in my head. *He betrayed you. He should pay for his treachery.*

Sharur wanted me to kill Alex, but as angry as I was, I refused to do it. I wouldn't allow the axe to influence my actions, although now that I knew at least some of what it was capable of, I couldn't leave it behind for Alcina either.

If it could get into my mind, I should probably be

able to get into its consciousness.

Shut. The. Fuck. Up. I thought to it slowly with deadly intensity. *You will not control me. My mind and actions are my own. If you ever try to do it again, I will see you buried in the deepest pits of hell or, better yet, melted down and turned into a garbage truck.*

The voice fell quiet, and I ran for the elevator.

"Stop her," Alcina screamed at my fleeing back.

I didn't know if Alex made a move to obey her, because he didn't come after me, and his signature water and ice powers didn't manifest. However, Alcina wasn't about to let me go quite so easily.

I slammed into an invisible wall, stopping in my tracks, and blood flowed freely from my nose due to the impact. I stumbled back a couple of steps as something wrapped itself around my neck, constricting my airflow. I reached up to claw at it, but nothing was there. My nails dug into my skin, drawing more blood.

Alex screamed at Alcina to stop, but I knew she wouldn't. She had been looking for the chance to kill me for weeks now, and she finally had motive and opportunity; therefore, she wasn't going to let this moment go. Alex wouldn't be able to help me this time. I still had Sharur, though.

As terrified as I was at what it represented and how it could influence me, I needed it right now. I also knew this was the first step on a slippery slope. If I couldn't win my battles without it now, I would only grow more and more dependent on it until I lost myself, but I didn't have a choice.

I stopped struggling and tried to focus my mind,

which was rapidly growing fuzzy. *Help me*, I thought.

All you ever needed to do was ask, it said, satisfied.

At my request, my mind flooded with what could only be described as part of the user manual for the weapon. It didn't escape my notice that Sharur only gave me the instructions on what I needed for this specific situation. He wanted me on the hook, like a drug dealer giving away the first taste free.

Following his instructions, I reached out with my senses and found some of the energy Alcina used to power her magic. It was like strings of glowing light in iridescent, ever shifting colors that undulated through the air. Her magic was thick and corded, as strong as rope. I drew on it, pulling the strands apart and unraveling them. Then I siphoned the magic away, deconstructing it, and turning it back on her. While she gasped at the sudden shift of her power, the invisible wall and constriction around my throat vanished, and I doubled over, gasping, but I didn't have the luxury of time to catch my breath.

Going for some dramatic flair, I turned on my heel and stood up to my full height, towering over Alcina's miniature frame and piercing her with a stare that promised vengeance. She paled at the unspoken threat and the real possibility that I could actually back it up. I wasn't so sure, but I wasn't about to let her know that. I could make an impression, though, which might get her off my back for a while.

I raised the axe and pushed energy into it, causing its gem to glow a brilliant aqua. With a toss of my arm, I threw the energy toward her, purposefully shifting my aim at the last moment to miss her by mere inches. As much as I hated her, I didn't need another death on my conscience tonight.

The light flashed by her head and hit the wall behind her. There was no explosion, but when the light faded, a crater the size of a city bus was left in the wall. It was as if the energy had eaten away at the stone, not even leaving rubble in its wake.

Alcina and Alex stared wide-eyed at the damage, and I took advantage of the distraction, slipping into the elevator and leaving behind my most formidable enemies — Alcina because of the power she could wield and Alex because of the hold he had on my heart.

Chapter Seventeen

EMMA

I didn't remember how I got there, but at dawn, I somehow stumbled back to Eddie's place and collapsed into my borrowed bed in the attic. I curled up under the blankets, clutching Sharur to my chest and draping one leg over the staff, as if it was a lover. Exhaustion and the effects of adrenaline depletion overwhelmed me, plunging me into the depths of sleep as soon as my head hit the pillow. My desire for a deep, dreamless sleep wasn't meant to be, however.

I dreamt of a hall of white marble, its great, colorless expanse that splattered with deep red crimson. I heard a woman scream then saw the faces of betrayal and destruction: Alex, Zane, Marduk, and Connor. They morphed into the faces of monsters, surrounding and suffocating me with their nearness, and then they converged on me with gnashing teeth and jagged claws, chewing and slicing through my flesh.

I awoke with a start to the shrill ringing of my cell phone. The ringer was set to the sound of an old wired telephone with its sharp trilling bells. I groaned, making a note to myself to change the ring tone. *Something like "Happy" by Pharrell Williams would be better… or not*, I thought sarcastically.

The sunlight was dim beyond my thin curtains. Without looking at the clock, I figured it must be around eight p.m. if the sun was starting to set. I had slept the entire day away.

The ringing stopped to my relief, but then started up again immediately. So much for staying curled up in my cocoon of self-pity as I had been planning to do for the next few days… or maybe weeks.

I picked up the offending device and, pressing a button, answered the call. "What?" I said with more hostility than I intended.

"You know, if you keep saying such sweet things to me, people are going to start to talk," Sam said.

A combination of relief and disappointment filled me when it wasn't Alex on the other end of the phone. I fell back against my pillow, draping an arm across my still heavy eyes.

"Hey, Sam. Sorry about that. I just woke up."

"Yeah, I guessed that. How long will it take you to get dressed? We're hunting the Syndicate tonight."

"Right, um… I can be ready to leave here in about an hour."

"Okay, I'll pick you up at nine." With that, he hung

up, leaving me wondering how the hell he knew where to pick me up. I guessed my safehouse wasn't as safe as I had thought.

With that disturbing idea, I pulled back the covers, preparing to get out of bed, and my eyes fell on Sharur lying by my side. I cringed away from it, exiting the bed on the opposite side, not wanting to touch the weapon. I needed a shower to clear my head.

Why in the fuck had I slept with it? The act felt almost intimate, dirty even, knowing that the axe was sentient.

I spent the next hour avoiding looking at the bed, not wanting the reminder of last night. However, the knowledge of the axe's mere presence was like a physical weight pressing down on me, straining muscle and bone, threatening to snap me into pieces. I couldn't hide from it and couldn't pretend it wasn't there, though I could keep my distance from it for a little while.

I showered and dressed in black yoga pants to give me flexibility of movement, paired with a *Goonies Never Say Die* T-shirt. When I could no longer avoid Sharur, I stepped to the bed, looking upon my nemesis. I wanted to stop myself from grasping the handle, yet I watched my hand close on the shaft as if it had a mind of its own.

You should not be upset with me, I heard in my head. The ease and simplicity in which it invaded my mind was disturbing.

"You killed Ronin," I said, my voice sounding loud in the silence of the bedroom.

No, Ashnan. You killed Ronin. I only helped you to protect yourself from him. He would have killed you if it hadn't been for me guiding and focusing your defensive response.

"So you have the ability to take over my body and make me do things against my will?" I asked, my heart pounding in fear.

No, of course not. I am not a demon that can possess you. I can only work with what is already there.

"So you are trying to tell me that I already wanted to kill Ronin, and you only guided my actions to make that happen?" I wasn't sure that was a better answer.

Something like that.

"But I didn't want to kill Ronin. I had nothing against him personally."

Is that so? You forget how much you still don't remember. Believe me when I say there was a part of you that wanted him dead very badly.

If that was true, how could I trust myself? How many other people from my past might have wronged me so much so, that I subconsciously wanted to kill them? I didn't know whom I harbored murderous intent toward or why, and that meant I was putting everyone around me at risk every time I took up the axe.

"How do you know about my past when I don't remember?"

I have access to parts of your mind that are closed off even to you, but before you ask, I am not able to tell you the secrets that lay hidden there. I only have access to those memories when they are relevant to the situation at hand, bringing them closer to the surface of your mind where there are cracks that I can reach through to grab them. I didn't know anything about Ronin until he was standing before you, trying to kill you on that subway platform, and I still don't know why you harbor animosity toward him, just that you do.

I felt more at ease knowing Sharur couldn't just randomly dig into any memory he wanted to access at any time, but that also meant he couldn't help me very much in learning more about my missing past. Nevertheless, Sharur's access to my mind might have some advantages. I remembered the information he gave me to fight Alcina.

"You might be able to access my thoughts, but it seems to be a two-way street. You can push your knowledge into my mind, can't you?"

Yes, but I have lived a very long time, and I have more memory and knowledge than your brain is capable of processing. It would be like filling a balloon beyond its capacity. You know what would happen.

I imagined my noggin exploding under the immense pressure of Sharur's knowledge. It was not something I was interested in experiencing.

Therefore, I can only give you what you need at a particular moment.

"Your power, it's based on deconstruction, isn't it? I saw how your magic tears apart the fabric of existence, destroying something by pulling apart the building blocks of matter."

It is your power too. And, yes, that is the essence of how it works.

"That's how you were able to create that crater in the wall of the subway station and how you can tear a rift between Earth and Urusilim."

Between this world and Urusilim, as well as others, but again, I do not act alone. These are your abilities, as well.

"I don't have any abilities without you. I just channel what you give me."

The doorbell rang downstairs, cutting off Sharur's response and signaling Sam's arrival. I needed time to absorb everything Sharur had just told me, but it would have to wait.

"I don't want you doing anything tonight unless I consciously ask for your help. Got it?" I felt kind of silly threatening an inanimate object, but the words needed to be said.

As you wish, it responded, although its tone held a trace of disappointment.

It wasn't easy concealing a battle axe. I slipped it into its holster on my back and for good measure, tucked my Glock into a shoulder holster. I put on a lightweight jacket a few sizes too large to hide all of the hardware I sported. I wore my hair loose to help further conceal the bulge. It wasn't perfect, and wearing a jacket in the middle of summer wasn't comfortable, but it would do.

I met Sam at the door, and he eyed me critically. "That's not obvious at all," he said.

"If you know of a way to discretely carry around a three-foot-long battle axe, I'd love to hear it," I grumbled to his back as he led me to the waiting black sedan parked alongside the curb. This time, no G-men tagged along; it was just Sam and I.

"Don't worry about it. New Yorkers tend not to look at the people around them too closely, and where we're going, there may be some benefit to displaying that you are armed and ready."

I climbed into the passenger seat next to him. "So

where are we going?" I asked, buckling my seatbelt.

"I followed the lead Gwen gave us and called the woman, Pearl. She was more than a little cautious, but ultimately fell for my charms and gave me an address, so that's where we're going. Let's hope she's not sending us down a rabbit hole."

We survived the forty-minute drive through bumper-to-bumper New York City traffic and insane taxicab drivers until we arrived at a modern office building twenty short blocks away. It stood like a soaring sentinel, wearing an armor of glass, reflecting the night sky so clearly I could make out constellations in its windows.

"Why didn't we just walk or take the subway?" I complained, feeling on edge after that drive. I could square off against a chimera, but nothing felt like I was taking my life in my hands more than driving through the streets of Manhattan.

"We don't know where she is going to send us, and we might need a car to get there. Anyway, it helps to have a trunk. I like to be prepared." He gave me a half grin.

"What do you have in there?" I asked, intrigued.

"Hopefully nothing we'll need to use." Sam held open the glass entry doors for me, and we stepped into a stark white cavern of smooth marble, clean lines, and gleaming surfaces. A simple, glass-topped table was placed in the center of the otherwise empty vaulted space. A young woman sat behind it.

I could tell she was petite even though she was seated. Her blond hair was pulled back into a neat bun, and she wore black rimmed glasses framing eyes the color of the Caribbean Sea. She wore a smart, navy blue skirt suit with a white blouse and sat with perfect posture. I could imagine her conservative dress and beautiful face made her every guy's fantasy of the librarian by day and vixen by night.

"Good evening. My name is Pearl. How may I help you?" she asked in a melodic singsong voice.

Sam flashed his government identification badge and said in an official tone, "I'm Sam Powell with the FBI. We spoke on the phone earlier. I'm sure I don't need to tell you how important it is that you cooperate fully and answer my questions."

She appeared completely unfazed by his veiled threat, continuing to stare at him with large, beguiling eyes.

"Yes, well… um… we are here to meet with the head of the Syndicate," Sam said, flustered under her intense gaze.

Pearl didn't respond, and her expression didn't change as her eyes shifted to me. "And you are?"

"Emma Hayes. I'm assisting Agent Powell in his investigation."

She nodded, as if expecting this response. Then she picked up the lone pen and square of yellow Post-It notes on her desk and wrote something on the paper in flowery handwriting. I had always wanted that kind of beautifully feminine handwriting with lots of loops and swirls, but I was stuck with chicken scratch that would make a doctor proud.

She handed me the paper. "Good luck, Miss Hayes."

Then she stood, circled her desk, and walked past us, out the front door, disappearing into the late evening crowd of pedestrians.

Sam and I watched her go, equally dumfounded.

"What the hell was that?" I questioned.

"I have no idea. What did she give you?"

I looked down at the paper in my hands. "A name and address."

"That was too easy."

Before he could back out of the plan, I said, "Well, it looks like someone is expecting us, so it would be rude to disappoint them. Why don't you show me what's in the trunk before we pay them a visit?"

Chapter Eighteen

EMMA

J expected an organized crime syndicate led by monsters to be holed up in some decrepit warehouse on the seedy side of town where skells and perps hung out, keeping themselves and their misdeeds hidden. Therefore, I wasn't prepared for the address to lead us to another sleek skyscraper on Park Avenue with businessmen and women in tailored suits coming and going continuously throughout the day.

Whereas the building Pearl occupied was cold and bare, this one was warm and inviting. The lobby housed comfortable couches for those waiting for their appointment times. The security staff wore suits instead of uniforms and kept approachable smiles on their faces. There was even a Starbucks kiosk in the lobby, filling the air with the heavenly scent of roasted coffee beans as we approached the reception desk. I was feeling underdressed in my yoga pants and T-shirt, and my hyperawareness of the bulge on my back didn't help matters. I shifted uncomfortably as the stocky security guard behind the desk looked up at our approach.

"May I help you?" he asked with a friendly smile under his bushy mustache.

"Emma Hayes to see Duncan Macalister," I said, trying to convey confidence as if I came here all the time.

The security guard typed something into his computer, and I half expected an alarm to start blaring as the building went on lockdown before monsters jumped out at me from all directions. Instead, the security guard handed Sam and I VISITOR badges and said in his chipper voice, "Fifty-sixth floor. Elevators are on the right. Have a wonderful day."

"Thank you."

We found the elevators and piled in with the other suits taking the long ride up. As we stopped at the different floors on our way up, my anxiety grew, not knowing what would be lying in wait for us at the top. By the time we reached our destination, the elevator was empty except for us, and my blood buzzed as knots settled into the pit of my stomach.

Sam and I exchanged glances, and I gave him a nod, letting him know I was prepared for whatever lay beyond those elevator doors. I slipped a hand inside my jacket and took hold of the handle of my gun. I saw Sam also reach for his weapon. Then the elevator dinged, and the doors slid open.

We were prepared for war, had anticipated it.

Instead, a lithe young man in a tan suit, pink shirt, and frameless glasses greeted us. He had high cheekbones and shoulder-length red hair, looking to be no older than twenty-one.

"Hello, Miss Hayes, Mr. Powell," he said with a thick Irish brogue. "My name is Derrick Smith. I am Mr. Macalister's personal assistant. If you would, follow me please."

My hand slipped off my gun, and I returned the smile, although it didn't reach my eyes. It was certainly possible they were trying to lull Sam and me into a false sense of security so they could attack with the element of surprise, and I wasn't about to fall for it.

"Lead the way," I said to Derrick, stepping out of the elevator.

When Derrick turned his back to us, Sam and I were confronted by an astonishing set of iridescent wings protruding from slits near the shoulder blades of his suit jacket. They shifted through shades of blue and green with just a touch of pink along the edges.

I would have stood frozen to the ground, just staring at them in utter fascination, but Derrick retreated down the hallway, and Sam nudged me in the ribs to get me moving. I shot him an irritated look, but the point was taken—I was in an office full of Monere, so I had better get my act together and expect the unexpected.

We followed Derrick and his wings down a hallway lined with expensive-looking, original artwork. Although I didn't know anything about art, these pieces were unframed modernist paintings, illuminated by small spotlights running along the ceiling. It reminded me a little of Nathan Anshar's museum-like apartment, but where Nathan was surrounded by ancient cultures and historical pieces, Duncan Macalister was clearly a fan of everything contemporary.

At the end of the hall was a set of frosted glass doors etched with a stunningly beautiful depiction of a tree. The roots of the tree twisted around each other, forming a tangled knot and weaving themselves into an elegant circle that surrounded the tree. Its branches split off from the main trunk into more, which further split off until it was too difficult for my eyes to follow the hundreds of graceful lines. Heart-shaped leaves sprouted from the branches, too numerous to count. It was an amazingly intricate piece of artwork.

Derrick paused briefly to knock on the doors yet didn't wait for a signal to enter before pushing them open. Rather than walk in ahead of us, he stood aside, allowing us to pass. The doors closed behind us, and Derrick was gone.

With the absence of light from the hallway, Sam and I were plunged into semi-darkness. A small lamp sitting on a glass-top desk cast the only illumination in the room. Floor-to-ceiling windows lined two sides of the corner office, offering a stunning view of the river and the city as far as midtown.

I was immediately on edge, alert to even the slightest sounds of movement. I heard nothing except for Sam's even breathing next to me, telling me he was either strangely unconcerned or had immense control over himself. I didn't feel nearly so comfortable knowing I was likely in the presence of a dangerous monster that I couldn't see or hear.

After a minute or so, my eyes began to adjust, and the shadowed figure of a man took shape, standing at the windows, gazing at the glittering lights of the skyscrapers. His hands were clasped in front of him, holding something that glowed softly, and he stared at it with a transfixed intensity.

"I apologize for the darkness," he said absently. "I have a condition."

"Yeah, I'm sure you do," I responded with an unladylike snort. I knew this guy's "condition" was that he wasn't human. "Let's just be straight with each other, shall we? What are you?"

He gave a soft chuckle, and without looking up at me, he said, "It seems reports of your... directness have not been exaggerated. I actually just see a bit better in the dark. Give me a second." He shook a small box in his hands, twisting it from side to side. Then he threw his arms up in the air in a triumphant shout. "Yes!" It was then I realized he had been playing a Nintendo DS video game system. "Pokémon Sapphire," he said, referring to the game he had just been playing. "I just beat the final gym leader and got a shiny Pokémon." I didn't even pretend to know what he was talking about as Duncan stepped into the dim lamp light. "Not what you expected?" He waved his hands down the front of his body in his best imitation of a fashion model showing off her new, designer outfit.

The man standing before me looked like he should work in a computer call center or maybe for Best Buy's Geek Squad. I stood at least two inches taller than he did, in my bare feet. As it was, my boots put me at a good four to five-inch advantage. He had tousled, mouse-brown hair that looked like it refused to be tamed and wore ripped jeans with a T-shirt that read "*Zombie Apocalypse? Keep Calm. Video Games Have Prepared Me For This.*"

"Is this some sort of joke?" My mind raced with possibilities of what was going on here since there was no way this guy was the leader of anything except maybe the computer club at his college. Perhaps we had been lured into this building as a trap or were brought here as a distraction while the real Duncan Macalister made his escape.

"I assure you, Emma, I am Duncan Macalister. Not all great men are large. I don't need brawn and violence and an expensive suit to lead my organization."

"I've never heard of a crime syndicate being led by a pacifist nerd," I challenged, still not ready to accept him at his word.

He laughed. "I'm a geek, not a nerd." He must have read the confusion on my face because he clarified by saying, "I do have a social life."

Sure, that cleared it up, I thought.

"What makes you think this is a crime syndicate, and what makes you think I'm a pacifist? Just because I don't lead with fear and violence, it doesn't mean I don't call on it when I need to."

I opened my mouth to spit something back at him, but nothing came out. Why had I assumed this was a criminal organization? As I searched my memory, I realized Gwen hadn't described them as criminals. However, she did say she worked for the Syndicate's dating service.

"Gwen. She is essentially a prostitute. Last time I checked, prostitution is illegal in New York."

"I suppose prostitution is in the eye of the beholder. Sure, Bill paid for a few dates with Gwen so she would accompany him to charity galas and the like, but they genuinely fell in love with each other. As soon as it became more serious, I refused to accept payment from him and gave them my blessing to pursue their relationship with no strings attached."

I had nothing to say to that. I certainly couldn't prove prostitution was involved. All I knew for sure was that the Syndicate ran a dating service and a bodyguard business, neither of which were outright illegal.

I glanced at Sam for help, but he merely shrugged his shoulders. When I looked back at Duncan, I noticed he stared at Sam with an odd expression on his face, as if he couldn't believe what he was seeing. I turned back to Sam who acted as if he hadn't noticed Duncan's confusion.

"Do you two know each other?" My eyes narrowed. Why would Sam hide something like that from me?

"Not that I can recall," Sam said, "although Mr. Macalister doesn't look particularly memorable. No offense," he said to Duncan.

"Um … right, none taken. You just looked familiar for a moment. Perhaps we met somewhere before in passing or maybe you just reminded me of someone else I know. But never mind that. Please, have a seat." Duncan waved us toward a set of worn leather armchairs around a recycled cork coffee table. "Now, what can I help you with?"

"Mr. Macalister—" Sam began.

"Please, call me Duncan. We're all friends here."

"Duncan, we're here investigating the deaths of three of your employees, Monere hired as bodyguards."

"Ah, yes. Jace, Magnus, and Leon. It was a devastating loss for their families and for the Syndicate," he said.

"Their families?" I cringed, imagining creatures procreating. Why hadn't I thought of that possibility before? They could be multiplying like rabbits as we sat here. What if they could have litters of little monsters all at one time? The city would be overrun in a matter of a few short years.

"Yes, families," Duncan said, shooting a cold look at me, "whom they love very much. Don't you have a family, Emma?"

His question pierced my heart, the barb hitting home. No, I didn't have a family anymore. Even though I had no memories, I knew in my soul I never grew up with love. The only person who had ever made my home life bearable—that I could remember—was Daniel. Could Monere really feel the same way about their families as humans did? Could monsters love? Certainly not in my experience.

"What can you tell us about your employees and the people they were hired to protect?" Sam continued, unfazed by the exchange.

"As far as I could tell at the time, there was no connection between those men. They were all wealthy executives, but so are many of my clients. They were employed at various companies, although mostly in the scientific and engineering fields. I don't know much beyond that. I'm sure you understand that, given the nature of my business, maintaining the privacy of my clients is critical, and the best way to do that is not to ask too many questions."

"Did they give you any idea why they needed the services of a bodyguard, and a Monere bodyguard at that?" I asked.

"Not in great detail, but my employees do need to know what they could be going up against. These men gave me the corporate espionage story. They feared someone might come after them for company secrets. You'd be surprised at how often I hear that one, especially when companies are being acquired or developing some innovative new technology. However, seeing as how these men have disappeared, and my employees have been murdered, I can only assume thieves got the information they were looking for. But they haven't gotten everything."

"What do you mean?" I prompted when he paused.

"Under normal circumstances, I would never divulge the name of a client, but since he is potentially in grave danger, I am willing to share the information if you agree to do everything in your power to try to protect him."

"Yes, of course. That's what we do," Sam said reassuringly.

"There are two other clients who hired bodyguards the same week as the others and are still alive as far as I know: Hiroshi Takai and Nathan Anshar."

Jackpot! I thought. How the hell was Nathan wrapped

up in this mess? I had been trying to contact him for weeks, ever since I had recovered Sharur. He had paid me — and quite handsomely at that — to retrieve the axe for him, but as soon as I had it in my possession and tried to hand it over, Nathan disappeared. Had he gone into hiding, knowing he was being hunted, or had he been purposefully avoiding me? I planned to ask him when I found him.

"Do you know where Nathan is?" I tried unsuccessfully to keep the eagerness from my voice. If one of Duncan's employees were with Nathan at all times, surely Duncan would know where they were.

"No, I'm sorry. I don't."

Disappointment sucked all the hope from my marrow.

"What about Mr. Takai?" Sam asked.

"Um… yeah. I think I can tell you where his bodyguard is, which should be the same place as Mr. Takai. Give me a second." He pulled out his iPhone and tapped on the screen, his thumbs a virtual blur. "Here he is. I have trackers on some of my employees."

"And why is that?" I asked with scowl, accusation dripping from my voice. I was certainly no fan of Monere, but I happened to have a deeply moral opposition to treating any living creature like slaves. I had seen enough of such abuses during Special Forces missions to last me multiple lifetimes. Some of my most satisfying successes were destroying human trafficking rings, but I quickly learned that one person, or even one tactical team, was not enough to change governments in countries like Bangladesh. Turning my back on those people, knowing I couldn't help them, would leave a stain on my soul forever.

Duncan could read the disgust on my face and frowned at the unspoken accusation. "I track my people just in case they get in trouble and need back-up or extraction. It's for their safety ... and it's voluntary," he added like a slap in the face. "That's why Nathan's bodyguard can't be tracked. He chose not to be."

I wondered if Nathan knew that, leading him to choose that particular bodyguard.

Moving his attention back to his phone, Duncan said, "It looks like Snake is only five blocks away."

"Snake? How did he get that name?" I asked, almost afraid to ask.

Duncan only smiled and winked. No doubt, he hoped Snake would show me exactly how he had gotten that name.

Sam's annoying ring tone interrupted the poisonous glares that Duncan and I were shooting at each other. "Yeah," he said into the mouthpiece, walking several feet away to have a whispered conversation with the caller.

Duncan lowered his voice. "I know you don't think very highly of me, my employees, or my business, but what is that human expression? People in glass houses shouldn't throw stones. I am willing to bet you have done worse things for money than go on a few dates or protect innocent businessmen. How many friends has that line of work earned you, Emma? Because I can assure you that my efforts in protecting the Monere and helping them make a life for themselves on Earth have earned me quite a few very powerful and terrifying friends."

I opened and closed my mouth a few times, trying to absorb what he had just said to me. No one had ever thrown the brutal truth right in my face quite like that before. He was right, though. I had done just as much evil as I had done good; my willingness to cross that line for the right amount of money was nothing to be proud of. Still, I didn't appreciate being called out on it.

Sam ended his phone call and returned to us. "Thank you, Duncan," he said, once again interrupting the glares Duncan and I shot at each other. "You've been very helpful. If we have any more questions, we'll be in touch." Sam clamped down on my arm and, with a rough yank, dragged me out of the Duncan's office.

"What the hell are you doing?" I fought his grip and wrenched my arm free. "I was just about to kick his scrawny ass."

"We have more important things to do right now than have a pissing contest with one of the most dangerous men in the city," he said, throwing me a sharp look like a mother would give to a misbehaving child.

"First of all, that pissant is far from—"

"Don't be stupid, Emma. He might not look like much, but he commands the loyalty of dozens of monsters that could rip most any human limb from limb. How do you think he got that kind of street cred? And he's a smart kid. Don't underestimate him."

"Fine," I said with a childish pout. "So what is he, then? I mean, besides a total geek?"

"He's a ghoul, and he survives by eating human

flesh. I don't think you want him to make a meal out of you."

"What?" I asked in stunned disbelief. "He kills and eats people? Why the fuck are we teaming up with a guy like that? We should kill him." My stomach lurched at the thought of Duncan gnawing on a mouthful of bloody flesh.

"Actually, he is the ghoul equivalent of a vegetarian. He can't survive without eating flesh, but he has chosen to eat the flesh of the dead instead of the living. He has contacts in local morgues and purchases bodies under the guise of using them for medical education."

"And then what? He cooks them up on a grill and has human burgers?"

"No. He doesn't eat his meat cooked."

Needing to shake that image and steady my stomach, I decided it was time to change the subject. As long as Duncan didn't kill what he ate, I would give him a pass, but I intended to keep an eye on him. "So what's the hurry? Where are we going?"

"I just got a call that there is an altercation in progress right now only a few blocks away. It sounds like it might be our guy, Mr. Takai."

"What? Why the hell didn't you just say that in the first place?" I said, picking up the pace. I pulled off my jacket and tossed it to the ground. Having ready access to my weapons trumped being discrete. I had a feeling I would need them.

Chapter Nineteen

EMMA

Thank goodness for nosey neighbors. Sam's team had been monitoring police scanners and heard the report of a mugging called in by an onlooker. The dispatcher conveyed that the caller was probably high on drugs because he thought he saw a ten-foot tall monster that looked like The Thing from *The Fantastic Four*. It sounded like a stone giant to me.

We needed to get there before the cops showed up and crashed our party. A short five blocks away, we came upon the scene within minutes. We heard the scuffle before we saw anything: scratching and scrabbling interspersed with pained grunts and deep thuds then high-pitched wails of pain and fear, followed by terrified begging.

"Please, please, please. Don't kill me. I'll tell you

whatever you want."

I heard a deep chuckle that lifted the fine hairs on the back of my neck. A shiver of familiarity ran down my spine at the same time a feeling of dread settled deep in my stomach. Something about that voice affected me.

Sam and I turned the final corner and came to a skidding halt as we took in the scene in front of us. We had stepped into the front courtyard of a very beautiful high-end apartment complex. The wrought iron gate surrounding the park-like space swung forlornly from a single hinge. The space was small, like everything in New York City, but filled with the fragrant scents of blooming lilac, roses, and cut grass. The path lighting that illuminated the area had been cut, turning the space into a garden of shadows.

A dark figure was giving one massive beat down to what I assumed was the Monere bodyguard, and the whimpering human I had heard cowered in a corner a few feet away, powerless to intercede on his bodyguard's behalf. The man was trapped in the corner by a steel beam that had pinned his leg firmly in place, no doubt positioned there by his attacker so he couldn't escape.

The current target of the attack was a massive, hulking shape that looked like it could win a fight just by showing up and watching its opponents run for the hills. The creature was humanoid — two arms, two legs, a head, and a torso — but its skin was lumpy and mottled gray. It had the same rough texture of the remains I had seen the night before. It was impossible to imagine this ten-foot and maybe five hundred pound beast — if its skin really was as solid and heavy as rock — could be turned into a gelatinous mass.

The stone giant's attacker had his back to me, so I wasn't able to identify him, but he appeared to be human. He moved with the fluid grace of water flowing over river rocks, smooth and inexorable. The guy had mad martial arts skills, landing almost every punch and kick he delivered. He was strong and nimble, but the stone giant's size alone was just too formidable to defeat with a few well-placed kicks. However, a creature that had to carry around that much bulk during a fight didn't have much staying power. The giant was probably used to taking down an opponent with the first blow.

The human wore down the giant with his relentless attacks. The man never seemed to slow, tire, or even need to catch his breath. He blocked every attack and returned each attempted blow with three more of his own. I had the feeling he was actually drawing out the fight for his own enjoyment.

As I watched, tingles erupted at the base of my neck and traveled down my spine, pulling my attention from the struggle unfolding before me. I twirled around, my eyes seeking the source of the magic that triggered my senses, but I could see nothing.

Whimpers drew me back, emanating from the darkened corner where the trapped man still struggled unsuccessfully to free himself. Catching sight of Sam and me as we cautiously approached the scene before us, the man pleaded, "Please help me. He's going to kill me."

Tears streaked down his face, but before I could take a step toward him, the attacker paused for a moment in his assault on the giant, realizing he now had an audience. Then the attacker decided to speed things along and put an end to playtime. Without further ado, keeping his back to us so he couldn't be identified, he plunged his hand into the creature's chest, and bones cracked as a wet sucking sound reached my ears.

The creature drew in a shuddering breath before letting out an agonized roar full of pain, anger, and regret. Pink-tinged foam frothed from its mouth, spilling past its jaws, and dark, viscous liquid leaked out from around the attacker's arm where it was still impaled inside the creature's body. The discharge started slow and thick, but in moments, a free flow of blood mixed with fat and puss.

The giant dropped to the ground, convulsing violently. As the creature fell, the attacker's arm slid free of the body, leaving it covered in blood and chunks of flesh and organs. The creature's insides were being liquefied, pouring from its body in pulsating waves.

I couldn't pry my eyes from the horror I witnessed. After what seemed like years of torment, the creature stopped moving. Relief flooded through me, not because I was happy to see the stone giant dead, but because I didn't want it to keep suffering. No one deserved that kind of death.

Still in a state of shocked stupor, I fumbled for my Glock with clumsy fingers and pulled it free, training it on the killer's back. My movement snapped Sam out of his immobility, and he did the same.

"Federal agents. Don't move," Sam yelled at him. "Very slowly, put your hands on your head and turn around."

To my surprise, the killer obeyed. His hands clasped together on the top of his head, and, facing away from us, he unfolded himself to his full height with the grace of a ballet dancer or MMA fighter. His slow, purposeful movements were thick with power and beauty. He wasn't as tall as I expected, and he was quite lean, almost thin. Something both foreign and familiar about him niggled at the back of my mind.

His willingness to comply with Sam's instructions put me on edge. I didn't trust him. Sure enough, our killer spun around in a blur of movement and leapt for us, hands outstretched. The darkness kept his identity hidden, but his movement seemed very familiar. I had seen what those hands could do, so I shrunk away from them, not wanting to be touched. Then I looked up from his hands, and my eyes landed on a face as familiar to me as my own.

"Daniel," I breathed, my voice caught by the lump in my throat.

The gun suddenly felt like it weighed three hundred pounds, and I could no longer hold it up. I lowered the Glock to my side, but Sam pulled the trigger on his. The report of the weapon exploded in my ears, and a wave of disorientation hit me.

Daniel stumbled backward, and I knew he had been hit.

Moving on unsteady feet and driven by desperation, I plowed my full body weight into Sam. He got off another shot, but it went wide, hitting the wall with a small explosion of dust and debris.

"What the fuck?" Sam growled, circling his arms to keep from falling on his ass. He caught himself and turned the brunt of his anger on me, but I wasn't paying him any attention.

"Daniel!" I screamed at the fleeing form of my little brother, but he never slowed.

As he ran past the trapped man who was now quiet and looking relieved at the turn of events, Daniel reached out and slashed him across the throat with nothing but a deadly hand. His hand melted flesh and bone as if they were butter.

The man stared blankly into space with a stunned look on his face, and then he spluttered, a spray of blood passing his lips.

"Sam, help him," I ordered, taking off on foot after Daniel, who had never been much of a runner, as he far outpaced my flat-out sprint.

I would have lost him had it not been for the blood trail he left behind. I hoped the wound might slow him down a bit, so I could catch up, but no such luck. However, it did give me some measure of comfort that he couldn't have been too seriously injured if he was moving like the wind.

Fresh air pumped through my lungs, fueling burning leg muscles and cooling my overheated skin. Daniel was alive and within my reach, and I felt like I could fly with that knowledge. Elation pushed me on and infused me with energy. I pressed harder, reveling in the sensation of tearing up the ground beneath my feet as my muscles strained with the increase in stride and pace.

No matter what had been done to Daniel that

allowed him to turn his victims into puddles of goo, I swore to myself I would fix him. The sound of my own blood rushing in my ears helped to drown out the nagging little voice that asked how I planned to cure Daniel when I couldn't do it for Zane.

As the volume of blood splatters on the sidewalk increased, I heard pounding footsteps ahead of me. Daniel was slowing down, his injury taking a toll, while I felt like I could easily run another twenty miles.

I heard the crash of metal garbage cans hitting concrete, and rounding a corner, they came into view, rolling in front of my path. I was over them in one smooth leap.

Daniel had stumbled into the cans, dizzy and unsteady on his feet from blood loss. He staggered to the side, falling into a hedge of boxwood. They were tall and full enough to hold him upright until he found his balance again. He stopped a few feet ahead of me, leaning heavily against the wall of the nearest building as if he was trying to hold it up. He panted, cradling one arm against his chest with the opposite hand while trying to catch his breath. Blood flowed freely down his arm from the bullet wound in his shoulder, soaking his black T-shirt.

As I stopped several feet away, every fiber within me wanted to run to him, hug him, tell him that I loved him and would fix everything as I always did. However, I knew he would bolt like a skittish cat if I came too close, or he might try to kill me.

"Daniel, it's me, Emma," I said in the same soothing tone I had used when we were kids, and I tried to lull him to sleep after a bad run-in with our sadistic asshole of an adoptive father. "I want to help you."

He laughed, with a mirthless sound full of contempt. "I don't need any help," he said in a voice that was almost unrecognizable. I had never heard Daniel use such harsh tones with me before.

"Daniel, please, look at me," I begged, needing the eye contact, needing to see whether my baby brother was still in there somewhere. The thought of Marduk doing to Daniel what he had done to Zane sent my stomach roiling.

Daniel took a deep breath and turned to face me. I knew that face had looked upon every curve and angle almost every day for years, yet it was completely alien. His features were hard and glacial, revealing no sign of his emotional state upon seeing me again. This wasn't the warm and open Daniel I had known for half my life.

"Your shoulder," I said, reaching out without touching the wound, but he flinched away from me, anyway.

"I'll be fine. Hurts like a bitch, but it didn't hit a major artery. It'll heal."

I couldn't hold myself back any longer and launched myself at him, fates be damned. If I were to die tonight, I would much prefer it to be at his hands than anyone else's.

Daniel stiffened when my arms wrapped around his neck as I pressed my cheek to his. I counted the seconds. One... two... three... Almost a full twenty seconds of agony went by before I felt Daniel's body relax against mine, and tentative arms closed around me.

He melted against me then, and we squeezed each other even tighter, clinging together as if we were the last two people on Earth facing our imminent destruction. He was the first to break the hold, but only after several minutes.

I gazed into his eyes, my soul set free from the horrendous burden it had been under since Daniel had been taken weeks ago. "Oh, my God, Daniel. Are you okay?" I asked, clasping the hand on his uninjured arm in a death grip, needing the proof that he was actually standing in front of me. "What happened to you? What did Marduk do to you?"

"Nothing," he said. "Well, not nothing, but not what you think. He didn't torture me or anything like that... well, not really."

"He must have done something to you unless you've always been able to turn people into jelly and just forgot to mention it to me," I said, the sarcasm coated with fear and concern.

"He made me better, Em. He made me one of his people, a Monere, hoping that would convince you to fight on our side."

"What side is that, exactly?" I asked, wondering just how much Kool-Aid Daniel had drunk.

"He's fighting for creature equality," Daniel said.

A harsh laugh bubbled in my throat at the ridiculousness of that statement, but I choked it back, realizing he was dead serious. Marduk thought himself the Urusilim equivalent of Martin Luther King Jr.? How could Daniel buy into such absurdity? It was more likely that my little brother had been brainwashed by Marduk, just as Zane had.

"Okay." I plastered on a poker face, not wanting to upset Daniel right now or get into an argument with him about how wrong he was. "Tell me what he did to you," I said, softening my voice.

He looked away and seemed to withdraw into himself. "I don't really remember."

Lie, I thought. He remembered more than he was letting on, but whatever had happened to him had left him changed, traumatized. I didn't want to open that wound until he was ready to deal with it, so I decided to let it go... for now.

"If Marduk wants creature equality, why are you killing those stone giants, and what are you doing with the men you are kidnapping?"

"I'm just following orders, Emma. I don't ask questions, same as my arrangement with you."

Ouch, that hurt. If I had ever kept him out of the loop on anything, I had done so to protect him. It was bad enough he worked for me as a mercenary, but I had tried my hardest to keep him from being exposed to anything he didn't need to know or see.

"So, what were your orders from Marduk?"

He sighed in resignation. "You're just going to nag me to death until I tell you something, aren't you?" I merely smiled. "Look, all he told me was to find those men and deliver them to another Monere. I don't know why or what is being done with them. The bodyguards are just collateral damage."

"Who are you delivering the men to? Where are you taking them?"

"Look, Emma, you are the strongest person I know, but this thing is beyond anything you are capable of handling. You wouldn't survive going after this thing. I'm sorry, but I can't tell you."

"I've learned a lot in the last few weeks, Daniel. You might be surprised at what I am capable of handling."

"Don't ask this of me, Emma," he begged, looking so forlorn I almost let him off the hook. Almost.

"Don't make me remind you of that time I saved your ass from the neighbor's Rottweiler. You owe me."

"All you did was distract the dog by giving him the burger you were eating."

"Hey, I love burgers. That was a major sacrifice I made for you." I thought I saw the hint of a smile before it disappeared like a wraith.

"Fine. This one is on you, Emma. Don't ever say I didn't warn you. You can find him—"

A pissed off growl erupted from behind me, and Daniel stiffened, looking over my shoulder.

"I know how persuasive she can be," said a voice behind me as smooth as silk and as hard as steel. It sent waves of liquid heat down my spine. "But you may want to reconsider what you were about to say," Zane said to Daniel.

"I… uh…" Daniel worked his jaw yet couldn't seem to find any words. What could he really say, though? He had been caught red-handed, selling secrets to the enemy, and Zane would kill him for that betrayal of Marduk.

Before I could come to Daniel's defense, Zane surprised me. "Get out of here, Daniel. You have a job to finish."

"No," I said before I could stop the word from spilling out of my mouth.

Zane turned a baleful glare on me, his jaw tightening, but if I let Daniel walk away now, I might never see him again. I couldn't lose my brother, and I couldn't let him continue to kill for Marduk.

"He's not going anywhere. You can let your boss know that Daniel is changing careers."

Zane gave me a half smile that kick-started the butterflies in my stomach. Here the man stood, threatening my brother and me, and all I could think about was what he looked like under those clothes.

"What say you, Daniel?" he asked without taking his eyes from my face, boring into me like he was thinking the same thing I was. He gave Daniel the choice, and my brother made his decision without hesitation.

"Don't worry about me, Emma. I'll be okay." Then he was gone, slipping away into the night as silent as a cat.

"Daniel!" I screamed after him, taking a step forward to follow before I was caught in the steel vice of Zane's arm around my waist, pulling me tightly against him.

I felt the hard length of him towering over me, soft skin over contoured muscle. Strength and power radiated off him like a sultry heat, and I felt myself lean into him as his arms tightened perceptibly around me, his hands brushing my hips and waist, sending pulses of electricity through my body.

Forcing myself back to my senses, I struggled against Zane, which only caused him to hold me tighter.

"Let go of me," I growled between clenched teeth, trying to keep the tears at bay. "I have to go after him."

"You're not going anywhere, Ashnan. That's what Marduk wants you to do. Why do you think he let Daniel come back to this world so soon? Daniel is being used as bait. Marduk is counting on you going after him, and when you do, Daniel will lead you directly into Marduk's trap."

"Daniel wouldn't do that to me," I said without hesitation.

"He would if he didn't know he was doing it. Marduk is playing Daniel like a pawn on a chessboard, so for now, the best thing you can do to keep your brother safe is to stay as far away from him as possible. Once Marduk has you, he doesn't need Daniel anymore."

I was so focused on Daniel that I almost overlooked one key question. "Why are you telling me this?" I asked, knitting my brows. "Shouldn't you be trying to kill me?"

He released his hold from my waist, but neither of us moved. He brushed his fingertips softly down the length of my arm, leaving a trail of goose bumps in his wake, and my breath caught in my throat. Then he took hold of my hips and, with a jerk, twisted me around to face him.

His full lips were so close to mine I could feel his breath. What was it about this man that kept me wanting more, even knowing I was in mortal danger every time he was near? He was my kryptonite, and I didn't even want to try to resist him.

Zane forced me backward until my back met the

solid surface of a brick wall. He pressed the length of his body against mine, his heat seeping into my skin and triggering a rush of pleasure.

Zane leaned in, brushing those sensual lips along my cheek then pressing them to my ear. "Why would I kill you when there are so many other things I would rather do to you?"

My breath caught in my throat as my knees turned to jelly, and I probably would have collapsed if Zane hadn't been pressing me against the wall, holding me upright. He pulled his head back, but only far enough to meet my eyes, and I saw the familiar war in them between desire and fear, love and hatred. Desire won out, this time.

Zane's mouth took mine, hard and desperate, kissing me like a drowning man gasping for air. I responded in kind, my arms reaching around his neck and pulling him even closer than I thought possible. He parted my lips with his tongue then deepened the kiss, and he tasted like fresh mint and danger.

He reached back and took hold of my wrists that were wrapped around his neck, pulling my grip apart and pinning my hands behind my back. A wicked sneer marred his beautiful mouth, and the crazy came back into his eyes with a vengeance. There was a fine line between passion and madness, and Zane had just crossed it.

A spike of fear ran though me at the vulnerable position he had me in as I mentally kicked myself for allowing this to happen again. Why did I think this time would be any different? The realization hit me that I had been stupidly clinging onto hope with a death grip that Zane would find his way back to sanity and to me.

Hope could change the tides of war and save the souls of men, but for me, it was a poison. My desires for Zane somehow to overcome what had been done to him, and regain himself, kept drawing me back to him. Each new encounter could be the one where he sheds Marduk's control and becomes mine again. It never happened, though, and I had to accept that it never would. I had to let him go.

I regained my composure, gathered my courage, and kneed Zane in the balls hard. He blew out a muffled *oomph* and loosened his grip on me. His eye closed as his ragged breathing gave away his struggle to work through the pain, and I wrenched out of his grasp then stepped outside of his reach. Instead of running, however, I turned to face him.

Forcibly choking back my feelings for the mage, I steeled myself and willed power into my hands, and they glowed with that now familiar blue light. Zane looked up then, his attention caught by the sudden illumination, and fearful recognition crossed his face. He knew what I could do, but how? If this worked, I might never learn the answer.

Raising my palms, I willed the destructive force that lived within me to end the man I once loved. The light burst forth, but before it reached Zane, it slammed into a wall of fire that Zane threw up to protect himself. When the fire met the light, hot sparks flew, sizzling and popping, dripping molten blue fire. My light consumed his fire and left us in a darkness that seemed even more oppressive than before.

Zane panted just as hard as I did from the effort. The edges of my vision wavered as I struggled to stay conscious. I was a one-hit wonder. Each time I used my magic, it drained me of strength and energy. I wanted to do nothing more than curl up on the filthy sidewalk and sleep for a few days.

Before I used that trick again, I needed to be sure I would win because I was way too vulnerable afterward. I could only hope Zane was equally as affected. Unfortunately, he wasn't.

Zane straightened and leapt for me, arms outstretched, going for my throat. In the moment before he reached me, he was thrown several feet away by a cold blast of arctic air, and I let out a shaky breath as I slipped the Glock I had pointed at Zane's heart back into its shoulder holster. I had pulled the gun while my magic engaged with his, knowing I wouldn't be in any state to fight him physically afterward.

Alex had just saved his friend's life and spared me a lifetime of guilt and heartache. Could I have really killed Zane? I was beyond grateful that I didn't have to find out this time, but dread filled me at the thought that I would probably have to make that decision again one day soon.

Regardless of my relief at the turn of events, I still wasn't ready to let Alex off the hook. The hurt of his betrayal was too fresh and too confusing. Had he been working against me from the very beginning, or did he choose to take Alcina's side at some point after our friendship had taken root? I wasn't sure which was worse, but they were both bad and perhaps unforgivable.

Zane struggled to his feet, rage transforming his features as he spun to face Alex, who had moved to stand beside me. I bristled, stepping away from him. I knew it didn't matter, but for some reason, I didn't want Zane to think I sided with Alex.

Zane turned the brunt of his anger on Alex. "I told you, if I ever saw you again, I would rip you to pieces and enjoy every minute of it."

Hurt flashed in Alex's eyes before he smoothed out his features again. I knew what Alex felt—the pain of someone you once cared for turning against you, becoming a stranger when you had once been the closest of allies. He deserved it.

"Zane, listen to me. I came here, looking for you," Alex said.

"So, you have a death wish," Zane snarled.

"No, I think I have a cure."

Chapter Twenty

ZANE

It took a moment for Alex's words to penetrate the haze of rage that clouded my mind almost constantly. It was a grueling effort to battle that demon, and most times, it felt like I was losing. Sometimes I couldn't remember why I tried to fight it. The effort was exhausting, and my will was slipping away from me. Soon, it would be gone forever, and maybe that wasn't such a bad thing. It would be so much easier to be nothing more than a mindless soldier, taking orders without thought or question.

Then I found Emma in that dark alley in New York City a few weeks ago, and I remembered why I needed to keep fighting to hold on to those last strands of myself. It still felt like a losing battle, but at least I was back in the fight.

When Alex came to me, begging my help to save Emma from captivity on North Brother Island, I would have done anything for her. Alex was injured, and I was the only one powerful enough to break her out. He gave me an antidote that time, albeit a temporary one.

It was a spell the mages had cooked up some years before when they tried in earnest to fix me. They gave up their efforts when they realized, each time they temporarily contained the madness, it returned with a vengeance as the spell eventually wore off. It became harder and harder to control myself, and my rages resulted in many innocent casualties. The effects of the antidote were worse than the disease.

In the throes of one of my earliest berserker rages, I escaped the mages and found my way back to Marduk, as if he was a homing beacon I couldn't resist. Marduk directed my madness toward a singular goal—hunting down his daughter, Emma. Then I found her.

She threw my already fragile world completely off its axis, as though the Earth was constantly shifting and tilting underneath me, and I couldn't find my balance. Her presence also sparked a new drive within me to keep fighting against the snarling beast inside that wanted nothing more than to break free and tear everyone's throats out.

That brief moment of lucidity Alex had given me with Emma was heaven on Earth. It was so much more than I deserved. I had both peace and happiness for the first time in a decade. Regardless, I knew even then that the crash was going to be a bitch, and I was right. I moved one step closer to the precipice of insanity, and once I fell in, there would be no coming back. It would only take one more time, one more antidote, and I would be lost forever, replaced by a mindless, unstable killer.

Given the mages' failed attempts at fixing me in the past, I couldn't manage to muster up much enthusiasm over the prospect of a new solution. It was sure to be only temporary, like all of their other treatments, and this time I had a feeling it would be my last. Maybe that was their intention all along.

Once the Mage Council could say without a doubt that the old Zane was gone, Alcina would have the unanimous backing she had been seeking for years to have me killed. The only thing that had been stopping her was the few holdouts on the Council who thought I could still be saved. When that hope was gone, they would have no choice other than to hunt me down.

As strong as I might be, I was like a toothless, declawed kitten against the full power of the Council. Now Alex, my old friend, had been sent as the harbinger of my demise.

Maybe I should let him do it. I was so tired, and I didn't want to hurt any more people or creatures in the name of Marduk. If he failed, the only way to stop me would be to kill me.

Then my eyes were drawn to the vision of strength and beauty standing beside him. Ash looked at Alex with disgust and disappointment. The pain in her eyes took me by surprise, and a flutter of jealousy spread through my chest. That much resentment could only be felt for someone you loved who had betrayed that love.

I saw a shadow of hope ignite in her eyes at Alex's

words. She still had feelings for me even after all I had done to her. I knew I should be noble and selfless, letting her have an eventual happily ever after with Alex, who was by far the better man. However, I couldn't lose her, not when I had just found her again. She always was my weakness, the one person who could simultaneously create my world and destroy it.

"Please, let me help you," Alex said, dragging my attention away from Ash, who hadn't even noticed me staring at her.

"Are you fucking kidding me?" I spat. "You mean like you and the Council helped me in the past? How many times did the Council promise me they had found a cure, only to make me worse? They are more to blame for my present state than Marduk is."

Alex held up his hands in a placating gesture, trying his best to diffuse my anger. *Good luck with that*, I thought.

"I'm not here on behalf of the Council," he said. "I am here on my own. I bargained with Alcina for the cure… the real cure." Alex's eyes darted to Ash, and the look of guilt and remorse he conveyed to her in that glance was unmistakable.

Her eyes widened a fraction before narrowing to slits, as she pierced him with a glare that contained mistrust and suspicion. What the hell had he done to her? The last time I had watched them together, they were close, maybe a bit too close for my comfort. Alex was loyal to a fault, so I couldn't imagine he would ever do anything to hurt her. Or did he do something out of loyalty to me? Would he really have chosen me over her?

As much as I wanted Ash for myself, I was surprised by how much it bothered me to be the destroyer of their friendship. It was that friendship that had kept Ash alive for so long. She couldn't have survived the last few weeks without Alex. I needed her to be protected. As much as I didn't want them to be together, I knew she was safer with him.

Alex's sense of loyalty was also dangerous when it was misplaced. His drive to constantly please Alcina made him dangerous and untrustworthy, even if he was an unwitting player. Alex had always thought of Alcina as the parent he had lost when he had joined the mages, and she had cultivated that relationship carefully, knowing she needed powerful mages like Alex whom she could manipulate.

She tried that bullshit with me too, when I first joined the mages, but I didn't need a replacement mommy. I had gotten along just fine without one. Anyway, there was always something disingenuous about Alcina.

Sure, she was the strongest of all the mages, but she had become that way by wielding dark magic forbidden to everyone else. She would never admit to it, but I had seen some of the things she could do, and they didn't teach that kind of stuff in school.

How did I know Alcina wasn't behind this cure of his? She could have easily manipulated the situation to make Alex think he had a real cure when, in fact, it could be the final bullet through my brain. As much as I wanted to cling onto the last vestiges of hope in actually having my life back, I had come to accept a long time ago that either I was destined to help destroy the world, or be destroyed while trying. I could only pray it was the latter, and soon.

"Why should I believe you?" I said, more exhausted than threatening. "Alcina is probably manipulating you as she always has. You fall for it every time, my brother. Even Ash doesn't trust you anymore. What did you do to her?"

Alex shifted his gaze to Ash yet remained silent.

"Tell him, Alex," she said. "Tell him how you gained my trust just so I would lead you to Sharur. Then you called in Alcina so she could take me out, and you could both ride off into the sunset with the axe."

"I know that's what it must have looked like, but please believe me when I say I did it for all of the right reasons," Alex pleaded with her.

"And what the hell reasons were those? What could possibly justify almost getting me killed and giving Alcina the power to access worlds at will?" Ash spat back, not giving him an inch.

"Zane was the reason," Alex said quietly, my name falling off his tongue like a prayer. That naive son of a bitch had done this for me. He had put Ash's life in danger for the completely impossible notion of trying to save me. Would he never learn?

"How many times do we have to do this before you finally accept there is no hope for me?" I growled, expending a momentous effort to keep my emotions in check.

"If our roles were reversed, you would never give up on me. I will keep trying until one of us breathes our last," Alex said, an edge of determination strengthening his words.

How could Alex have been so stupid as to lead Alcina to Sharur? Heat flared to life within me, emotions clashing and warring: anger at Alex for betraying Ash, frustration at his continuing blindness to Alcina's manipulation, jealousy at the strength of Ash's feelings for Alex, and desire to fulfill my mission to Marduk and recover the axe myself.

My skin burned and the air shimmered around me as my body temperature intensified. My emotions were inextricably tied to my powers, each feeding off the other like parasites. Trying to control the beast awakening within me was like attempting to battle a tornado, and Alex could see it happening.

"Emma, get out of here," he urged.

"Tonight, Alex, you will breathe your last, and I will finally put an end to your childish hopes," I said.

Ash could stay or go; I didn't care. If she ran, I would find her another night and finish this. If she stayed, I would take her down, but not before I learned where Sharur was. It was time for me to fully embrace the monster Marduk had created and end this mission so I could go home to Urusilim.

Ash's eyes turned as hard and determined as stone. Through gritted teeth, she said, "As much as I want to kill you myself, Alex, I'm not leaving you."

All I heard in my rage-addled brain was "*Alex, I'm not leaving you,*" and jealously exploded in my chest as I struggled to take a breath. It felt like my heart was being squeezed in a vice. Dead or alive, she was mine, and I would take her either way.

With a roar, I let loose an inferno of hellfire.

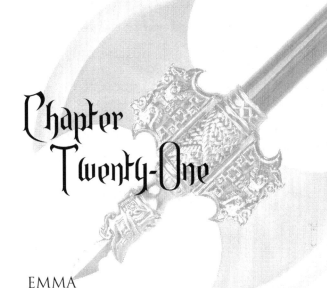

Chapter Twenty-One

EMMA

"Holy shit!" I screamed just before throwing myself to the ground.

A blast of searing heat scalded my back, followed by an oppressive wave of hot air that seemed to suck all of the oxygen from the environment. I heaved and gagged, trying to swallow clean air while I kept my eyes shut tight against the stinging heat to prevent my eyeballs from melting out of my skull. I could only hope Alex had reacted just as quickly and dodged out of the way.

As the smoke began to clear, I felt a tingle at the base of my neck and knew another blast was about to come at me. I rolled to the side, only narrowly avoiding the flames that lit up my vision behind closed eyelids. The acrid smell of burning hair reached my nose. My eyes flew open, and I frantically beat at my ponytail to put out the smoldering strands. On the bright side, now I didn't need to get those dead ends trimmed off.

Leaping to my feet, I fell into a fighting stance, unsure how I would be able to punch or kick my way out of this situation. Nevertheless, I found that I already had a shield.

Alex stood in front of me, using his magic to hold a steady torrent of liquid fire at bay. He sweated from the effort or the heat, probably both.

I wanted to help him, but I stood there, feeling useless. Then I remembered what I had done to Alcina. I reached out with my senses, feeling for the magical energies swirling and colliding all around me like glittering threads. It was impossible to tell where one thread started and the other ended. I tried pulling gently on one, and Alex grunted as his shield wavered.

Jerking my senses back, I realized I couldn't determine which threads belonged to which mage. If I pulled harder on Alex's thread, his shield would collapse, and both of us would be barbecued. I couldn't take that risk.

I could wait until one of them faltered. Then I would know whose magic threads were left, but there was a very good chance Alex would be the first man down. He was strong, but Zane was the superior magic user. I thought the only reason Zane hadn't been able to defeat Alex yet was because the two of them had probably grown up sparring with each other, and Alex knew all of Zane's tactics and capabilities. However, being prepared wouldn't always be enough to save his life.

I could just shoot one of them. I fingered the gun

holstered at my waist, taking comfort in the familiar feel of the grip. A non-fatal hit wouldn't be too difficult to pull off, but knowing Zane, he would either shrug it off or fight through any minor flesh wound. I would have to create a serious injury to put him out of commission, and I wasn't prepared to risk his life just yet.

The only option left to me was the axe strapped to my back. Its weight suddenly felt heavier with the knowledge that I hadn't learned enough about its capabilities to be a real threat, and given how much the axe's magic took out of me, I didn't have unlimited chances to get it right. Even if I had learned all of its secrets, would I dare use them? I also didn't want to draw the mages' attention to Sharur, knowing they were both after the axe.

Then again, why did I even care about what happened between Alex and Zane? Maybe I should let the two of them simply battle it out until only one remained standing. This wasn't my fight after all. If Alex wanted Zane, I should let them figure it out and slip out of here. On the other hand, how would I feel if one of them didn't make it out of this alive? Whose death would affect me the most?

I reached back and gripped the axe's handle as if it was the only thing stopping me from falling into an abyss, but froze in indecision. Then I caught movement in my periphery under a nearby street lamp. Turning in that direction, I saw something familiar—three somethings, in fact—and I flashed back to the incident in Mexico that had changed my entire life.

After I had escaped from Vincent Darko, I had

been chased down hallways and out the front door of a Mexican mansion by a creature that reminded me of the gargoyle dogs in *Ghostbusters*.

Three of those gargoyle-like beasts crept toward me on all fours. They were the size of grizzly bears with dry, scaly skin, a mouthful of sharp teeth, and two tusks extended from their mouths like saber-toothed tigers. The pack raised their heads in unison and bellowed a threat from deep in their throats, and Alex and Zane startled at the sound then broke off their fight, turning their attention to this new threat.

The gargoyles didn't attack, only pawed the ground, and swished their massive heads restlessly. Then they stepped aside, opening a path, and Daniel came forward. As he passed the beasts, he petted each of their gnarled heads tenderly as if they were adorable puppies. The beasts lifted their heads higher in pride at the acknowledgement of a job well done. The lead gargoyle snarled at me with spittle dripping from its tusks, as if telling me he was the biggest, baddest, and most capable of his pack.

I drew the axe by instinct and only afterward realized I should have gone for my gun, instead. In my defense, I already had a grip on Sharur, and my poor Glock had been forgotten.

When Sharur cleared its sheath and came into view, there was a collective gasp, followed by utter silence. I could feel covetous eyes boring into the weapon, desire pressing in on me like a palpable thing, and I realized my mistake immediately. I held the one thing they all wanted most in the world. I had just made myself the target of mages, madmen, and monsters. *Oops.*

Well, I couldn't put the genie back in the bottle, so I had better work some magic, both literally and figuratively, if I was going to get out of this mess alive.

I spun in a slow circle, watching the greedy expressions closing in on me. My muscles tensed, and I crouched low, waiting for the first sign of attack.

Could I count on any of these men to defend me? Did I have any friends among them? Until last night, I would have bet everything I had and more on Alex standing by my side and protecting me through hell and back. However, he had proved his loyalty to Alcina trumped all, and he would do anything to get the axe for her.

And what of Zane? I knew I couldn't trust him, but I didn't believe he would stand by and allow me to die either. There was still something between us, a spark that remained hidden from the effects of the torture and dark magic Zane had endured at Marduk's hands. I had seen it, felt it. That amazing night we spent together less than a month ago had to have stayed with him in some way. I knew it had replayed in my head once or twice or maybe a dozen times a day. I couldn't rely on Zane to have my back though.

Then my eyes landed on Daniel, my foster brother, the little boy I had practically raised myself. I had spent my youth protecting him from a brutal adoptive father, purposefully pissing the man off so I would take the brunt of the beatings. I had never made it easy for the bastard, fighting back as best I could. By the time he had been done with me, he had been so drunk and exhausted he hadn't possessed the energy to go after Daniel.

As soon as Daniel had turned sixteen, I had taken him out of that house and rented us a place together. It had been tiny, filthy, and in a gang-infested neighborhood, but we had been safer there than we had ever been. I enrolled him in a variety of martial arts and fighting classes so he could defend himself, and it had turned out he was a savant at Brazilian jujitsu and had become equally skilled at Krav Maga.

When I had left the military and gone into the mercenary business, I had hired him for my team. He was more than capable, but I had also wanted to keep him close.

When Marduk had taken him, it had felt like someone had ripped out my soul and destroyed my world. I would have followed them to Urusilim immediately, but I had known I would lose the battle. As a soldier, I knew the only way to win was to know what I was getting into and have a plan. Therefore, I had spent the last several weeks trying to learn all I could from Eddie about Urusilim and its creatures so I could go in and get Daniel back.

Now he stood in front of me, and Marduk had done something to him. I didn't know if this man was still my baby brother or something else entirely, and until I found out, I couldn't count him as being on my side. As a result, I was on my own against three snarling beasts, two incredibly powerful mages, and a man who could melt a living being with a single touch. To say that I had faced better odds was something of an understatement.

Then my feelings of defeat washed away on an

unexpected tide of anticipation, excitement, and raw enthusiasm. Adrenaline and endorphins flooded my system, filling me with a heady sense of strength and a desire to draw blood. I had been in plenty of fights and was familiar with the feelings—fear, anticipation, anxiousness—but this was like nothing I had ever known. I felt like I could take down an entire army of monsters singlehandedly with a smile on my face. *Shit*, Sharur had just hijacked my nervous system.

The lead gargoyle—the one that had snarled at me with the promise of death—let out a bark, and on his command, his two brethren leapt at me while he stayed behind. I heard a shout escape from Daniel, but I couldn't tell if he was trying to stop them or egg them on. My brain could no longer recognize words or perform higher-level cognitive thinking.

I slipped into the mind of a ferocious, wild animal, both foreign and familiar to me at the same time. My senses narrowed, recognizing and reacting to movement, speed, sights, and sounds only. Words were unnecessary.

The weight of the axe balanced perfectly in my relaxed grip as I spun, twirling the blade over my head, and slicing it through the air. I felt resistance slow its graceful arc, but only for a moment. Then the blade came free of flesh, and it glided unencumbered through the air again.

Without a pause, I used the axe's momentum to bring it back up over my left shoulder and slam it down on the second gargoyle, my full bodyweight behind the swing. The crack of bone and scream of pain reverberated through me as hot blood splattered my face. The taste of it on my lips was salty and metallic, and my pulse quickened as my tongue slipped out, gliding over the thick liquid on my lips like it was chocolate.

As I looked up at the gargoyle leader from under my lashes, a smile curled at the corners of my mouth, and I bared my teeth. From a far corner of my brain, I realized I must look utterly insane and terrifying, but that was the point.

A shadow of doubt flittered across its monstrous features before it met my unspoken challenge. The dark space was illuminated by flashes of red and blue light, fire and ice. Alex and Zane were at it again. Zane gave the gargoyle a chance to take me down by keeping Alex otherwise occupied. Daniel stood to the side, watching both fights, perhaps waiting to see where his assistance would be most needed.

Taking advantage of my momentary distraction, the gargoyle lowered its head like a bull and charged. This one was smarter than the other two. He had been watching me fight and anticipated my swing of the axe and, thus, sidestepped the blade with ease. He lashed out with a claw, and my head whiplashed around on my shoulders. The world spun as something wet trickled down my cheek. Its talons had scraped the skin and drawn blood.

I stumbled yet stayed on my feet. A blow like that should have taken my head off or, at the very least, knocked me unconscious. Instead, I merely shook my head to clear the ringing from my ears then brought Sharur around for a wicked upswing.

The gargoyle hadn't expected me to recover so quickly. The axe bit deeply into the muscle under its arm just as the creature prepared another blow.

I had cut through tendons and ligaments, its arm falling limp and useless, but it didn't seem to notice the injury. After all, who needed an arm when you had a mouth the size of a great white shark, filled with six-inch razor blades?

The gargoyle lunged for me with open jaws. Its rancid breath was hot on my face, and the smell of rotting meat overwhelmed my senses. I fell backward, holding out the axe in front of me like a shield. Teeth snapped shut on the wooden shaft, but the handle held. Whatever wood it was made from was as strong as steel, though I would contemplate that mystery another time.

The creature reared up on its hind legs, pulling me off my feet as I refused to release the axe. I dangled in the air a few feet off the ground. I could have easily let go of the axe and landed safely, but I knew the creature would bolt the minute I was free then carry its trophy right back to Marduk. I had no doubt there was a magic user holed up somewhere in the city whom Marduk used to periodically open and close gates for his people.

The gargoyle whipped its head from side to side, trying to shake me off. It slammed me into a wall, knocking the air from my lungs and loosening my grip, but I held on to Sharur by not much more than my well-manicured fingernails. With another hit like that, not only would Sharur belong to the gargoyle, but I would likely be dead. I knew my newfound zest for battle and my ability to take a beating had been given to me by Sharur. If I lost the axe, I would lose those gifts, and without the axe's protection, I would end up a tasty gargoyle snack.

When the creature reared back, preparing a repeat performance, I levered my body back and forth like a kid on a swing set, building momentum, and swung up and over the gargoyle's head, straddling the back of its neck. I had to release my grip on the axe handle so I wouldn't be draped helplessly over its face. All of that artificially induced adrenaline left my body in a rush, replaced by tremors of withdrawal.

The gargoyle howled in triumph when it realized I no longer had possession of the axe. Before it could gloat too much, though, I pulled my Glock. At point blank range, a steady hand and good aim was entirely unnecessary.

Pressing the gun to the back of the gargoyle's head, I squeezed the trigger. *Pop. Pop. Pop.*

The creature froze, stunned. It shook its head as if trying to clear away a fog of confusion. Then its jaw relaxed, and Sharur clattered to the ground right before the beast collapsed.

I slid off its neck, stepping lightly to the ground, and then moved toward Sharur, but someone else got there first. A tall, lean figure lifted Sharur from the ground with an expression of awe, not believing his amazingly good fortune to have retrieved such a valuable artifact without even having to try. I stilled, afraid any sudden movement would cause him to flee.

"Daniel," I said gently. "Give me the axe… please. You don't know how dangerous it is in the wrong hands."

Daniel tore his eyes from the beautifully etched blade and met my gaze. "Dangerous?" he repeated, sounding like he was in a daze. "No, it's the answer."

"The answer to what?" I asked, taking a step closer.

He clutched the axe closer to his chest then took a step back, and I lifted my palms to tell him I wouldn't come any closer.

"You have no idea what it's capable of," he said. "It's wasted on you. You're just a soldier, completing one small mission after another, never looking at the big picture." He didn't speak with anger or animosity, but his words still stung. Was that how he had always seen me, or was that Marduk speaking? "In the hands of a true leader, Sharur can help bring freedom and equality to all Monere."

"How can it do that?" I asked, trying to hide the hurt in my voice.

"Nothing as noble as freedom has ever been won without bloodshed. This axe is a symbol of power, and the Monere will follow the person who wields it. It is also a key that will open the gateway for the Monere to find a new home where they will be feared and respected instead of oppressed and enslaved as they are on Urusilim. They will come to a world where they are stronger than the native population. The Monere will rule Earth."

"Have you gone insane?" I spurted before I could stop myself. "What the hell did Marduk do to make you betray the human race and your entire fucking planet? These are your people."

He looked at me with genuine surprise. "No, Emma, humans are not my people; you are my people. You always have been." The little boy I had loved and raised stood in front of me then, and I wanted to weep with relief and wrap my arms around him in a fierce hug. "I am doing this for you, for *your* people."

Before I could respond, a ball of fire exploded at my back, heating the air around me to oven-like temperatures before it dissipated. I spun, lifting my gun in a fruitless attempt to protect myself, but the blast hadn't been directed at me.

The smoke cleared, revealing a writhing form, huddled in singed rags on the ground. Low moans came from the figure, and I saw it was Alex. Before I could remember how pissed I was at him, I raced over and fell to my knees at his side.

"Alex!" I hesitated before touching him, afraid I would cause him pain, but when I gently rested a hand on his shoulder, he relaxed under my touch. "Oh, God. Alex, are you okay?"

He simply moaned again in response.

"What did you do?" I screamed at Zane in horror. "He is your best friend, and he was trying to help you, for fuck's sake."

"How can you possibly defend him?" Zane snarled. "He is lying. He would do anything for Alcina. This is all a set-up so the mages can kill me. Getting me out of the way takes out the competition so they can steal Sharur from you without interference. He has proved to you that he can't be trusted."

It was difficult to contradict his words. It made

sense. Alex had proved he was capable of betrayal. Therefore, who was to say his desire to "cure" Zane hadn't been some elaborate scheme to get inside Zane's head and take him out permanently? If that happened, Alcina would have eliminated Marduk's number one attack dog, her greatest competition for the axe, and left me without my sometime defender. It would have made her job a whole lot easier. If that was the motive, though, was Alex aware of what he was doing, or was he a hapless pawn in her game?

Then Zane's gaze landed on Daniel… and Sharur in his hands. His eyes narrowed and lips thinned in anger. "Give that to me, boy," he said, sneering the last word.

Daniel took a moment to consider the demand, but decided he would take his chances against Zane. After all, Daniel had newfound abilities of his own, and Zane had just expended a tremendous amount of power by fighting Alex.

"I'm the one who retrieved it, so I will bring it to Marduk," Daniel challenged.

"Looking for all the glory, huh?" Zane said, stepping closer to him.

Zane stood at Daniel's height, but his broad shoulders and the corded muscle that wrapped his arms, chest, and abdomen made him loom menacingly over the slimmer man. My money was on Zane, even in his weakened state.

Zane shot out and grabbed the axe, moving almost quicker than my eyes could follow. After a brief tug-of-war that looked ridiculously like two dogs pulling on a knotted rope toy, Zane wrenched the axe to the right, trying to twist it out of Daniel's grasp. Zane didn't anticipate Daniel's martial arts background though.

Daniel repositioned his hands on the handle, using the momentum and his body weight to keep twisting the axe until he wrenched Zane's arms, forcing him to release it. Then Daniel slammed the staff into Zane's jaw, and as Zane doubled over, he swept it under Zane's knees, dropping him to the ground.

I gaped, sisterly pride competing with worry. When Zane didn't rise right away, my anxiety grew. I knew it was a trap.

Daniel leaned over Zane to check on his status, and I took a breath to call out to my brother. Before the words passed my lips, Zane leapt from his prone position, grabbed both sides of Daniel's head, and channeled power into his hands. While the glow emanating from his palms grew in intensity, Daniel gritted his teeth, his face a mask of agony. Then a wail of pure anguish rose from his throat and ripped through me as he dropped the axe.

I should have grabbed Sharur, but in a mindless fury, I ran forward and leapt onto Zane's back, knocking him away from Daniel who fell to his knees, gripping his head. Zane threw back an elbow and caught me in the ribs, knocking me loose, and then he spun on me, lost in his rage. I knew he was beyond reason, but I couldn't bring myself to shoot him. Still holding the Glock, I slipped it back into the shoulder holster to remove the temptation.

His hands flared with fire again, but this time, they were directed toward me. How was I supposed to stop magic without the help of Sharur or Alex? He would burn me alive, and I would essentially be letting him because I was unwilling to shoot him.

"Zane, don't do this," I pleaded.

He rubbed his hands together, gathering a ball of white-hot power in his palms. I looked around for an escape route, but I was trapped in a corner with my back to a solid wall and Zane blocking any path of escape. I was a fish in a very small barrel.

He pulled his arm back in a pitcher's stance and threw the ball in a perfect line that ended at my head. I waited for the searing pain, to smell my own hair and flesh cooking, but it never came. The ball simply fizzled out in mid-air before reaching me.

What the hell happened? Looking up, I saw Zane was just as confused as I was.

"How did you do that?" he asked with murderous intent.

"It wasn't me," I said quickly.

I frantically scanned the space for my savior, but Alex was still lying on the floor, huddled into himself. The only sign of life from him was an occasional twitch or tremor rattling his frame. Daniel was similarly absorbed in his own pain, still clutching his head, his hair burned off in patches.

Zane decided to give up on the fireballs and turn to a more substantial weapon. He bent down and retrieved Sharur, which had been resting on the ground close to his feet. Lifting the weapon over his head in both hands, he prepared to split my skull with the very axe I was supposed to use to save the world. *So much for that prophecy,* I thought, throwing up my arms in front of my face in an unconscious effort to block the attack, as if that would even remotely help me.

I wanted to look away, but I couldn't. My wide eyes were glued to the man I had once loved and maybe still did. Instead of feeling fear or hatred toward him, an overwhelming sense of sympathy bubbled up at all he had been through and suffered. It must have required tremendous brutality to break the mind of a man as strong as he was. I hoped someday he would find peace, and if that happened, I prayed the guilt of having killed me wouldn't eat him alive.

Then the axe fell.

Chapter Twenty-Two

EMMA

Before the blade reached me, an unseen force slammed into Zane, knocking him off his feet and tossing him like a rag doll almost twenty feet away. His back slammed into a metal stairway railing with a sickening crack, and Zane crumpled to the ground in a heap, unmoving.

I could barely comprehend what I was seeing. Zane couldn't be hurt. He was the strongest man I knew. Hell, when he was carried out of Citi Field by a shape shifter in dragon form, he killed the creature, and walked away without so much as a scratch. I had convinced myself he was nigh indestructible, but now he looked so small and broken. Who could have done this to him?

I wanted to run over and check for a pulse, but I was too terrified that I might not find one. As long as I couldn't confirm his death, he was still alive to me. Why was I so intent on his survival though? In actuality, the real Zane — the one I had loved once upon a time — had died a decade ago. Maybe this was for the best. Maybe I should let him go.

I turned to face who or what had been able to stop Zane with one blow and came face-to-face with Sam. My eyes darted around him, looking to the right, left, behind, and even above the FBI agent, searching for Zane's attacker and my savior, but there was no one else.

I stared at Sam in incomprehension, my brain frozen. *What the hell?*

"The axe," said Sam.

"Huh?"

"Sharur. The axe," he hissed.

Oh, crap. Where was it? Zane had it when he was… what? Killed? Hurt?

I forced myself to look in the direction of his body. He lay as still as death, and I swallowed the lump in my throat. Then movement nearby drew my attention away from Zane. Daniel stirred.

He struggled to his feet, leaning heavily on a wall until he stood, albeit not too steadily. He shook his head, trying to clear it, and noticed Zane's body. Like me, he looked around trying to figure out who could have felled such a strong mage, and then his eyes alit upon Sharur. I followed his gaze and saw it at the same time.

The axe had rolled free of Zane's fingers when he had hit the ground and come to a rest underneath a nearby trash bin. It would have gone completely unnoticed except for the spike at the top of the axe head poking out from underneath the bin. Daniel and I both started for Sharur at the same time, but he was much closer and reached it first.

He pulled it out, clutching it in a double-fisted death grip, and then spun on me, looking as if he was preparing to fight. He would never beat me. We had sparred countless times, both for fun and for training, and he rarely won a match. He clearly didn't like his odds because, when he saw me coming for him, he turned and ran.

His flight caught me by surprise, and I slowed for a step or two. Then I hit the gas and shifted into an all-out sprint. Racing down a quiet residential street with its darkened windows and gated shops, I ground to a halt at the first intersection, looking right then left then straight ahead for any sign of Daniel, but he was nowhere to be seen.

I took my chances and turned right. When I reached the next corner without finding him, I turned back and took a different street. Still no Daniel. I randomly ran down block after block until I finally accepted that he had eluded me. He knew the city as well as I did, and there were thousands of hiding places for whoever knew where to find them. He could have lost himself in a crowd of pedestrians on one of the busier avenues, descended into a subway station, ducked into a building, or even laid on the sidewalk and tossed some newspapers over his face to pass as a homeless person. Maybe I had run right by him without noticing.

I closed my eyes and nudged my tracking magic to alertness. Reaching out with heightened senses, I searched through nearby streets, buildings, and subway tunnels. Nothing. There was no telltale signal alerting me to Daniel's presence. Perhaps my magic didn't work on him because he wasn't technically a Monere. He was a human who had been endowed with a magical ability. That thought actually gave me some hope that maybe it wasn't too late to undo what Marduk had done to him.

With a defeated shuffle and hunched shoulders at having lost Daniel, I made my way back to the street where I left Sam. When I found him, Sam had one of Alex's arms draped across his shoulder, trying to help him into a standing position. I ran over to them, wrapping an arm around Alex's waist to help support him.

Alex's skin was smudged with black soot, and angry blisters covered the palms of his hands and forearms as a reminder of his struggle to hold back Zane's fire. I could smell the pungent odor of burnt hair and flesh. His eyes were red and watering, and he blinked rapidly to clear them. Those were only the injuries I could see. From the way he struggled to breathe, I guessed he had at least a couple of cracked ribs, and who knew what other internal injuries.

"Alex, we have to get you to a hospital," I told him, trying to hold him as gently as possible, but he still winced with every shifting movement.

"No, I'll be fine. Just call Lilly. She can help me," he said, panting from the strain of standing and talking at the same time.

"Why not the mages? Surely Alcina could heal you just as well as Lilly could." I didn't want to drag Lilly into this if I didn't have to. I also couldn't help getting in another jab at Alex, just in case he had forgotten how pissed I was at him. There was nothing like kicking a guy when he was down. How wonderfully noble of me. I winced at my own spitefulness.

"Emma, I can't tell you how sorry I am for what happened, but believe me when I tell you I did it for a good reason. If it makes you feel any better, Alcina removed me from the Council for my role in helping you escape the subway tunnel at Grand Central or, at least, for my role in not trying to kill you. She believes I am, too... taken with you, and she's right. I will spend the rest of my life proving myself to you if I have to."

"Won't Alcina want to know about... about..." I nodded toward Zane's still form, unable to say the words.

Alex followed my gaze then took a step toward Zane. I forgot Alex had been unconscious when Sam took Zane down, so he hadn't known of his friend's fate. My heart broke for Alex, knowing the emotional pain would far exceed his current physical agony. Sam and I helped Alex stagger to the body and lowered him to his knees.

Zane was pale and still, curled in upon himself as Alex reached out a shaky hand and placed it on his friend's pulse point at the neck. I wasn't sure whether Alex's hand trembled from pain or the fear of what he might find.

His fingers settled on Zane's skin, and he held them there for what felt like a year and a day before saying, "He's alive." Then Alex let out a breath and rocked back on his heels in relief and exhaustion.

I shut my eyes and let powerful waves of emotion rip through me while keeping my poker face firmly in place. I didn't want anyone to see what Zane truly meant to me and how much his almost death had affected me. I was suddenly very tired and wanted nothing more than to go home and bury myself under the covers of my bed for days. There was one more piece of business to attend to tonight before I could clock out, though.

I turned to Sam and shot him a glare. "We need to talk."

To my surprise, he nodded in agreement. I expected evasion or, at the very least, a few lies. I supposed I shouldn't get my hopes up yet. Just because he was willing to talk, it didn't mean he would actually tell me anything. I pulled out my phone and texted Lilly our address with a brief message, letting her know we needed her healing abilities. She responded immediately.

"Lilly is on her way. She will be here soon."

Alex nodded his thanks.

"So what happens to Zane?"

"I will take him with me. Lilly will be able to heal him as well... his physical condition, at least."

"And his mind? Were you telling the truth about a cure?"

Alex took my hand in his as we sat side by side, his large hand almost completely engulfing mine, soft and warm, reassuring. It felt nice.

"I overheard a conversation I wasn't supposed to hear," Alex started. "They thought I was recuperating in my room, but I was tired of being cooped up, so I decided to go for a walk. I walked past the library doors when I heard Alcina talking to Ronin and some other Council members. They mentioned Zane's name, which caused me to stop and listen." Alex stopped speaking and shook his head as though he couldn't find the words to continue.

"What were they saying about Zane?" I urged, keeping my voice soft and encouraging.

"It took me a long time of listening before I could even get a grasp on what they were saying and then even longer for me to actually believe it. *They* did this to him, Emma," he said, throwing me a look filled with grief and anger.

"What do you mean? I thought Marduk was responsible for Zane's condition," I said, my pulse quickening from Alex's accusation.

"He was... They all were. Marduk twisted Zane's mind, but the Council didn't do anything to stop it even though they could. I heard them admit there is a cure, but they purposefully withheld it from Zane. They wanted Zane to gain Marduk's implicit trust, and the only way to do that was to ensure Zane was completely under Marduk's influence. Anything less and he would have been discovered."

"They wanted a spy," I breathed, catching on.

"Yes. They planned on curing him at some point when it most suited their needs. Then they would have him continue in Marduk's employ as a spy for the mages. Marduk would never suspect him as a traitor after Zane had given so many years of dedicated and loyal service."

"And they just assumed Zane would agree to stay on as a spy after everything he has been through?" I asked, shocked at the size of the Council's balls.

"Well, the old Zane probably would have. He was completely committed to the cause until he met you. You have thrown the Council's plans into complete turmoil. Zane's behavior with you over these last few weeks has threatened Marduk's trust in him. Zane has failed his mission of capturing or killing you and recovering the axe due in no small part to his feelings for you. He is fighting Marduk's hold on him, and chances are that hasn't escaped Marduk's notice. Not only that, but if the mages do cure him, they can no longer trust him to take their side over yours."

"So what are the mages planning to do about that?" I asked, although I could guess the answer.

"Well, number one on their list is your imminent demise. Taking you out of the picture stabilizes all of their plans. If that doesn't happen, Zane becomes too much of an unknown quantity, and they are prepared to kill him if necessary."

I sucked in a breath. I knew Alcina would happily kill me. In fact, she had already tried. However, I didn't expect they would kill one of their own, especially if there was a chance they could get Zane back. I guessed that little bitch had no real sense of loyalty and was only interested in what people could do for her. That was just another reason I had for her dethronement.

"You can't let them kill him, Alex," I said. With Zane in such a vulnerable position, should I worry that Alex would turn him over to Alcina?

"I have no intention of letting that happen. I can no longer stand by and participate in what the Council has been doing. I have my own agenda. I am going to help my friend. I had to coerce Alcina into revealing the cure by promising I would lead her to you and the axe. I didn't have anything else to leverage. I had to do something," he said with equal parts remorse and determination.

"I understand why you did it. I just wish you had let me in on your plan so I was better prepared for when she came after me. I killed Ronin, Alex. That didn't have to happen."

"Yes, it did. She needed to see what you are capable of. She needs to think twice before coming after you again. I hope you made her feel fear for the first time in her life."

My eyes widened at the venom in Alex's voice. I didn't think he was capable of that kind of hatred. Then again, betrayal was a perfect fuel for rage.

"How can you trust that she gave you the cure? Hell, she could have given you a spell that will kill everyone in a ten-block-radius."

"It's possible," Alex said, his mouth forming a grim line, "but that's a chance I have to take. This charade ends now. I will either cure him, kill him, or possibly kill us both. Regardless, I won't fight against my best friend anymore."

The sadness in his voice weighed me down, threatening to suffocate me. I wanted to argue with him, to stop him from taking such an enormous risk, but maybe this was for the best. No one should have to spend ten years witnessing someone he loved spiral into a void of suffering, slowly being twisted and poisoned. How could he let his best friend continue to deteriorate when there was a possibility for a cure?

"Okay," I said with a nod.

He looked at me with gratitude. I knew he had been steeling himself for an argument, but he wasn't going to get one.

"Just do it somewhere safe, where no one else can get hurt if things go wrong."

"I promise," he said, holding my gaze, his blue eyes deep pools of warmth into which I could feel myself falling. He wrapped an arm around my waist then pulled me closer, and I could feel his breath on my neck as he leaned close to my ear. "I'm going to lose you whether I fail or succeed, but before that happens I need to know something." He pulled back slowly, his lips brushing my cheek until they found my mouth.

There was nothing tentative about the kiss. He took my mouth with a desire and desperation I had never felt before, as if he had been waiting his entire life for this and knew he would only ever have this one moment. I met his passion with my own, warmth flooding my body and turning my insides to liquid. His hands moved over my waist, and I wanted to feel them caressing every inch of my body.

I leaned into him and opened my mouth, deepening the kiss. He moaned, and I melted at the sound, returning it with my own whimper. My right arm wrapped around his neck, drawing him even closer, and my left hand wandered over his shoulder, his bicep, forearm before moving to his waist and his hard abs, exploring the ridges and planes of his body.

"Ahem," came an intrusive voice.

Shit. I had forgotten Sam was still standing there.

Alex pulled back from me, albeit reluctantly.

"I'm sorry," Sam said, and it sounded like he actually meant it. "But, Emma, it's time to go."

"Yeah," Alex said, his voice deep and rough. "I need to get Zane out of here and secured before he wakes up."

"Let me help. I'll come with you," I pleaded.

"No, Emma. This is something I have to do alone. This is between me and Zane, and I'm not going to put your life in danger."

"How are you going to get him out of here? You're not exactly in the best condition."

"Mage, remember?" he said with a wink, the corner of his mouth curving up.

I was just stalling, trying to find a solution that would keep them both safe. I didn't want this to be the last time I saw either of them. These two men had only come into my life a few weeks ago, but since then, they had both brought my withered heart back to life and taught it how to beat again. Although it happened without my notice, now that I faced the prospect of losing both of them, I finally realized how much they meant to me.

I also knew this next battle was for them and them alone. Alex needed to fulfill his promise to his best friend, and I needed to get Sharur back, save Daniel, and find out what role Sam played in this whole thing. It was time for us to go our separate ways. I could only hope I would see them again.

With a silent nod, I stood and took a few steps away

from Alex before I turned and asked, "What did you mean when you said you needed to know something? What did you need to know?"

This time, his smile held a trace of sadness. He ducked his head, looking up at me through his long lashes. "I needed to know... if... maybe... you had feelings for me."

"And what did you find out?" I teased.

Chapter Twenty-Three

EMMA

I probably should have gone back to Eddie's place where I had been crashing for the last few weeks, but I was homesick. My heart hurt and every muscle in my body ached. I wanted to go home. I had moved out of my apartment because of the risk that I would be found by my enemies, but now that Zane was out of the picture, and I no longer had Sharur, I figured there wasn't much danger that anyone would be coming after me.

Sam and I made our way back to his car and drove to my place in Greenwich Village. We rode in silence, the air heavy with unspoken questions, but both of us were too wrapped up in our own thoughts to initiate a conversation. I couldn't stop thinking about that kiss with Alex. It was erotic and exciting, opening up a door of possibility that had been previously shut tight, but guilt wafted around the memory, tainting it.

It felt like a betrayal to Zane, even though he and I weren't exactly together. Alex also seemed to think we had no future together. He said that, whether he failed or succeeded, he would never have a chance with me. I could only guess that meant, if he failed in curing Zane, it could mean his death, and if he succeeded, it meant Zane could win back my heart.

Was that even a possibility? If Zane was cured, was there really a chance for us? I wasn't so sure. After all of the rage and violence, I didn't think he could ever go back to being who he once was. There were no guarantees as to what kind of person he would be if he regained his faculties, and I might not want that person. I wasn't exactly the forgiving, nurturing type. I didn't know if I was prepared to take on all of that baggage, no matter how hot and sexy it was.

I had been through a lot. Maybe I should think about settling down, leading a quiet life with someone steady, reliable, and loyal. Someone like Alex?

I shouldn't short-change him. Alex was gorgeous with his fair hair and sky blue eyes. He was the light to Zane's dark, both literally and figuratively. Regardless, that kiss proved to me that he wasn't all Boy Scout, and that prospect sent warmth rushing into my abdomen.

My musings could be entirely moot if the cure failed in epic fashion. Since it was Alcina's cure, that was a very real possibility, given her interest in having him killed.

Tears stung my eyes at the prospect of losing them both, but I blinked them away and buried my fear and sadness. I wasn't going to mourn them just yet. There would be plenty of time to worry about my romantic future if we all survived the next couple of days.

Once Sam found a parking spot and we walked up to my apartment building, I drank in the familiar sight like water to a person dying of thirst. I had missed it so much. It was my haven, my sanctuary, and it had been off-limits to me for weeks. As grateful as I was to Eddie for putting me up in his place, staying there chafed my nerves like rough spun wool. It just wasn't home.

I took out my phone and shot Eddie a quick text, letting him know where I was and that I wouldn't be back to his place that night. Then I turned off the phone before he could start berating me for my decision.

We entered my building and John, my doorman, greeted us. "Miss Hayes, how are you?" he asked. "I haven't seen you in weeks. Thought you may have moved out."

"Hi, John. It's good to see you. No, I would never sell my apartment. I was just away on an extended business trip."

"Well, welcome home, then."

I smiled at the sound of those words. "It's good to be home."

Sam and I rode the elevator to the penthouse in silence. I turned the key to my apartment door and swung it open, revealing the airy space with its sixteen-foot high floor-to-ceiling windows filling the opposite wall. The familiar sights and smells of my apartment washed over me like a warm bath, and the tension left my body for the first time in weeks.

"Nice place," Sam said, closing and locking the door behind us.

The apartment was long and narrow, the main level essentially one large great room with a modern, open-concept kitchen and living room/dining room combination. A wrought-iron staircase climbed up exposed brick walls covered with framed movie posters, leading to my loft bedroom with its coveted walk-in closet.

"It's home," I said, feeling more content in that moment than in my entire life.

I threw myself onto the sofa, kicking up my feet and reveling in the sensation of the cool, soft leather against my skin. Sam took a seat in the overstuffed armchair across from me.

"I'd offer you a drink, but I haven't been grocery shopping in a while."

The thought occurred to me that drinking with this man might not be a good idea. After all, I had no idea who he was or what he was capable of. As badly as I wanted a drink right now, leaving myself inebriated and vulnerable in his presence was just stupid. However, he had more than enough opportunity to harm me over the last twenty-four hours, and hadn't made a move against me.

I didn't get a threatening vibe off him; no tingles at the back of my neck warning me of danger. Even so, I felt the comforting weight of the Glock in its shoulder holster and kept my hand within easy drawing distance. I had no idea if a gunshot would have any effect on him. He looked human enough, but I knew by now that looks could be deceiving. Nevertheless, I was prepared to shoot first and judge its effectiveness later.

"So, who the hell are you?" I gave him a sharp look that contradicted my casual pose.

He chuckled softly. "What, no small talk to warm up to the big conversation?"

I shrugged. "I offered you a drink."

"No, you didn't."

"It's the thought that counts."

"If you say so," he said, before turning serious. "Emma, I think you have already guessed that I am not from around here."

I smirked. "No kidding."

The corner of his mouth quirked up briefly. "My name is Shamesh or Sam for short. I came here through the rift you opened a few weeks ago."

My eyes widened at the revelation that he had been among Marduk's army that stormed onto Earth via Citi Field. My hand inched closer to my gun. "You've been working for Marduk this entire time?"

"No," he insisted immediately. "I simply saw an opportunity to get to Earth and took it."

I knew the non-verbal cues that signaled someone was lying: blinking, fidgeting, licking the lips, swallowing, touching the face. None of those tells were present in Sam. Either he was a very good liar, or he happened to be telling the truth.

I had no doubt that he was, in fact, quite a good liar. He had been able to fool me into believing he was nothing more than a very human government agent was. However, that didn't necessarily mean he was lying to me now. My gut told me he could be trusted, and I put a lot of faith in my instincts.

"Okay." I nodded, removing my hand from my weapon. "So why did you choose to come through the rift?"

"I was sent here to make contact with Nathan Anshar."

"Nathan? I knew it," I declared, feeling vindicated. "I knew there was more to him than just a glorified hoarder."

"Indeed, there is significantly more to him, or at least, there once was. He is not of Earth. He was stripped of his powers and banished to this world where there is no magic for him to draw upon. Such a punishment is worse than death for our people, and many don't survive beyond the first few weeks of banishment. Yet, Nathan has been here for almost thirty years and has done quite well for himself."

"He was banished from Urusilim? Why?"

"No, not from Urusilim. We are from a different plane. Gateways can be opened between countless worlds, but ours is of the highest order. Your people and many others call us gods."

I sucked in a breath. "Are you telling me Nathan was a god? That *you* are a god?"

"Well, I am a lesser deity, but Nathan was one of the thirteen, an Original. Now he is essentially human, but he has been trying to help you."

"Help me how? He disappeared weeks ago. He sent me to recover Sharur for him and then just vanished when I tried to return it. If he's trying to help me, he's doing a pretty lousy job."

"Is he?" Sam asked with a pointed look. "You were given possession of one of the most powerful weapons to ever exist. You made contact with it, did you not? It showed you how to start channeling your powers. And you have faced down and defeated some of the most dangerous creatures ever to walk this world or any other. I'd say Nathan has helped you learn a lot."

"Well, when you put it that way…" I conceded. "So why was Nathan banished?"

"Alas, that is not my story to tell. Nathan must be the one to tell you that tale. What I can tell you is that I have been working for Nathan these last few weeks. He used his connections to create a false background for me and to secure me a job at the FBI."

"Why did he need you in the FBI? And what does this have to do with the murdered creatures and missing scientists?"

"Nathan needed information on this case, insider information. He only has a small piece of the puzzle, the one component he was contracted to develop. When he noticed that other scientists on this project started disappearing, he contacted them and recommended they hire protection from the Syndicate. He thought they were dealing with standard corporate espionage and that the Monere bodyguards would be more than enough protection against a human threat. But, when the bodyguards started turning up murdered, Nathan realized something much bigger was going on. It isn't just anyone who can kill off creatures, especially in that manner."

"So why did you pull me into this? I'm not an investigator, and I don't have any inside information. Besides, after what I saw tonight, you certainly don't need any protection."

"It's nice of you to notice," he said with a teasing smile. "But, seriously, Nathan asked me to involve you. I don't know exactly why, but he must have thought either you would be able to help, or you would get something valuable out of the experience. Regardless, I think we make a good team. You have been invaluable to this investigation."

"It's nice of you to notice," I threw back at him with a wink. "Where is Nathan? Why did he just disappear on me?"

"He knew someone or something very dangerous would eventually come after him, and he didn't plan on making it easy for them to find him, but I would also bet he has been avoiding you. The best way for you to learn is through experience, and I'm guessing his intention was to throw you in the deep end and see if you would sink or swim."

"Gee, that's so very supportive of him." For some reason, Nathan's avoidance of me stung, and his willingness to throw me to the lions sparked more hurt than anger. I barely knew the man, yet I craved his attention. "Well, now I know who the killer is, and he has Sharur," I said with a pang of regret.

I felt like I had failed Daniel. He had landed in the hands of a monster, and I hadn't protected him. Now he was a killer and could be the tool to unleash hell on Earth.

"He could be handing Sharur over to Marduk as we sit here," I said. "Waves of monsters can pour through a rift at any moment, flooding the city and killing thousands of people before anyone knows what is happening. We have to stop him." I dreaded voicing my fears, not wanting to make Daniel a target. I had no idea how to fix this. Maybe I could just convince him to give me Sharur back.

"He's not going to be able to use the axe to open a gateway," Sam said. "Only you can do that."

"What do you mean?" I asked, feeling a glimmer of hope alight within me.

"Sharur is bonded to you. He won't respond to anyone else."

I flashed back to that night in Citi Field when Zane had disarmed me and taken Sharur. He had tried to use it to open a rift, but in the attempt, pain had ripped through him, doubling him over into a helpless mess. Zane might not have expected it at the time, but now he knew the axe was virtually useless to anyone except me.

"Then why does Marduk want it if he won't be able to use it?"

"Well, just because he can't use it right at this moment, that doesn't mean he won't figure out a way. The boy who took the axe from you, Daniel, will have to return to Urusilim through a single rift opened by a mage. Chances are, they have a pre-arranged date, time, and location to open the rift to bring Daniel back through. It's possible that we're not too late. If we can find him before he returns, we may be able to retrieve the axe."

"Is it possible for Marduk to find a way to use Sharur?"

With a thoughtful sigh, Sam shifted in his seat and propped his feet up on my glass coffee table to get more comfortable. "It's possible, but it won't be easy. It would take tremendous power that Marduk doesn't have. Even the mages in his employ couldn't do it. There are only a few people I know of who might be able to do it. Alcina might be the only one from Urusilim capable of such a feat, which is why she wants the axe for herself, but she's certainly not going to help Marduk."

"So we have nothing to worry about," I said. A tremendous burden released from underneath my skin, leaving me feeling lighter, and I rested my head back on the arm of the couch then took a deep, cleansing breath.

"We don't have Marduk to worry about," Sam corrected, "but he was never my concern. His master, on the other hand, is."

This time, I sat up straight, my feet hitting the floor with a loud *thunk*, and all of the stress and anxiety that had left me only moments before returned with a vengeance.

"His master? I thought Marduk was at the top of the food chain."

"On Urusilim he is, but his, or maybe I should more accurately say 'our,' master rules over many realms and works to ensure his people are placed in positions of the highest authority on those worlds he wants to rule. Marduk is nothing but a puppet for the real monster." A look of disgust and revulsion was plastered on Sam's face as he spoke. His hands were knotted into fists at his sides, as if he struggled to contain the violence he so desperately wanted to inflict.

"Are you telling me Marduk's master is yours, as well? I thought you were working for Nathan."

"I am now, thank the gods, but before I came to Earth, I was in the employ of Adad, who is considered a god on many worlds, and his cruelty and power know no bounds. He is the ruler of the original thirteen, and the one who banished Nathan, stripping him of his magic. Before he was forced through the rift to Earth, Nathan made me promise to stay behind and keep working secretly on his behalf in our world, and that's exactly what I have been doing for the last twenty-eight years."

Something niggled at the back of my mind. "You said you were sent to Earth. Who sent you?"

Sam visibly blanched. That was a piece of information he must not have intended to reveal, and given the way his eyes darted around the room, searching for the right answer, it must have been a fairly critical piece of information. "I'm sorry, Emma," he said, shaking his head. "I am not authorized to say anymore."

"Authorized by Nathan or someone else?" I pressed.

Sam held his ground and remained silent.

"Fine," I conceded. "No more questions."

"Emma, I know this is frustrating for you, but trust me when I tell you that Nathan will answer all of your questions at the right time. For now, though, we must recover the axe and solve this case for him. He won't rest until it is done."

"Why not? What is it about this case that is so important?"

"We aren't positive yet, but if the government would go to such lengths to hide what they are trying to build by piecing out components to competing companies, and there is a creature-killer working for Marduk, trying to obtain information on it, it's not something we can ignore."

I understood his point, but now that I knew Nathan could answer all of my questions, I had a hard time being patient. I needed to help Sam solve this case so Nathan felt safe to come out of hiding, and then he could finally tell me everything.

Weariness overcame me then. It was too much to take in all at once. I had so many more questions for Sam, but I knew they would remain unanswered for the moment. Even if Sam was willing to be more forthcoming with information, I'd had enough for one night. I didn't think my overloaded brain could take much more.

"I need to get some sleep. What's the plan for tomorrow?"

"Tomorrow, we interview our only surviving victim and see if we can find out what they are building."

Satisfied with that plan, I dragged myself off the sofa and lumbered up the stairs to my loft bedroom. Calling down to Sam, I said, "Feel free to crash on the couch. There are pillows and blankets in the hall closet." Then, without further ado, I tumbled into bed and plummeted into a restless sleep.

Chapter Twenty-Four

EMMA

The sunlight flooding through my apartment's floor to ceiling windows urged me awake against my will. I was still wearing my clothes from yesterday and smelled of sweat with undertones of trash. Just lovely.

I kicked at the covers tangled around my legs and, after a few tries, finally managed to free myself. I stripped my now stinky sheets, peeled off my clothes, and made my way downstairs to the shower. When I reached the bottom of the stairs completely naked, I suddenly remembered the man sleeping on my sofa, except he was in my kitchen, making breakfast.

With a squeak of surprise, I tried in vain to cover myself with my hands. Sam glanced up, chuckled, and then turned back to the pancakes he was flipping. I wasn't sure if I should be offended or relieved by his lack of reaction. I stopped trying to be modest and simply walked by him as nonchalantly as possible to the bathroom.

After my heavenly shower, I emerged from the bathroom, wrapped in a white terry cloth robe, and the sweet smell of hot pancakes smothered in butter and syrup wafted toward me. "How did you make pancakes? I have no ingredients in the house."

"I've been awake for a few hours, so I hit the bodega down the street and picked up a few things." He placed a plate full of heaven on the breakfast bar in front of me.

"Oh, my God. Can you move in with me please?" I said, trying not to let the drool escape down my chin.

Taking a huge, very unladylike bite, I moaned as the flavors hit my tongue. I finished the first stack and asked for more before I could even start engaging in any conversation. He seemed quite pleased at my reaction, smiling broadly, flashing his white teeth.

"I'm glad you like them," he said. "I just learned how to make them two weeks ago from Nathan's cook. It's the only thing I can make, but I would love to learn more. The food here is amazing."

"Wow, I've been making pancakes for at least a decade, and they have never come out this good," I said, polishing off my second helping. "So, what's first on the agenda?"

"All business, huh?"

I shrugged unapologetically.

"We are going to New York Presbyterian Hospital to question Mr. Hiroshi Takai. He's the guy who almost got killed in the alley last night. He's the first person who made it out of these attacks alive, so hopefully he can shed some light on what Daniel has been after. Then we'll see Nathan."

"Where is Nathan exactly?" I asked, trying to appear casual and uninterested, but Sam saw right through me.

"Don't worry about it. I'll get you there," he said just as casually.

Smartass, I thought.

I changed into a pair of black jeans that were a little harder to button than I remembered, probably due to the amount of pancakes I had just eaten. I pulled on a T-shirt that read, *"I Taught Your Boyfriend That Thing You Like,"* and my favorite black military boots. Then I slipped my Glock into my boot and pulled my jeans over it. My T-shirt was too tight to hide any bulges, and it was too damn hot out to put on a jacket.

We stepped into an oven as we exited my building. The oppressive heat and humidity were like being hit in the face with a frying pan. I stepped back involuntarily, throwing my arm up to block my eyes from the glaring sun, my body unwilling to proceed into the inferno. I slipped on dark sunglasses and forced one foot in front of the other as we walked into what felt like the gates of hell.

Sam and I caught a cab to the hospital on the Upper East Side of Manhattan. I was a little jealous at Sam's all-access pass as he flashed his FBI badge at each nurses' station, and we were ushered through without delay. I needed to get myself one of those. I knew a guy who was great at passports. Maybe he could do badges too.

Mr. Takai was in intensive care, but was well enough

for visitors. Thankfully, the ICU patients had private rooms, so we could talk without being overheard. Mr. Takai was hooked up to an IV and heart rate monitor. He was already a small, Asian man, but he looked positively shrunken in the hospital bed surrounded by so much medical equipment. He was bruised and had bandages wrapped around his head and neck, and his eyes were glassy as he struggled to focus on us through a haze of pain medication.

Sam flashed his badge at Mr. Takai then introduced me as his partner. Mr. Takai was in no condition to question anyone's credentials, so he merely nodded with blind acceptance. I was relieved he wasn't feeling well enough to ask me to produce identification then felt guilty for wishing him ill. Heck, in his condition, even if he had asked for ID, I could probably flash him my library card, and he would accept it.

Mr. Takai stared at us intently, giving a small shake of his head to clear out the fog. Some brightness returned to his eyes as he said, "I remember you two from last night. You saved my life. I can't thank you enough." He barely got the words out before he choked up as tears spilled down his cheeks. "My wife and daughter, they'll want to thank you too."

"No need," said Sam, softening his stern G-man expression. "We're just glad we were in the right place at the right time."

He turned to me, desperate hope in his expression. "Did you catch him, the man who tried to kill me? I saw you go after him."

"Um… No, I didn't catch him."

Mr. Takai deflated as fear crept back into his eyes. It was highly likely Daniel would make another attempt at the man's life since he hadn't gotten what he had come for the first time. As a result, I didn't blame Mr. Takai for being terrified.

Trying to reassure him, I said, "But we know who he is, and we are working very hard to locate him."

"Would you mind answering a few questions for us?" Sam asked. When Mr. Takai nodded, Sam continued, "Do you know why this man came after you?"

"I think it may have something to do with a government contract my company landed recently. He told me he was going to take me someplace where no one would ever find me and pry every detail about Project Hades out of the deepest recesses of my brain. And, if I didn't cooperate, he would kill me." Mr. Takai sobbed at the memory.

Taking a seat on the bed beside Mr. Takai, Sam gently prodded, "Project Hades?"

Mr. Takai sniffled and hiccupped, trying to regain some semblance of propriety. "Yes, that's what Ed Connor, the government representative leading the project, called it."

My hackles rose at the sound of that name. "Ed Connor?" I almost shouted, my voice rising to a soprano.

Both Sam and Mr. Takai turned to stare at me as if I had gone bonkers. At least I had distracted Takai from his crying.

"Um… yes," he said cautiously, as if afraid of provoking another insane reaction from me. "I believe that was his name."

Sam shot me a death glare that said, "*Shut up and let me do the talking.*" I stepped back and leaned against the farthest wall, lowering my head and trying to disappear. I had just screamed at a terrified man. Not my finest moment.

"What is Project Hades?" Sam asked in his soothing baritone.

"Well, I don't know exactly. I was given a blueprint and asked to follow the specs exactly. It required some very rare materials that have been incredibly costly to procure, and the parts were so custom I had to build many of them from scratch. Since I am the only person authorized to work on the project, I haven't even finished it yet. Even so, I couldn't tell you what it is. If I had to guess, it's only one small piece to a much larger technology, but I couldn't even guess at what it might do."

"Do you know why your attacker would be interested in information on this project?" Sam asked.

"I can only assume he wants to be first to construct the fully assembled device before the government does. Do you think he's a terrorist?" Mr. Takai's eyes grew wide. "Am I building a weapon of mass destruction? Oh, my God, I'm going to be remembered as the engineer who killed thousands or maybe tens of thousands of innocent people." He grew frantic, hyperventilating. His heart rate monitor increased, the erratic beeping alerting the nursing staff.

"I'm sorry, but you're going to have to leave. Mr. Takai needs to rest now," said a particularly stern nurse who reminded me of the Wicked Witch of the West from

The Wizard of Oz, without the green skin, of course. She prepared an evil-looking syringe of what I could only guess was something to help Mr. Takai sleep. "You can come back later during normal visiting hours."

"Thank you," Sam said, "but I think we're done here."

"Well, that didn't tell us much that we didn't already know," I whined, sounding like a petulant five-year-old even to my own ears.

Sam shot me a withering glare. "Are you always this annoying, or did I just get lucky?"

"Believe me, you would know it if you had gotten lucky," I said around the straw in my mouth.

Sam and I sat in a Starbucks, planning our next move. With the oppressive heat bearing down on me, I was in desperate need for an iced mocha latte. Sam had ordered a hot coffee, black. How the hell did he do that? Not only was the coffee the same temperature as the surrounding air, but it wasn't even sweetened. Just yuck.

As I was about to nag him for the millionth time in the last five minutes about what we were going to do next, my cell phone rang. I could almost see Sam's shoulders visibly relax at the welcome interruption.

I didn't recognize the phone number on the caller ID, so I answered it with a tentative, "Hello?"

"Emma," came a boisterous voice that required me to pull the phone back from my ear by a few inches.

"Who is this?" I didn't think I knew anyone with that much energy except maybe Lilly, but this definitely wasn't Lilly unless she had started taking steroids recently.

"And here I thought I left more of an impression on you."

"Duncan," I said, finally recognizing the leader of the Syndicate. Sam perked up when I said Duncan's name, paying attention. I was slightly offended he didn't take me quite as seriously. "What's up?"

"Oh, you know, kicking some Pokémon ass and taking names. Same old, same old."

"That's good. Well, it was great catching up with you. Thanks for calling…"

Sensing I was about to hang up on him, Duncan said, "I know where your killer is holed up."

That got my attention. I straightened, and Sam noticed my shift in position and leaned in, his arms crossed on the table in rapt attention.

"I'm listening," I said.

"Emma, before I tell you what I know, just remember this was all to help you find the killer."

My browns knit together. "Why? What did you do?"

"Well, I sort of had you tailed."

"What?" I shouted into the phone, drawing stern glares from nearby patrons. "I knew someone was following me," I hissed. "I just didn't know who. I never saw anyone."

"I had my best guy on you, a shade who can blend into shadows and all but disappear, so don't feel bad that you didn't spot him. No one ever has."

"And why the hell did you have me followed?"

"I needed a lead, and I figured the best way to find one was to follow the woman who attracts trouble like dog hair to a lint roller." I wasn't sure I appreciated the analogy, but it was hard to argue with the logic. "And my instincts paid off."

"What did you find out?" Hope bloomed within me at the prospect that he might have actually found something useful.

"When your killer escaped from you at the last crime scene taking the axe with him, my guy stayed on him."

I sucked in a sharp breath, my knuckles turning white as I squeezed the phone in a death grip. "Did you find out where he went?"

"I sure did." I could almost hear his Cheshire cat grin through the phone.

"Tell me."

"First, I need you to promise me something," he said, turning serious.

I wasn't in the mood for demands or ultimatums, not when I was so close to finding Daniel and getting Sharur back. "What do you want, Duncan?" I said. The warning in my voice came through loud and clear, although I was prepared to give him almost anything he wanted for this information.

"I want my team to go in with you. You can learn what you can about what this murderer has been after, but the guy is ours. Nobody hurts Syndicate members and gets away with it."

Shit. I would have agreed to almost anything but that. Even with his newfound powers, Daniel was no match for that many monsters. Duncan's creatures would tear my little brother limb from limb and eat his entrails for breakfast. Duncan was asking me to lead Daniel to the slaughter, stand by, and watch it happen. I simply couldn't do that.

However, if I didn't agree to his terms, Duncan would go in without me and do it anyway. At least this way I might stand a chance of intervening to save Daniel's life. It wasn't beneath me to break my word if it meant saving someone I loved. Duncan wasn't someone I wanted as an enemy, and I would surely place myself in the Syndicate's crosshairs if I went back on my agreement, but I had no choice.

"Yeah, okay, I promise, but I have one condition. I am in charge; your team has to follow my orders while we are on this mission. If we try to go in there without a coordinated plan, this thing will turn into a shit storm of epic proportions."

"Agreed. The shade scoped out the building where our killer is hiding and can give us the lay of the land as well as their security precautions so we know what we're walking into."

"Good. Sam and I will be at your place in twenty minutes. We make a plan and go in tonight." Nathan would have to wait.

Chapter Twenty-Five

EMMA

I had never been so grateful to be surrounded by a gaggle of supernatural creatures. Was "gaggle" the right term? Maybe a group of monsters should have been called a "bevy" or a "brood." Well, whatever you called them, I felt strangely comforted by their presence.

Duncan had been true to his word. We met him in a sleek, modern conference room in his office building with a killer view of the New York City skyline framed against the Hudson River glittering in the sun's rays.

Sitting around the conference room table was quite a diverse team of Monere to help us come up with a plan of attack, and across from me was the shade Duncan had hired to follow me. He actually turned out to be a lot less creepy than I expected. I thought I would see a black, cowl-garbed skeletal creature that sucked all hope, kind of like a Dementor from *Harry Potter*. Instead, the shade was more like a ghost. He was difficult to see, being almost completely translucent. The black-leather conference room chair was clearly visible through his humanoid shape. He had vague facial features, but I got the feeling he shaped himself to look more human to put us at ease.

My senses were on fire as I sat in the conference room, surrounded by almost two dozen supernatural creatures with their eyes boring into me. The frenzied tingles at the back of my neck worked their way down my spine, causing me to squirm in extreme discomfort. Out of sheer necessity, I managed to push my senses inward and turn down my internal creature sensor to more bearable levels. It made me wonder what else I was capable of doing should the need arise. That was when it dawned on me that maybe Nathan had a point in leaving me to learn on my own, and my anger with him subsided.

I found myself sitting amongst giants, shades, fairies, shifters, harpies and other creatures I couldn't identify, and I felt safer than I had in a very long time, especially when looking at what lay before me.

The shade had tracked Daniel to 5 Beekman Street, a building that stood in all of its red brick and terra cotta glory on the Manhattan side of the Brooklyn Bridge near City Hall. I had passed the building's shuttered doors and barred windows many times, always surprised that such a beautiful structure could remain abandoned for more than sixty-five years, especially in a city where space was at a premium, and real estate was snatched up quicker than a kid pilfering a freshly baked chocolate chip cookie.

However, the building wasn't abandoned anymore. A bevy of Monere had decided to squat there and make 5 Beekman their home. I should have known Daniel would pick that location. He had been as taken with the building as I. We had even tried to explore its interior once.

We had been planning to run away from home and were scoping out potential places to live until we could find jobs and pay for an apartment. We were caught by the cops as we tried to break in. They thought they were doing us a favor by returning us home rather than putting us in jail. After that punishment, I would have preferred jail.

According to the shade, Daniel had placed security on every interior floor of the building, but avoided putting any creatures outside for fear of attracting unwanted attention. After all, the building was supposed to be abandoned, and downtown Manhattan wasn't supposed to be populated with monsters. That meant the Syndicate could surround the exterior of the building without being spotted by Daniel's team.

Once the plans were set, we made our way to the location, and the Syndicate positioned themselves at seemingly random locations along the sidewalks surrounding the building. We selected creatures with human or mostly human appearances for street level and had them perform mundane and unremarkable tasks, such as reading a newspaper, collecting soda cans for recycling, and selling knock off purses.

The more conspicuous creatures scaled the rusty fire escape that threatened to tear free from the brick wall at the slightest movement with Sam, Duncan, and me. I cringed with every creak and vibration. It didn't help that dozens of other feet pounded up those same steps behind me, but we somehow survived the climb without incident.

When we reached the top, we expected to find a standard, flat roof with HVAC units and a door that would allow us to access the building. In its place, we were amazed to find a skylight that soared up from the roof in graceful arches of iron and glass as if trying to touch the heavens above. It was enormous, taking up almost the entire rooftop.

I stepped up to the edge of the glass and peered inside. Nine floors surrounded by ornate cast iron railings spiraled downward to a lobby floor only faintly illuminated by the moonlight filtering down through the glass. It was stunning, or would have been if not for the monsters prowling every floor. There must have been triple the number of Monere down there than were in our company, all of different shapes and sizes, but all with razor sharp teeth and wicked claws.

I squinted into the dimly lit atrium as movement on the lobby floor caught my attention. I couldn't make out what was down there beyond brief glimpses of something dark, shiny, and massive. The thing was restless, continually crisscrossing the lobby. The sound of a guttural rumble floated up from the mysterious beast and rattled the glass panes in their iron frames.

"There he is," Sam said beside me, drawing my

attention to the top floor of the building about twenty feet below us. I could only hope our black clothing against the night sky kept us invisible to any observers below. Then again, the patrolling creatures seemed more focused on potential intruders coming in through the lobby and not from above. Their obvious neglect of the roof nagged at me, but we had scoped it out, and it was clear.

Daniel just stepped into view, walking to the ninth floor balcony and clasping the railing with both hands. He had shaved his head bald to even out the patches of burnt hair that Zane had left him with. The skin where Zane had laid his hands was red and angry, but it looked like it was healing nicely. I had to admit, Daniel could pull off a shaved head pretty well. It took away the youthfulness of his features and left him with a more mature and slightly badass edge.

Daniel peered over the edge of the balcony, his shoulders sagging as if he was bearing a great burden. A hunched over, goblin-like creature with pockmarked skin came up from behind him, carrying a simple metal table and two folding chairs.

When Daniel heard the scrape of metal against tile, he straightened his back and jiggled the railing, as if testing it for structural integrity, and the four-foot segment of iron wiggled precariously, its bolts just barely holding it in place.

The goblin set up one of the chairs so its back just touched the loose segment of railing, and the other chair was placed at the metal table a few feet away. A knot formed in the pit of my stomach as I guessed at what they were doing.

Two more creatures then came into view, dragging a human man between them. The man was middle-aged, lean, and balding with pale skin and frameless glasses.

They tossed him into the chair as if he was nothing more than a sack of trash and proceeded to duct tape his ankles to the front legs of the chair then tape his wrists together behind his back. I recognized the man as Bill McNeill, the CEO of Global Mechanix who disappeared a couple of nights ago from the parking garage on Park Avenue. He was Gwen's boyfriend.

They were going to question him. If they had wanted to kill him, he would already be dead. He must not have revealed everything they needed yet.

"We have to get in there and help him," I implored Sam and Duncan, who stood, pressed against the sloping glass skylight on either side of me.

Sam pursed his lips as if what he was about to say tasted sour on his tongue. "Emma, we need to find out what Daniel wants from him. If we go in there now, we may never learn what is going on. My first duty is to Nathan, to find answers for him that will keep him safe. I promise, as soon as we learn what Daniel is after, we will go in there and save that man if at all possible."

I gaped at Sam, shocked at his callous view toward this poor man's situation. "But you're an FBI agent."

"No, Emma, I'm pretending to be an FBI agent. I am one of Nathan's soldiers, and I have my orders."

Duncan snorted quietly and said under his breath, "That's one hell of an understatement."

I didn't know if Duncan was referring to Sam being

one of Nathan's soldiers or having his orders.

"What does that mean?"

Duncan merely shrugged in response, but I didn't have time to argue with him, with either of them.

"We have to get in there, now."

"Sorry, sweetheart," Duncan said. "I'm with Sam on this one, and my team follows my orders. If you go in, you go in alone, and I think we all know how that will end."

"You made me a deal that your team would follow my orders tonight," I said.

"You're right, I did, but you've been outranked."

He didn't call Sam out or even look in his direction, but I knew Duncan viewed Sam as the leader of this operation. Sam had told me he was considered a minor deity on Urusilim, Duncan's home world; I supposed I couldn't fault Duncan for choosing to side with his god against me. In any case, Duncan was right. I would never survive going into the building on my own. I needed the backing of Duncan's team, and I didn't have it.

"We need to hear what they're saying," Sam said, looking at Duncan.

Duncan waved over one of the members of his team, and a beautiful woman with feathered wings and the lower half of a bird stepped forward. Duncan had introduced her earlier as Iris, a harpy. Her wings and leg feathers were an iridescent green against her white-blond hair, and her hands and feet ended in sharp talons.

She stepped up to the pane and scraped one wickedly sharp claw against the glass in a small, circular motion. The glass let out a quiet screech like nails on a chalkboard, causing my teeth to ache, but it wasn't loud enough to draw the attention of those below us. When she had repeated the circle several times, she dug her nail into the grove she had made and pried out a perfectly cut circle of glass. Then Iris launched herself in the air, taking an aerial position over the building. Duncan, Sam, and I leaned close to the hole she had made and listened as Daniel's voice floated up to our ears, faint but clear.

"Hello, Mr. McNeill. It's good to see you again. Are you ready for another session?"

Bill moaned in response.

"Well, as I have said before, if you'd like to conclude these little interviews of ours, you must share with me all of the information in that brilliant brain of yours. If you keep holding back or passing out before we can finish, these sessions can go on for quite some time. Believe me, neither of us wants that to happen. Let's see if we can finish this up tonight, shall we? Inkvis, if you would do the honors, please."

Daniel stepped back, and a creature I hadn't noticed before — presumably named Inkvis — scuttled toward the man. It was tall, close to seven feet, and skeletal. It moved on limbs that appeared segmented into multiple joints, much like a spider. It wore human clothing: tan cargo pants with a touristy *I Love New York* T-shirt and a Panama hat. It looked awkward, like something alien was living under human skin. The Bug from *Men in Black* instantly came to mind, and I hoped I didn't need to let it swallow me in order to kill it.

The creature lifted the hat off its head to reveal

a misshapen skull. It was lumpy and bulbous, and I marveled at how its matchstick neck could hold up such an oversized melon. It placed its free hand on the top of its head and grasped the skin, peeling it clean off along with a large chunk of flesh. Left behind was a smooth skull more proportionate to its body. There was no blood and no apparent pain resulting from the scalping. Then the mass it held in its hand wriggled and stretched, sprouting thin tentacles that moved like an octopus, yet more threaded, similar to jellyfish tendrils.

Bill began to scream and buck, straining against his bonds to no avail. The creature slapped the writhing flesh onto the back of Bill's head, and the mass instantly wrapped its tendrils around the man's forehead, face, and throat, locking itself into position. I pressed harder on the glass, wishing I could fall through it like Kitty Pride from *X-Men* and help the poor man, but there was no help for him now.

Tendrils sunk into the flesh at the base of his neck, and Bill went rigid just before every muscle in his body fell slack as his eyes rolled back in his head. He slumped in the chair, held in an upright position only by duct tape.

At first, I thought the parasite's job was to make Bill more compliant so he would have no choice but to answer their questions. However, Daniel never asked him anything. He simply waited.

The parasite attached to Bill's head pulsated and throbbed in a steady rhythm like a heartbeat as it undulated, its jelly-like sack expanding. I didn't want to know what it was filling up with.

Daniel's eyes moved around the space, landing on the ornate moldings around doorways, the floral and sunburst patterns in the wrought iron railings, the cast iron dragons that held up each of the balcony floors. He looked everywhere except at what was happening to Bill. It gave me some small measure of comfort that he didn't seem to want to be doing this.

After the parasite's sucking slowed then stopped when its bag was full, the skeletal creature pried the bloated thing from Bill's skull and placed it back on its own head. The parasite latched its tentacles into its original host and deflated like a balloon losing its air, and the walking skeleton collapsed itself onto the empty chair at the small folding table. It wasn't designed to sit in human chairs, so it struggled to fold its body into a comfortable position as bone rubbed against bone with a grinding noise. When it had finally found a position it could tolerate, it picked up a sharpened pencil and began to draw.

I couldn't make out what was on the paper, but its hand moved furiously, sometimes in large swirly movements and, at other times, in small, tight scratches. Daniel stalked behind it, stopping occasionally to watch intently over a boney shoulder.

After about thirty minutes of drawing, the skeleton put down the pencil and sat back slowly, stretching out the fingers of its cramped writing hand.

"Is it done?" Daniel asked.

"Yes," the creature said, its voice as dry and raspy as sandpaper on metal. "That was the last treatment. I have it all now."

Daniel nodded, his expression grim yet determined. He rolled up the large sheet of paper, handling it as if it were fine china, and then walked through the open doorway from which they had brought out their prisoner earlier.

Bill struggled to rouse himself. He kept trying to lift his head, but it would fall forward onto his chest as if it weighed a thousand pounds. After several tries, his neck was once again able to support the weight, but his eyes kept rolling in their sockets as he struggled unsuccessfully to focus.

Daniel stepped up to him and placed gentle hands on the engineer's shoulders, leaning down to whisper something in his ear. Bill's mouth opened and closed, his lips trying to form words, but nothing would come out.

When Daniel stood, he placed a single foot on the seat of the chair between Bill's legs and pushed.

I sucked in a breath and leaned farther into the glass as the chair rocked back against the wobbly railing that had been unbolted for this purpose. The railing gave way, and Bill fell backward in utter silence through the center of the nine-story atrium. When he hit the bottom, I heard a sickening combination of metal slamming against marble and a wet thud. Then a slithering noise reverberated through the open space, bouncing off walls and echoing up the atrium shaft until it reached my ears.

The creature at the base of the atrium lobby was the cleanup crew.

I pressed heavily against the cool surface glass, taking

in deep gulps of air to hold down the bile threatening to
rise up. I glared at Sam and Duncan with the full force
of my fury, ready to unleash hell on them for allowing
Bill to die. Duncan had his arms crossed over his chest
with a bored look on his face, while Sam at least had the
decency to look regretful, if not entirely unapologetic.

I opened my mouth to rail at them then heard the
faintest of sounds, like the crackle of a candy wrapper.
It was the oddest thing. The world around me came
grinding to a near stop, moving in slow motion.

I saw Duncan uncross his arms, his face morphing
into surprise, eyes wide and mouth shaped into an O.
Sam's jaw was set in a determined frown as he reached
out to me with his long, powerful arms, but he didn't
grab onto me in time.

The glass I was pressed against simply disappeared,
and then I was falling, falling. Shards of leaded glass
accompanied me down the infinitely long atrium of the
building, rainbows of light glinting off the prisms. I fell
past the top balcony, and Daniel's horror-filled eyes met
my own as he ran toward the edge of the balcony in a
vain attempt to catch me.

And down I went, knowing I wouldn't die from
hitting the bottom. I would die in the jaws of the beast
whose hot breath I could feel at my back as he waited
eagerly, mouth wide open, for his next meal.

Chapter Twenty-Six

EMMA

As I plummeted helplessly to my awaiting fate, something flashed toward me faster than my fall. End over end, I glimpsed flashes of burnished wood then steel then wood again. Reaching out, terrified of missing this lifeline, my hand wrapped around the shaft of Sharur that Daniel had thrown to me with all of his considerable strength.

Using the axe's momentum, I twisted my body to face into the fall, wind rushing past my face and whipping my hair out behind me. With two stories left, my eyes met the ferocious, yellow glare of a dragon. Although its inky black body melded into the shadows of the darkened lobby, I could see the outline of its hulking, scale-armored form. Sharp ridges ran from between its eyes, along its back to the tip of its tail. It was the size of two double-decker tour buses, and I thought it gave me a toothy grin in anticipation of my arrival.

Since it just had a Bill dinner, I planned to deprive the dragon of an Emma dessert. I gripped the axe and sliced the air beneath me. A rift opened and I fell into it. I hadn't given much thought as to where I would end up or if I would continue to fall to my death, just in a different realm, but I didn't exactly have the luxury of planning my destination.

Before my fears could fully form, I was through the gateway and hitting solid ground. I came in at an angle, which helped to lessen the impact, but it was jarring, nevertheless. The breath left my lungs in a rush as I rolled over a hard floor, coming to a stop after what felt like forever. Eyes squeezed tight, I remained pressed against the wall that had halted my momentum, sucking in oxygen and waiting for the pain wracking every inch of my body to subside.

I needed to lift my lids and test the condition of my limbs. I might have just fallen from the frying pan into the inferno and needed to be prepared to move if I was in imminent danger.

Fighting against my body's desire to stay curled in a ball I stretched my arms and legs and found everything surprisingly intact, albeit extremely sore. My eyes fluttered open as the thought occurred to me that I might have died after all. All that hit my retinas was a luminous white light, soft and diffused but uncomfortably bright. I couldn't decide if I would be able to see better by squinting or opening my eyes wider.

I blinked a few times, trying to clear my vision until

outlines and variations of color took shape. I was in a large room the size of a ballroom. The walls and floor were made entirely of white marble, and they glowed softly with their own luminescence. I did not see an external lighting source.

I heard scuffling and cursing along with the rattle of chains coming from the far side of the room.

Placing my palms on the unusually warm marble tiles to push myself up, I was relieved to see the axe still in my hand. I rose unsteadily to my feet, trying to fight the dizziness, but staggered back into the wall. With a deep breath and my feet placed squarely under me, I stood and turned to face the noises I had heard… and froze.

Two men stood before me, dressed in full medieval military regalia. It sort of reminded me of the costumes I had seen during a visit to the New York Renaissance Festival with Daniel when we were teenagers. Each suit of armor was painted gold with overlapping plates across the chest and down the arms. A heavy-looking plate hooked at the waist and hung low, protecting the groin. All the soldiers wore thick, leather gauntlets and leggings as well as full helmets that covered the entire face with nothing except narrow slits to see through.

The men held massive, shining broadswords, all drawn and pointed in my direction. However, it wasn't the odd dress or even the weapons that had me rooted to the spot. It was the woman who was chained and on her knees between them.

She was stunning, with long, dark hair that fell in waves around her shoulders, almost sweeping the floor. Her skin was golden, radiating a vibrant glow, even given her imprisonment. Her eyes, the color of dark chocolate, hid intelligence and strength behind a mask of obedience. And she stared at me with the same intensity, shock, and interest I knew must be reflected in my face.

I stepped forward, drawn to her as if an invisible thread pulled me closer, despite the danger posed by the two guards. They barely registered in my consciousness. To me, they were nothing more than a minor inconvenience that I would cut through as easily as scissors through paper. I spun the axe deftly, enjoying the perfectly balanced weight in my hand. The guards braced themselves, preparing for a fight.

Then the woman's eyes shifted to something behind me, breaking the spell. I heard the deep creak of a heavy door swinging open, and male voices preceded the sound of footsteps into the room.

There was nowhere for me to hide in this vast, white space. It was entirely empty other than a throne that sat upon a dais behind the woman. The throne appeared to be formed of clear crystal shards that thrust up violently from the ground, fanning out dramatically so the chair looked much larger than it really was. It absorbed the ethereal light in the room, refracting it into a rainbow of color that seemed to live inside of the crystal.

I turned to face the visitors and came face-to-face with Gabriel Marduk and a man whom I didn't recognize. They were caught off-guard at my unexpected presence and halted just inside the doorway. Marduk's mouth was agape, while his companion showed no emotion beyond a slight furrow of his brow.

The man with Marduk was tall, probably close to six and a half feet, with broad shoulders, and his chest narrowed into a tight waist. He had close cropped, blond hair and steel gray eyes the color of the sky during a harsh, winter storm and a gaze just as cold. He stood with the deadly confidence and arrogance of a leader who had never been defeated. He didn't have to move or say a word for me to know he was the most dangerous thing I had ever encountered.

A frantic whisper cut through my stupor. It came from the woman behind me, and based on the panic in her voice, she must have been trying to get my attention for some time.

"Go back," she hissed. "By the gods, get out of here." But it was too late.

"I have searched worlds for her, and she appears right before me like a precious gift left on my doorstep," Marduk's companion said, almost salivating over his good fortune. "Take her."

When he issued the command, I realized two things. First, Marduk wasn't the man in charge here, so the other man must be Adad. Second, a troop of soldiers in formation waited outside the doorway, and the command had been issued to them. *Shit.*

Dozens of vampire soldiers poured into the room. They had no need for the heavy armor that the other two guards wore. They probably had little need for weapons beyond their own strength and fangs, but they all pulled wickedly curved daggers as they charged me. Behind me, the two suited guards abandoned their post and came after me, as well.

Closer to me than all of them was Marduk. The magic permeating the air in this realm was dense and thick, almost a palpable, living thing in comparison to the anemic force I was just learning to identify on Earth. I could feel the magic coalescing around Marduk as he drew it into himself, preparing to unleash it against me.

I focused my thoughts on the threads of his power, trying to pre-empt his attack by mentally grabbing thick clumps of the stuff and pulling, unwinding it as fast as it was gathered. With a howl of frustration, he came after me. I couldn't fight them all. The distraction of any physical fight would make me vulnerable to a magical attack.

The woman's voice was almost lost in the din of running feet and clattering weapons, but I heard, "Sharur, take her home."

Then that familiar voice in my head with its strange accent said, *You heard the goddess. It is time for us to depart.*

As the first soldier reached me, my arm lifted of its own accord, sweeping the axe across the soldier's throat and taking its head clean off. The remaining troops were only a heartbeat away, but it was all the time I needed.

Under Sharur's influence, my legs pumped and I flew over the white marble floors toward the still open rift. Marduk and the vampires were right on my heels. Then I was through, stepping into air. The ground fell away beneath my feet, and this time, I braced myself for impact, knowing I would arrive near where I had departed, giving me about a ten-foot drop.

I hit the ground and rolled, leaping up into a fighting

stance as if expecting to be attacked by a fifty-foot dragon at any moment. However, the lobby was empty.

Marduk fell to the ground in a heap behind me, followed by two soldiers who landed lightly on their feet. *Fuck!* I needed to close that portal before I brought dozens of bloodthirsty vampire soldiers onto Earth, right down on my head. Alcina had closed the portal in Citi Field a few weeks ago by blasting it with her magic, damaging its structural integrity, so I decided to take a page from her playbook.

Using Sharur to channel my energy, I drew the indigo light into my palms, preparing to release it onto the gate, but I was too late. A swarm of at least two dozen soldiers poured through the opening behind Marduk. There was no way I could take them all on. If Sam, Duncan and the rest of the Syndicate joined the fight, we stood a chance, but I didn't think I could stay alive long enough for them to arrive.

The soldiers were coiled, daggers held at the ready, prepared for whatever battle awaited them on this side. However, what came for them was completely unexpected, and they were nearly helpless against it.

Marduk was back on his feet and stalking toward me with the two vampires who had come through the gate with him. The larger group of soldiers swiveled their heads toward me when they noticed where their master's attention was focused. Before they could coordinate their attack, a snuffling sound hit my ears, like the chuff of an old-fashioned steam locomotive. The others noticed it as well, and looked around in confusion searching for the source of the strange noise.

It was only then that I became aware of how the space felt like a sauna. The lobby was oppressively hot, the air thick with suffocating moisture. Rivulets of water dripped down the walls, and the damp, marble floor was slick. While the vampires were distracted by trying to identify the sound, I carefully backed away from the new threat, trying to keep my footing while staying silent.

I had taken only a few steps when a massive, black beast consumed my vision, moving like quicksilver. In the time it took me to take a breath, the dragon had opened its massive jaws and torn into the squadron of soldiers. Chaos erupted in the space, punctuated by screams of pain and terror. Blood splattered the walls and pooled on the already slick floors, making them even more treacherous to traverse.

I spun and ran, losing my footing, yet turning it into a slide that brought me closer to my destination. Scrambling to my feet, I dove behind a weathered rotting security desk at the backside of the lobby then peered over the top, taking in the scene.

Only six soldiers remained alive, and Marduk was nowhere to be seen. The soldiers stumbled over the pieces of their fallen comrades littering the floor, but managed to regroup and coordinate their attack. They moved around the creature so that they stood between it and the front door of the lobby, randomly lunging forward to slice at it with their daggers before leaping back out of its range. The dragon roared more in frustration than in pain as it spun, trying to catch the swift vampires.

The dragon was both beautiful and terrible, stealing my breath with its sheer magnitude and otherworldliness. I couldn't believe I was actually seeing a real life dragon. Its shimmering scales were like a suit of armor, easily protecting it from the dagger strikes. The vampires would never bring it down that way. They had to know that.

Then Marduk charged out from a corridor on the left, joining his troop in the fight, urging them on. He tossed bolts of magical energy at the dragon, but they deflected off its armored scales harmlessly. Some of the soldiers sheathed their daggers and, using their superhuman strength, hurled old furniture and debris at the creature: sofas, chairs, wooden beams, chunks of concrete.

As the dragon reared back in irritation, moving away from the annoying yet relentless attack, I realized they weren't trying to kill it; they were trying to drive it toward me. They must have seen me take cover behind the desk, realizing I wouldn't be able to defeat the dragon any more than they could.

I was a dead woman.

Marduk stood at the entrance of the lobby, tall and proud, herding the dragon back with short bursts of energy, as if he was in no danger from it at all. "You stupid beast, do your job and kill her. Need I remind you of what is at stake?"

My neck tingled with the dangerous, magical energy colliding in the enclosed space. The muscles at my shoulders and back were bunched so tightly they ached, both hands clenching Sharur like he was my last hope, and he might very well have been.

The dragon's great head swung in a graceful arc, and its slender tongue tasted the air, searching for its prey. It would find me. In this heat, I was a sweaty, smelly mess. The dragon would catch my scent easily.

As if it heard my thoughts, the dragon turned in my direction, yellow eyes piercing mine, freezing me in place with the intensity of its reptilian stare. I held my breath and waited for it, waited for the beast to lunge at me and crush my skull in its jaws, but the dragon didn't move. It simply continued to size me up.

"What do I do?" I asked under my breath to Sharur.

You could start by bowing, it said. *By the gods, no one has manners anymore.*

I blinked, not sure if I had heard him correctly through his thick accent.

The beast roared, the sound shaking the foundation and causing dust and debris to fall from the upper balconies. I covered my head in a lame attempt to protect myself, but a large chunk of plaster hit the desk and burst it into splinters. I staggered, falling to my knees as a wave of dizziness overtook me from the concussive force.

When voices floated down to me from above, I looked up to that vast glass ceiling and saw Duncan leaning into the empty space I had fallen through when the glass fractured.

"Emma, we're sending help. Hang in there."

The only help close enough to get to me on time was the Monere Duncan had posted outside on the street. They were nearest to the front doors of the lobby, but none of them would be a match for a dragon.

"No, don't send them in," I shouted back to Duncan. "It's too dangerous. I've got this." I didn't really have it, but it was wrong to think they were expendable, and my life was more valuable than theirs was. I didn't want innocent blood on my hands. "Duncan, you need to take your team and get out of here. The mission is over."

I didn't wait to see if he listened, because the dragon chose that moment to make its move. Its head struck at me like a snake, so fast it was almost a blur. Jaws full of jagged teeth snapped shut only inches from my face, and I leapt back, hitting the wall behind me.

With only one place to go, I ran toward the beast, taking it by surprise. It lashed at me again, but I dropped into a slide underneath its heavy body, the slick floors carrying me easily across the expanse of the lobby. I lifted the axe as I slid, leaving a bright red trail across the dragon's abdomen as the axe bit into its tender underbelly.

The dragon roared, more in anger than in pain since I was careful not to cut too deeply. The wound was no more than an annoying scratch to the beast, but I needed this to look good.

My slide carried me to the opposite side of the lobby where the soldiers were crouched, waiting eagerly to further antagonize the dragon if needed. The creature swung its great body around, more gracefully than should have been possible for such bulk. Its massive tail swept across the entire width of the lobby, completely flattening the remains of the check-in desk and clearing the floor of all debris.

Getting to my feet, it occurred to me that I was

the deli meat in an "oh, shit" sandwich. The dragon stood in front of me, the vampire soldiers behind me, and they were all salivating. Once again, Marduk had disappeared from view.

The vampires grinned madly, their lips pulled back to reveal gleaming white fangs. All they needed to do was keep me where I was so the dragon could take me, and maybe they would even be left with some bloody scraps as a nightcap.

As the dragon pulled back, sucking in a great breath of air, I could feel the draft flow past me as it was drawn into those massive lungs. This was no fire-breathing dragon; otherwise, the whole place would have gone up in flames already.

With a great heave, the dragon opened its jaws. That was my cue to duck. I dropped to the floor and rolled back under the creature's belly, emerging on the other side of it, just as a cloud of blistering steam hit the vampires, roasting them alive… or undead, as the case might be.

Their high-pitched wails echoed through the lobby, reverberating off the marble walls as the stench of sizzling meat hit my nostrils. I wasn't proud to say it, but they actually smelled a bit like pork, and my mouth might have watered just a little.

The dragon had me dead to rights as it spun to face me. There was nowhere left for me to go.

Marduk appeared behind me pressing in so close I half expected him to shove me into the dragon's waiting jaws. The dragon blocked any possible exit through the front doors and into the street. I had no space to maneuver, and I certainly couldn't outrun the creature. Even if I tried, Marduk could turn his magic against me and do the job if the dragon couldn't catch me. I mentally crossed my fingers, praying my gamble of not slicing open the dragon when I'd had the chance would pay off.

I stood, facing the terrifying beast, steeling myself for the possibility of death, and tried one last tactic. I bowed deeply from the waist.

While I waited, bent over, my eyes on the marble floor, it felt like ants were tap dancing down my spine as the dragon's eyes bored into my back. Time slowed to a crawl while I anticipated the killing blow, but it didn't come. My lower back started to ache from trying to hold the bow, so I finally decided to take my chances and straighten up.

I stood slowly, peeking at the dragon from under my lashes. Every muscle in my body was tensed and ready to react to the slightest movement. When my eyes finally connected with the dragon's, that yellow reptilian glare softened, and I could have sworn it nodded at me. I thought it was safe to say I wasn't going to be eaten today.

"You will regret that, beast," Marduk said from behind me.

I turned to see him standing, red-faced, glaring at the dragon with fists clenched at his sides, breathing heavily. "How does it feel to know you have just issued a death sentence to the last of your kind?" he growled.

The dragon bellowed with rage and torment, its emotions tumbling out of it along with that Earth-shattering roar. However, as hard as it tried, it seemed impotent to attack Marduk. Something—a spell maybe—must be holding it back.

I raised my hand toward it, palm up. "Allow me. I've got this." And this time, I meant it.

Chapter Twenty-Seven

EMMA

The dragon, knowing it could offer me no help in this battle, retreated into one of the corridors off the lobby. It hunkered down just around a corner where it could stay out of the way yet still observe the proceedings.

I faced down Marduk in the moment I had visualized countless times. I didn't care if he was my father. He certainly didn't deserve the title, and I felt no kinship toward him. I didn't care enough about him to be disappointed, angry, or regretful at a lost parental relationship. Don't get me wrong; it was something I had craved for a very long time—dreamed of, longed for—but never from him. All I felt was joy and satisfaction... at the prospect of taking Marduk's head off.

Sharur thrummed in approval, vibrating with

anticipation. I could taste victory. Marduk raised his hands, preparing to hit me with his magic, but I was faster.

I swung the axe at Marduk's throat, and it moved in a perfect arc, cutting through the air directly toward his jugular, but Daniel stepped in front of the blade. I couldn't have stopped the momentum on my own. Sharur stilled my arm before my brain could process this development.

A choking noise escaped from me and my knees went weak as terror flooded my body, turning my joints to jelly. I had almost killed my brother. My arms fell limply to my sides.

"Daniel," I choked. "What are you doing?"

"I can't let you do this," he said in an imperious voice that didn't match the pleading in his eyes. *I'm sorry*, he mouthed so Marduk, standing behind him, couldn't see the communication.

Marduk's lips turned down into an exaggerated pout. "Poor, Ashnan. It must hurt to know I have taken both your boyfriend and your brother." A wicked grin spread across his face as he placed one hand possessively on Daniel's shoulder. "Oh, yes, and your mother. You have no one to blame but yourself, you know. If you had just been a dutiful, obedient daughter, none of this would have happened. Alas, you are too much like your mother. No matter. I will correct that. You will learn to cower under my hand just as she has."

So many questions bombarded my mind about my mother that I could hardly think straight, but I didn't want the answers to any of them from Marduk. He would probably just feed me lies. I couldn't trust anything that came from his mouth, so I stayed silent. Nonetheless, confusion and anxiety built within me, turning to anger.

What had he done to my mother? Whatever it was, I would make him pay. I could feel my insides turning molten as the energy coalesced in my core, growing and churning, and a glow emanated from my palms, becoming brighter.

"Marduk," Daniel said, shrugging the man's hand off his shoulder, "it's time to go." Daniel eyed my hands cautiously, holding his own out in supplication, trying to calm me.

"He's not going anywhere," I growled, taking a step forward and pulling my arm back, threatening to hurl my destructive power.

"Run!" Daniel yelled then grappled me, allowing Marduk to bolt for the stairwell. The dragon bellowed in frustration at being unable to take action to stop Marduk's escape.

Daniel and I struggled until I broke his hold, pushing him away. He tried to sweep my feet out from under me, but I jumped over his leg before he made contact. Daniel was a martial arts expert and could have put up one hell of a fight, but he didn't try very hard. He merely wanted me distracted, not hurt. I also didn't want to injure him, so it was a lot like the play fights we'd had when we were kids.

We danced around each other—dodging, lunging, blocking, grappling—but never really tried to overpower the other. The dragon must have sensed that I wasn't in any danger, because he didn't try to intervene. He simply paced the lobby floor restlessly, like a lion behind bars, the space too confining for his great bulk.

Having given Marduk several minutes head start, Daniel grabbed my arm and heaved me out of the way before running toward the stairwell himself. I caught myself mid-stumble and changed direction, sprinting after my brother. The stairwell was black with only the dim illumination of exit signs on each floor casting a faint glow.

Daniel's feet pounded on the steps ahead of me, and more faintly, I could hear the much slower steps of Marduk several floors above us.

My legs burned from the upward sprint, and Daniel's breathing was just as fast as my own. Then light flooded the stairwell, and I had to shield my eyes with my arm. Daniel pushed open the exit door, letting in the fluorescent lights that illuminated the top floor balcony. I burst free of the musty stairwell and caught a glimpse of a door closing farther down the hallway.

I reached the door and threw my entire body into it, but it wouldn't budge. The building's original flimsy wood entrance had been replaced with a steel security door, bolted into a reinforced frame. This was the only steel door in the hallway, so I knew it must have been protecting something important.

The dragon could have easily knocked the entire wall in with one swing of its powerful tail, but dragons couldn't fit into tight stairwells, and this one apparently didn't fly, much to my great disappointment.

Axes couldn't chop through steel, so Sharur wasn't going to be much help. I stepped back from the door and centered myself, reaching into my core with my mind and stoking the fire I found there. The heat grew within me, and I directed it to my hands. I had done this more than once tonight, and it was taking a toll. The magic came much more slowly, only grudgingly responding to my call. Weariness sunk into my bones, but I pushed past it.

Placing my palms on the door, I urged the energy out of me. This time, I tried to regulate how much I released. I only wanted to take out the door, not the entire top half of the building.

I must have been getting the hang of it since the door disappeared in a flash of white, leaving behind a smoking hole in the wall through which I stepped.

The entire left wall of the large room was wallpapered with schematics, diagrams, and engineering blueprints. They were all drawn by the same hand, most likely the skeletal creature that had sucked the information out of Bill's brain. All of this must have come from the heads of the kidnapped humans.

Daniel and Marduk stood near a familiar-looking machine that sat in the center of the open space. It was very similar to the technology the government had used in Citi Field to open a rift. I could only assume, when Marduk had come through the rift in Citi Field a few weeks ago, he had seen the machine and had been trying to rebuild it ever since. They must have been building it a piece at a time as they extracted the information from the scientists.

If he could make it work, he would no longer need me to wield the axe. All he needed were the last two pieces of the machine's design, known only to Mr. Takai and Nathan Anshar, and Sharur's gem to power the technology.

Thankfully, Sam and I had been able to save Mr. Takai before he could give up information on his piece of the machine, and Nathan had never been found. They also didn't have Sharur's gem so the machine wasn't complete; it would never work.

I looked down at the axe in my hands and noticed for the first time that the blue stone was missing. Daniel must have removed it while he had possession of the axe. However, if Daniel had removed the gem before returning Sharur to me, how had I opened a rift earlier when I fell through the atrium?

We are connected, came Sharur's voice in my head. *I can now draw power directly from you to open a gateway. I no longer need the stone.*

If Sharur was able to siphon power directly from me that meant the gem could be destroyed. Then no one would be able to use it to open a gate and I could still use Sharur to open a rift. That didn't solve my immediate problem though. The gem wasn't depleted and could still be used to power the machine and open a gate if Daniel and Marduk were able to finish building the device.

"Daniel, how could you be a part of this? Don't you know what you're doing?"

"I know exactly what I'm doing. Once the machine is built, we can go through and lead the Monere back to Earth, their new home world."

"You'll never finish it. You don't have the remaining

pieces from Takai and Nathan. Your plan is over."

"Is it now?" Marduk asked with a sneer crossing his features. "Haven't you heard the news? Mere hours ago, Mr. Takai suffered a terrible stroke that left him in a permanent comatose state." I tried not to let the shock show on my face, but it was impossible not to react. "It happened only moments after my colleague, Inkvis, visited Mr. Takai to wish him well."

It took me a moment to place the name before I recalled that Inkvis was the disgusting, brain-sucking squid creature. It must have put Takai into a coma by destroying his brain after stealing his piece of the machine's design. I tried to appear nonchalant, shrugging my shoulders. "It doesn't matter. Without Nathan, you have nothing."

"You are correct about that. How fortunate for us that we do have Nathan."

I heard the sound of footsteps behind me and then came a familiar voice that sent ice down my spine. "Hello, Emma. It is so good to see you again." I turned to face Vincent Darko.

"What the fuck?" I asked in disbelief. Darko held a gun to the back of Nathan Anshar's head. There were no words. I stood there, flabbergasted, my jaw slack. I wanted to run to Nathan and throw my arms around him just to prove to myself that he was there and not a figment of my imagination, but Darko's presence turned me to ice. I hadn't seen Darko since that fateful night in Mexico City. It felt like years ago yet was only weeks. Everything had started that night. It was my first introduction to all of this chaos.

I had thought so many times about what life would be like right now if that night had never happened, if I had never accepted that job from Darko to find his supposedly kidnapped daughter in Mexico. The girl had turned out to be a monster who incapacitated me with a single bite while I tried to comfort her, thinking she was merely a scared and lost little girl. That was after I had already escaped being mauled by a gargoyle.

Where would I be if none of that had ever happened to me? Most likely doing the same thing I had been doing for years: putting my life on the line, taking on mercenary jobs for the highest bidder. There was no way to form meaningful, lasting relationships, especially of the romantic variety, when the job required me to travel so much. Not to mention, I could get myself killed on any random night.

I might have fantasized once or twice about having a husband, someone I connected to, heart and soul. Being able to fall asleep every night and wake up every day with that person was something I longed for in the deepest recesses of my dreams. Those musings lived in places so deep that my waking mind could barely acknowledge them for fear they would never come true. Now that I was caught up in this mess and unlikely to make it out alive, those fantasies were completely unattainable. The anguish and loss of what never was and could never be washed over me as I looked at Darko.

"Thank you, Vincent, for finding and bringing me the last piece of the puzzle," Marduk said. "Please bring Nathan to Inkvis so we may begin."

Darko nudged the back of Nathan's head with his

gun, urging him on. Nathan took one small step to the side, out of the line of fire, and I saw Darko shift his weapon an inch farther away from Nathan. My eyes widened as understanding dawned. Daniel figured it out at the same time I did and shoved Marduk out of the way just as Darko depressed the trigger. The bullet tore through the space vacated by Marduk only a split second before, in which Daniel now occupied.

Daniel grunted as the bullet hit home, and he was thrown back into the machine. His head impacted with the metal before he crumpled to the ground, unmoving. I ran to him, dropping to my knees and running my hands over his body, looking for pulse points and injuries. He was still breathing, but my hand came away from the back of his head covered in blood. He had a superficial cut to his scalp from hitting the machine, but it would heal. He had probably suffered a concussion as well, which was also not life threatening.

The bullet wound was more concerning though. He was hit in the chest, just below his collarbone. It bled heavily yet wasn't pulsing or spurting like an arterial injury would. Still, he would bleed out eventually if he didn't get medical attention.

I looked around frantically for something to use as a tourniquet and my eyes landed on the electrical cables snaking out of the machine. I grabbed the closest one and yanked hard, pulling it free. I then lifted off my T-shirt, thankful I wore a sports bra underneath, and balled it up, pressing it against the wound to stanch the flow. Then I tied the cable tightly around Daniel's chest, securing the T-shirt. That would have to do for now. I pulled him away from the machine and propped him up against a wall to help further reduce the blood flow from his wound.

While I had been administering first aid, Marduk rose to his feet and turned his full attention on Darko. I could feel the magic coalescing in the air, raising the hair on my arms like static electricity. Tingles exploded at my neck and down my spine, causing me to flinch in discomfort. "Nathan, get out of here!" I screamed to him, knowing the room was about to erupt into a magical shit storm, and I didn't want him getting caught in the crosshairs.

Nathan looked at me with a small smile and winked. He winked! I knew at that moment that the bastard had planned all of this. He had orchestrated the entire encounter to play out exactly as it was. Darko had double-crossed Marduk because he had really been working for Nathan the entire time. Now Nathan and Darko were perfectly positioned to destroy the machine and take down Marduk at the same time. I would have been in awe of his planning if I hadn't been so pissed at having been played like a pawn in their game of Stratego. Regardless, Nathan was still without any powers of his own, which meant he was vulnerable, and I needed to get him out of there.

I got to my feet right as Marduk and Darko let loose the first barrage. Heat and electricity exploded through the air as magic was unleashed, and the brightness and concussive force blinded and deafened me. I blinked rapidly, trying to clear my vision. When the room came back into focus, I saw Darko and Marduk hadn't slowed in their assault.

Nathan staggered out of the room when the skeletal form of Inkvis appeared in the doorway blocking his exit. Inkvis took in the scene before him, and then his eyes landed on Nathan. I was separated from Nathan by a torrent of deadly magic, preventing me from helping him as Inkvis grabbed his arms and pulled him from the room. Visions of Nathan's brain being sucked dry and his body discarded like so much trash flooded my mind. I needed to get to him.

Requiring a distraction, I reached out with my senses and siphoned some of the magical energy in the room to power my own abilities. I was exhausted, but stealing power was much easier than trying to generate it on my own.

Blue light surged in my hands and that sense of euphoria flooded through me. I turned toward Marduk, still standing in front of the machine trying to protect it from being damaged. Darko noticed the glow from my hands, and when our eyes met, he nodded in understanding.

"Now!" I screamed, and in unison, we released a stream of energy toward Marduk. But that bastard was slippery.

He leapt to the side, barely dodging the attack, and our combined magic slammed into the machine, instead, which threw off sparks as its metal turned molten. The magic flowed through the wires and into the generator, which switched on and vibrated with the excessive power. It was going to blow.

Darko ran to me, grabbing me around the chest in a

vice grip and pulling me from the room.

I struggled against his hold. "No, I have to get Daniel." But he wouldn't release me. "Daniel, wake up! Daniel!" I saw him stir, but I wasn't sure he would come to his full senses in time. I kept screaming his name repeatedly, hoping my distress would trigger his fight response, which had been honed by years in the military and as a mercenary.

Then Darko had me through the doorway and I could no longer see Daniel or Marduk. However, I could now see Inkvis pulling the squid-like appendage off his head and moving it toward Nathan, whom he had by the throat and backed against the balcony railing. Darko also saw and released me like a hot potato. Then we lunged toward Inkvis at the same time.

I heaved the axe over my head and swung down hard on Inkvis' outstretched arms. Sharur cut cleanly through flesh and bone with ease, and the creature let out a high-pitched wail that pierced my eardrums. The parasite fell to the floor at Nathan's feet along with Inkvis' now detached hands, and its tentacles flailed wildly, seeking purchase on anything it could find.

Darko went for Inkvis' face, wrapping his hands around that gaunt skull. Darko's expression morphed from cold and brutal to euphoric as his hands lit up and burned into the creature's face. I was familiar with that feeling—the pleasure and ecstasy brought on by calling forth immense power. It could become addictive.

Inkvis' screams died as Darko melted his voice box. Searing heat flooded into the creature, its skin blackening as it cooked from the inside out. Then it crumbled under

Darko's hands, turning to ash and floating to the floor in a pile of black dust.

My awe at Darko's ability turned to nausea as I realized he could have done the same to me in that cave in Mexico. Before I could get too caught up in that thought, though, I felt a constriction around my calf.

Looking down, I saw the parasite had wrapped its tentacles around my leg and was climbing up my body. I couldn't hack at it with Sharur unless I wanted to cut my own leg off in the process, and I didn't want Darko trying to burn it off and turning me to ash by accident.

I flipped Sharur around, wielding the spiked end of the handle and then carefully pried the spike between my leg and the creature, twisting and wrenching, trying to pull the thing loose. The creature's tentacles flailed and held on tighter, but I got enough of a wedge that I was able to angle the spike into the creature's body and shove. The spike impaled it and the tentacles loosened as it tried to escape.

Before it could slide off the spike, I stabbed the end of the axe into the ground, holding it in place. Then I pulled my Glock from my shoulder holster and pumped four rounds into it. Black blood splattered the floor and the axe, but the thing finally stopped moving.

I pulled the axe out of the floor, wiping bits of gore off the handle with my boot until it was as clean as it was going to get. Then I holstered the axe on my back.

With Inkvis gone and Darko no longer restraining me, I raced toward the machine room, intent on saving Daniel or dying with him. Before I made it to the doorway, however, two figures emerged, stumbling and running.

Daniel, although more injured, had Marduk's arm draped over his shoulder and pulled the man to safety, but he didn't stop running. He pulled Marduk inexorably toward the balcony.

"Daniel, don't," I yelled to him. Then they were over the iron railing and the room exploded behind them.

The force of the explosion threw me against the railing, which gave way. I reached out blindly and managed to grab hold with one hand to a section of metal balcony that still clung precariously to the floor by a single bolt.

Looking down, I watched Daniel and Marduk fall through the atrium and into the rift that was still suspended in air.

Why? I screamed silently. Why was Daniel protecting Marduk? How could he do this? It felt like my heart was being shredded from hurt and betrayal. I wanted so badly to believe Daniel was still on my side, but he just blew our best chance at taking down Marduk.

Then again, perhaps there was still a chance. My fingers loosened their grip on the balcony and I slipped a fraction. If I could follow then through the rift, maybe I could still end this thing now.

Just as my fingers opened and I began to fall, a hand gripped my wrist and pulled me up until my feet were back on the floor. I collapsed into Nathan's arms.

"They went through the rift," I said, weak with both mental and physical exhaustion.

Nathan held me close. It felt good, comforting. "Vincent, please destroy the gate," he said calmly, as if it was merely another day in the office.

"Yes, sir," Darko responded, gathering energy to him.

"No," I protested. "We can follow them through. Marduk is weakened. This is the perfect time to press our advantage." I didn't voice my primary motive of going in to get Daniel back.

"I'm sorry, Emma," Nathan said. "As much as I want to end this, it is not the right time. We need to go through a different gate to a safer location. There is someone much more powerful than Marduk directly on the other side of this gate, and we are not ready to face him yet."

"Adad," I said, remembering the man I had seen on the other side.

"Yes, Adad," Nathan said just as energy exploded from Darko's hands, directed downward into the atrium. A pop and a flash of light signaled the gate had been destroyed. "I do intend to go to Urusilim, but our first step when we arrive will be to shore up our allies. When the time comes to face Adad, we will need an army at our backs."

I laughed weakly. "And where are we supposed to get an army?"

A loud slam echoed up through the atrium from the lobby far below. I sat up and crawled over to the edge, looking down to see Sam, Duncan and the Syndicate members pouring into the building, ready for a fight. I chuckled softly before calling to them, "You guys are a little late to the party."

"Emma, are you okay?" Sam asked, sounding

relieved.

"Yes, and so is Nathan. He's here with me."

"You've made quite a few new friends," Nathan said, joining me. "It looks like they would make a good army."

We exchanged a long look. My expression was uncertain, not eager to put any of them in danger; his was pleased. Then an Earth-shattering roar broke the silence.

"Crap, I forgot about the dragon," I said, painfully scrambling to my feet. Every muscle in my body ached, but I hadn't sustained any significant injuries, so I sucked it up and powered through it.

I raced down the stairwell, hoping I would be on time to avert the slaughter of my friends. That thought almost stopped me dead in my tracks. When had I started to think of Sam, Duncan and the Syndicate members as my friends? Had Nathan planted the word in my head, or did I really feel that way about them? I didn't have time to explore the nature of my feelings, nor did I even want to. I kept moving and practically flew into the lobby, throwing myself between the angry dragon and my would-be rescuers.

"Stop… wait," I managed to get out while trying to catch my breath. I took a deep inhale, gathering myself, and then bowed deeply in front of the dragon as I exhaled. The dragon's roars and chuffing fell silent as he eyed me. I stood and spoke to the beast. "These are my… friends. They came here to help me, but Marduk is gone; he escaped through a rift."

The dragon growled deep in its throat, displeased at

the news.

I heard Nathan and Darko approach from behind and Sam caught sight of his boss and stepped forward. The two men clasped forearms in an unspoken greeting, their faces betraying the depth of their friendship and relief that the other had made it through this alive.

"So what now?" I asked Nathan. "I have so many questions, but let's start with him." I nodded toward Darko, still uncertain of the man even though he had just saved my life.

"I'm sorry, Emma. I know how confusing all of this must be for you. Walk with me and I promise I will tell you everything." He held out his elbow, encouraging me to take his arm like a proper lady and gentleman. Before leading me away, though, he turned to the Syndicate leader and said, "Duncan, can you and your team please search the building and round up Marduk's remaining team?"

Duncan nodded and quickly organized his team into search parties, joined by Sam and Darko.

Nathan and I then walked slowly down one of the side hallways where we would have more privacy. "What will Duncan do with Marduk's creatures when he finds them?"

"Duncan will do his best to convince them there is a better path, and perhaps they will agree to join the Syndicate."

"And those who refuse to convert?"

Nathan sighed heavily. "If they are deemed to be a danger to human society, they will be… eliminated. It doesn't happen often, but sometimes it is important to remind the others of what will happen if they choose to endanger humans."

"Why do you care about humans so much? As I understand it, you're not one yourself."

"I see you have been learning. That's good. I have been living on Earth for almost thirty years. In that time, I have come to appreciate and even grow fond of the people of this planet. They are often petty, but capable of amazing greatness when the need arises. In any case, as a resident, I believe it is important to respect one's home."

"I thought you wanted to go back to your own home. Why didn't you use the gate Marduk and Daniel opened? Why are you even here? What is your role in all of this?" I grew anxious and frustrated as the questions tumbled out of me, my voice rising an octave.

Nathan led me along the balcony. "I'm sorry to have had to put you through all of this, Emma, but there was no other way."

"What do you mean 'no other way'? How much of this was your doing?" I asked with wide eyes, fearing the answer. I didn't want Nathan to be responsible for the last few weeks. For reasons still unknown to me, I wanted him to be one of the good guys. I wanted him to be a hero in this story.

"I arranged your... meeting with Vincent in Mexico. I waited patiently for years for you to manifest your abilities, but it wasn't happening. Even if you didn't know it, you subconsciously prevented yourself from using your powers after what you did in Urusilim. I can't say I blame you; I heard the destruction was... Well, let's just say it was impressive. But I couldn't afford to let you wallow in self-pity for much longer."

Ever since Zane had started to break down the walls blocking my memory, I'd had nightmares about an atomic level destructive force leveling towns, killing people and animals, setting fire to fields of crops, and leaving behind a wasteland. I had a feeling they were not just bad dreams, but memories. As a result, it didn't surprise me that I had shut down any ability to do something like that again.

"So what happened in Mexico was meant to trigger my abilities?"

"Yes. The cave Vincent took you to was a sacred place, and a celestial alignment that night increased the strength of remaining magical energies surrounding it. The magic required to activate your abilities was significant, so we couldn't just do it anywhere or anytime. We timed it just right. I regret that it was a negative experience for you, but you wouldn't exactly have gone along with it if we had just asked you to."

No, I supposed I wouldn't have, but I also wasn't ready to forgive him and wipe the slate clean.

"That night *was* horrific. You can't tell me all of that was necessary. Why would you have me attacked? They could have just drugged me and dragged me to the cave from the start."

"We needed to know what you were capable of and how much you would need to relearn. We had even hoped experience alone might trigger your memories and abilities so we wouldn't need the ritual in the cave."

"But the ritual didn't work. I didn't manifest any

abilities after that. Instead, I just became a monster magnet."

"Yes, that was one of the risks we had to take. Trying to enable your abilities also made you detectible to those searching for you, but there was a benefit. I needed you trained on how to fight them. We didn't have a lot of time, so I had to throw you in the deep end and hope you learned to swim." When my jaw dropped in hurt and disbelief at his callousness, he quickly said, "But I knew you could do it. I knew your military training and determination would not allow you to fail, and I was right."

I continued to scowl at him. "And what about Sharur? Why did you hire me to retrieve the axe, only to disappear before I could return it to you?"

"Because it wasn't meant for me," he said with a small smile. "Sharur is my gift to you. I knew he would help you to come into your abilities more fully and help you direct your power. You still have a lot to learn, and he will be your teacher, but as with most things, there is a double edge. Sharur is a significant asset, but he is also…" Nathan thought for a moment, chewing on the corner of his lip. "I guess you can call him amoral. He is not very good at deciphering right from wrong, and as you know, he is able to exert influence over you. You must be very careful."

"What is he? How can an inanimate object talk to me in my head?"

"Now that is a long story and his to tell when he is ready to reveal it to you. However, I will tell you he wasn't always as you see him now. He is ancient and was once a good man, but he lost his way and paid the ultimate price. Don't misunderstand me; he is not inherently evil, nor is he inherently good. Just take what you need from him and don't expect anything more."

The weight of the axe grew heavy on my back, and I was acutely aware that Sharur was probably listening in to this conversation. Nathan must have known that.

As we continued to circle the fourth floor balcony, I said, "Okay. So time for the big question. Why do all of this? What is your end game, and what does it have to do with me?"

Nathan heaved a sigh as if he had been carrying the weight of the world on his shoulders and was finally unburdening it, both with relief and regret. "I suppose, very simply, I did it all for love."

I blinked. Of all the answers I had anticipated he would give me, that wasn't one of them.

"Love? Of whom? Or what?"

"Your mother."

I stopped walking so abruptly Nathan jerked back as he hit the resistance of my arm still wrapped in his.

"What did you say?"

He took one step back to me and gently released the death grip I now had on his forearm. "I did this for the love of your mother," he said softly. "It's another long story, but I will give you the short version. Your mother is alive, being held as a prisoner."

An image of that beautiful woman in chains whom I saw when I went through the rift flashed through my mind.

"I think I saw her," I said as I pictured her brown

eyes and long dark hair, so much like my own.

Nathan grabbed my arms hard, jerking me out of my reverie. "When did you see her?" he demanded, his eyes bright with hope.

"About an hour ago. When I fell through the skylight, I opened a rift before hitting the ground and landed in a white marble room. There was a woman—" I hesitated before saying the next words, "in chains."

Nathan went very still as his face fell into an expressionless mask, but I knew that meant he was screaming inside.

"It didn't look like she was hurt," I added quickly. "I didn't talk to her. Marduk and Adad walked into the room, so I fled back through the gate. Tell me about him, about Adad."

"He imprisoned your mother, because he wanted her for himself. He banished me to Earth, stripping me of my powers so I would be incapable of helping her. That's why I need you. You are the only one who can free her, but I needed to try to prepare you for what you would face."

"Why didn't you just ask for my help years ago when I was in Urusilim and had full access to my powers?"

"You were under Marduk's control. That is why you were given to him to be raised. He is not your real father. He was, in essence, your jailer. You were too dangerous and too valuable to be trusted to anyone but Adad's first in command."

A part of me felt like cheering, *"I knew it!"* The relief of knowing with certainty that his blood did not run through my veins was palpable.

"If Marduk isn't my father, who is?" It was a loaded question that hung heavily in the air between us, and I held my breath, waiting for the answer, acutely aware of what I wanted to hear.

"Honestly," Nathan said, meeting my eyes, "I just don't know."

I deflated, surprised at how much hope I had been holding in my chest that he would tell me it was him. Why did I want it to be him so badly? Not ready to explore the depths of my daddy issues right now, I put those feelings on a shelf to be explored another time.

I cleared my throat, trying to loosen the knot that had lodged there. "What now?"

"Now, you have a choice to make. I have led you this far down the path to be sure you were prepared, regardless of what you decided. Now your fate is in your hands, maybe for the first time ever. I will not try to control you like Marduk and Adad, your human foster parents, and Ed Connor. Even though I may not be your father, I want you to have the freedom to direct the course of your own destiny."

I hadn't really thought of my life in those terms before, but I realized he was right. That was what I had been missing, had been searching for — freedom to make my own way in this or any other world.

Chapter Twenty-Eight

ZANE

Awakening was a long, drawn-out process. All I remembered was pain, a woman with red hair, blinding light, and more pain. I didn't know how long I spent in that half-conscious state — maybe hours, maybe days. However, at some point, the blessed darkness in which I had tried very hard to drown receded.

The first thing I noticed when I awoke was the rusty railroad spike through my temples. At least, that was what it felt like. The pain in my head was like nothing I had ever felt before, and I hoped to hell I would never feel again. I could hear the blood rushing through my skull with every heartbeat, and the noise was excruciating.

My eyes remained shut against the light pressing into my lids. I made a minute movement of my head, and a fresh wave of agony rolled through me. My stomach churned, forcing me to move so I wouldn't get sick all over myself. That was when I realized I was sitting up.

Dropping my head between my knees, I dry heaved, and a hand rubbed my back in methodic circles. When it became obvious that I couldn't manage to sit back up by myself, those hands moved to my shoulders and pulled me upright. My neck felt like a rubber band, completely incapable of supporting the weight of my throbbing skull. The steady rumble interrupted by occasional jolts that shook my weakened frame didn't help the situation any.

Someone pressed a cool hand to my forehead. "It'll pass. You're going to be okay," said a soft, female voice. The musical quality of her tone would have been pleasant at any other moment but this one.

All I could manage was a groan, and even the vibration of my own vocal chords was agonizing.

"Water," I managed to croak.

After some scuffling and the sound of a zipper, plastic was pressed to my lips, and cool elixir flooded my mouth. I sucked at the bottle greedily, desperate to sooth my parched mouth and cracked lips, but the woman would only allow me to take small sips. Unfortunately, I was in no position to argue with her.

"Is he waking up? How is he?" came a familiar male voice from far away.

"He's getting there," the woman said in her singsong voice.

The ache in my skull subsided a small fraction, but it was enough to allow me to open my eyes.

Fiery red hair blocked my vision until she pulled

back. Then I could see emerald green eyes and a startling tattoo of a flame in the center of her forehead. She tucked a lock of red hair behind her pointed ear. She was an elf. I hadn't seen one of those in a decade. I thought they had all gone extinct.

"Who...?" was all I could manage to release from my throat.

"My name is Lilly. I am a friend of Alex and Emma's. What's the last thing you remember?"

Trying to think was just too taxing, so I slowly rotated my head to one side in a lame attempt to signal I couldn't remember anything right now.

She seemed to understand what I tried to convey. "It's okay. Take your time."

Once again, I tried to get my brain working. The memories revealed themselves sluggishly, just vague recollections playing at the edges of my consciousness. I focused on them, trying to catch them like elusive fireflies: flashes of a city street, a fight, darkness, then mind-blowing pain, and finally waking up here. Alex had done this to me, but I couldn't remember why.

"Alex," I croaked.

The elf nodded approvingly.

"I'm here, my friend," the male voice said reassuringly, and I now recognized it as belonging to Alex. I didn't particularly want to see him, and knowing he was here didn't bring me any comfort. He had done this to me, caused me this pain.

Spears of light stabbed my eyes at regular intervals as I struggled to focus.

"Where am I?" My own voice sounded strange and

distant.

"You're in a car," said a clipped voice that wasn't Alex. This other man sounded annoyed, his tone cold.

"We're here," Alex said as the car rolled to a stop.

I heard two doors slam, and the car shifted as the weight of the two men in the front seat exited. Then the door next to me opened, humid air rushing in and flooding the cool air-conditioned space. I immediately felt like I was suffocating, trying to suck in the thick, viscous air.

A hand grabbed my upper arm, gentle but firm, and began to pull. From the other side of me, Lilly pushed, and between the two of them, they somehow managed to get me across the seat and to the car door.

The annoyed man then took Lilly's place, roughly grabbing my opposite arm. Between the two men, they managed to pull me to my feet. Lilly closed the car door behind us, and then they all but dragged me along between them.

"Is this the right place? It looks abandoned," Lilly said nervously.

"This is the address Nathan gave me," Alex said, breathing heavily at the effort of keeping my bulk from hitting the floor.

"I still don't understand why he insisted that Jason and I come with you," she said.

"We'll find out soon enough." Alex clearly wanted to end the conversation so he could put all of his energy into keeping me upright.

I willed my legs to move, but beyond a few useless twitches, they refused to obey. I gave up and allowed myself to be manhandled, my head lolling forward against my chest. I couldn't see anything except the ground beneath my feet: sidewalk, a short flight of concrete steps, the threshold of a door, a marble tiled floor.

As hot as I thought it had been outside, it was like a sauna in the building. The dampness permeated my clothes and hair, leaving a sheen of sticky moisture on my skin. The space also smelled oddly of grilled pork chops.

"Jason, Lilly," came a woman's excited voice, followed by the sound of stampeding feet flying across the floor. Then she stopped short in front of us. "Oh, my God. Is that Zane? Is he...?" Ash's voice caught in her throat, and she couldn't finish her sentence.

"Yes," Lilly reassured her. "He's alive."

The two men carefully lowered me to my knees. Then she kneeled in front of me. My Ashnan took my face gently in her hands and lifted my eyes to hers. Her face was the first thing I was able to focus on since waking up.

A massive shape loomed up behind her. All I could make out were yellow eyes shining brightly in a field of pitch-blackness so deep it absorbed all of the light in the room. Every molecule in my body urged me to get up and protect her, but I couldn't move.

Lilly let out a high-pitched scream that split my skull in two. I guessed the others had noticed it too.

Ash glanced behind her shoulder, entirely too unconcerned, and said, "It's okay, guys. The dragon is on our side... sort of. He won't hurt us in any case. Just treat him with respect, and he'll do the same to you."

I had to trust her judgment. It's not as if I had any other choice.

I refocused on her green eyes, the color of a lush rainforest. Her long, dark hair was wet from the dampness in the room, curling in loose rivulets. Her gaze bore into my soul as she searched for signs of... what?

There was an itching in my brain as a faint memory struggled to surface. I focused on it, pulling it to the front of my mind. A cure. Alex had been trying to cure me. Had it worked? I could only guess from my less than stellar condition that he had tried his damned hardest, and it had taken a toll.

It was hard to look inward when there was so much outward pain tugging at my focus, but something was different. That burning fury that consumed the synapses of my brain and every fiber of my being was still there, but it receded back into the recesses of my mind where it could be controlled or, at least, bargained with. Where my thoughts were once fragmented and as hard to hold on to as butterflies, they were knitting together. The yarn was fragile and left behind ragged seams, but those scars meant healing.

Still, I thought I had been healed before, and all of those cures had turned out to be only temporary. Who was to say this time would be any different? And, even if it was permanent, scars were ugly, and the wounds they hid even worse. I wasn't the same man I had been ten years ago. There was no rewinding the clock.

Until then, Emma couldn't know I was back. I had

broken her heart and her spirit too many times. I was the reason she was on Earth with no memory. I had turned her into a killer. If she looked at me again, touched me again as she had after I had saved her from North Brother Island, I would be lost. And, if the past was any prediction of the future, I would end up hurting her again, even inadvertently.

I needed time to figure out who I was, what was in my head, and if the cure was permanent.

No, she couldn't know the cure might have worked.

Chapter Twenty-Nine

EMMA

"Zane?" I prompted, holding my breath as I searched his face, looking for any sign of recognition, of the old Zane who only existed in my still fragmented memory.

Please be there, I willed silently.

I didn't realize until that moment how desperately I wanted him back. I had been holding my desires at bay behind a concrete dam, believing they would never come to pass. Even fantasizing about what could have been was too painful to contemplate.

The hope bubbling to the surface was both exhilarating and terrifying, something I wanted to cling to with abandon, but run from, fearing weakness and heartache. Regardless, I couldn't look away.

I rubbed my thumbs lightly against his softly stubbled

cheeks, waiting for some kind of reaction. My face was mere inches from his, as if my body was preparing itself to press my lips to his at the first indication the cure had worked.

Something flickered behind those glazed-over eyes. For a moment, I thought I saw him breaking through the surface of the torment he had been drowning in this past decade. Then it was gone, that elusive light receding. I deflated a little, leaning away from him and sitting back on my heels, my hands dropped from his face.

It felt hopeless, but I couldn't give up on him. He had been battling this demon for ten years; therefore, I couldn't expect him to snap out of it in only moments or even days. Maybe it would take weeks or months. No matter how long it took, I would be there for him when he emerged.

My gaze wandered to Alex standing in the background, trying not to get in the way of any potential reunion. He looked stiff and uncomfortable, shifting from foot to foot and glancing everywhere other than at Zane and me. He was a hot mess, exhausted, with dark circles under his eyes, a shadow of growth on his chin and cheeks, and his hair mussed. His face was a solemn mask, but his eyes churned with emotion. They shone with unexpressed grief and acceptance. Did he know the cure had failed and was mourning the loss of his friend? Did he feel guilty that he hadn't been able to make it work?

As Alex met and held my gaze, his blue eyes as deep and complex as the man, I thought about our kiss, warmth flooding my body. I remembered the sweet taste of him, his mouth soft, yet demanding. His arms had been strong and hard around my waist as they drew me closer. His lids grew heavy as if he knew what I was thinking, and his thoughts were in the same place.

I tore my gaze away before I was tempted to go to him and recreate that moment. It would be too easy to give in to my physical attraction for Alex, but I needed to be careful not to damage our still fragile friendship. I didn't think Alex could keep the lines between lust and love separate. He struck me as too much of a romantic.

A hand rested lightly on my shoulder, and I looked up to see Jason's concerned face. I hadn't even noticed he was there until then.

"Jason," I gasped. "What are you doing here?" After Citi Field, I had been trying so hard to keep him out of all of this for his own safety, and now here he was, right in the middle of the chaos.

I finally took a moment to look around me, and saw Lilly there as well. Sam and Duncan had returned to the lobby with their Syndicate search teams along with some new members, and Nathan stood behind me with one hand on the dragon's shoulder, giving me the impression they were old friends.

Jason pulled my attention back to him.

"Nathan called and said he needed to see me and Lilly immediately, and he was sending Alex to get us. Imagine my surprise when Alex showed up with enemy number one. I would have killed Zane right then, but I thought something had happened to you. I might be pissed at you, but I would never let anything happen to you if I could help it. Anyway, Zane didn't seem to be in much condition to run or fight, so I figured he wasn't going anywhere for a while." Jason took my hands and helped me to my feet.

I gave Jason a fierce hug, his familiar scent comforting me. He stiffened, trying to reconcile his anger with me against his desire to hold me close. His body relaxed after a moment and he brought his arms around me. I closed my eyes and just breathed him in, thinking back to a simpler time when I fought for money and not for my life and the fate of humankind.

When I pulled back, Jason only reluctantly released me. We both could have used a few more minutes or maybe hours to reconnect and find our center of gravity again. However, this wasn't the time, and it certainly wasn't the place.

I turned toward Nathan, who had so carefully orchestrated these events, and asked him, "So, what now?" He was the chess master and more than likely knew exactly what came next.

"You tell me, Miss Hayes," he said, leaving the dragon's side and coming to stand in front of me. I suspected he kept addressing me so formally as a way to erect a barrier between us. Maybe, like me, he also wasn't ready to acknowledge this connection we had to each other. "One option is for you to stay on Earth and go back to your life as a mercenary or take up whatever profession you would like to pursue. Duncan will be sure the Monere stay out of your way, and you will never have to see any of us again—well, except maybe for Jason. You can keep Sharur or give him to someone you trust. I will not demand him back from you. I know you will ensure he is kept safe from our enemies. All I ask is that you let us through the gateway before you leave."

Was he really going to let me simply walk away after everything I had seen and experienced? Could I even do it? I wasn't so sure it was possible just to pick up where my life had left off before I met Darko. Right then I wasn't so sure I wanted to.

My eyes fell on Zane, still kneeling in silence on the floor, gazing into space. Then they moved to Alex, stoic and unmoving, his arms crossed at the chest as if trying to shield himself from my answer. Accepting Nathan's offer would mean walking away from them both forever.

"And my other option?" I asked.

"Come home with us," he implored. "We need you. You can be so much more than just a mercenary fighting insignificant battles for humans. Help me return Urusilim and other worlds to their glory. Lead an army against our enemies. Bring our people back together so we can live in peace once more." He stopped speaking abruptly, probably because he noticed my jaw was on the floor, and I looked at him as if he belonged in a padded cell. "I'm sorry," he said. "I have been trying to get back for a very long time. I am just... enthusiastic."

"Um ... okay," I said. "What exactly is it that you need from me, Nathan? Because I am certainly not going to be leading armies."

Nathan looked sheepish, realizing he had overstepped. If those were his true ambitions, he could count me out. After Citi Field, my days of leading armies were over. I didn't like the idea of directing others to their possible deaths.

"You're right. I went too far. Truly, all I want or need from you is to help me free your mother from Adad and Marduk. Once that is done, you may choose your own path. You have Sharur, so you can also return to Earth at any time. I just ask that you please wait to do so until after your mother is freed. Believe me, I would do this myself if I still had my powers. I'm sorry to ask it of you."

He was telling the truth. I didn't know if the woman I had seen on the other side of the rift was really my mother, but the possibility that she might be was alluring. Even if I couldn't remember my childhood, I could feel that void inside of me that a mother's love should have filled. If she had been missing because someone was holding her against her will, didn't I have a responsibility to help her?

Her absence from my life was character defining. Would I have turned into a cold-hearted killer if she had been there to read me stories when I was little, protect me from the evils of the world, or help shape my moral compass? I could almost guarantee I would have been a very different person.

Then and there, I vowed to myself that the person who had taken her from me would pay the ultimate price. I would avenge the woman who'd had her child stolen from her, who hadn't been able to see that little girl grow up. I would also avenge myself for my lost childhood and never knowing the love of a mother.

I set my jaw and straightened my back. "I'll go with you," I said.

Nathan visibly relaxed, blowing out the breath that he had been holding and releasing the tension in his shoulders.

"But I am not bringing them with me," I said pointing to everyone gathered around me. "They are my friends, not an army. This isn't their fight, and I won't risk their lives."

My companions all burst out speaking at once.

"You can't stop us—"

"But I want to help—"

"I'm going with you—"

"Okay, okay," I said, raising my palms in surrender. "I will leave the choice up to each of you. You are adults and can make your own decisions, but know that this will be incredibly dangerous, and you may not see it to the end of the mission. I wouldn't blame any of you for choosing to stay."

Duncan stepped forward. "Emma, I think it's safe to say we're all behind you one hundred percent. We may each have our own reasons for going back to Urusilim, but we will help you free your mother before pursuing our own objectives."

I couldn't help wondering what those objectives were, but it wasn't my place to scrutinize. They would tell me when they were ready. In the meantime, I wasn't about to look a gift horse in the mouth. I needed as much muscle as I could possibly get if we were to be successful and stay alive. They also brought with them the advantage of knowing the lay of the land, the people, and the culture. Hell, I didn't even know if they spoke English in Urusilim.

"Thank you," I said softly, my eyes shining with unshed tears at their loyalty and friendship. "Is everyone ready?"

There were nods all around.

I pulled Sharur from its holster, hefted it above my head, and with a single thought, *Urusilim*, I swung downward. I felt that familiar resistance as the blade sliced through the curtain between our worlds.

Then, together, we all stepped through.

The End

Made in the USA
Middletown, DE
02 October 2015